P9-DBT-221

TERROR IN

Taffeta

TERROR IN
Taffeta

MARLA COOPER

MINOTAUR BOOKS
A THOMAS DUNNE BOOK

A THOMAS DUNNE BOOK FOR MINOTAUR BOOKS.
An imprint of St. Martin's Publishing Group.

www.thomasdunnebooks.com
www.minotaurbooks.com

The Library of Congress Cataloging-in-Publication Data
is available upon request.

ISBN 978-1-250-07256-6 (hardcover)
ISBN 978-1-4668-8438-0 (e-book)

Our books may be purchased in bulk for promotional, educational, or
business use. Please contact your local bookseller or the Macmillan Corporate
and Premium Sales Department at 1-800-221-7945, extension 5442, or by
e-mail at MacmillanSpecialMarkets@macmillan.com.

First Edition: March 2016

10   9   8   7   6   5   4   3   2   1

To Kay Bauer, who loved a good mystery and
would have been the most excited of all

ACKNOWLEDGMENTS

This book would never have been written if I hadn't met Ali Wing, who asked me to help her write a baby-gear guide for Chronicle Books. Or if my editor at Chronicle, Lisa Morris Campbell, hadn't reached out to me to ghostwrite a second book: a guide to destination weddings. Or if Alison Hotchkiss Rinderknecht of Alison Events hadn't taught me basically everything I know about destination weddings during the writing of said guide.

Once I started writing, my mystery writing group was a great source of inspiration, laughter, and bagels—and Diana Orgain and Laura-Kate Rurka proved to be awesome partners in crime. Not only did they make brilliant suggestions, they corrected my Spanish and reminded me that sometimes people and places require physical descriptions.

After I finished the book, the fabulous Marina Adair was kind enough to introduce me to her agent, Jill Marsal of Marsal Lyon

Literary Agency. I owe a huge debt of gratitude to Jill for believing in this book and for getting it into the hands of Anne Brewer at Thomas Dunne Books, who waved her magic wand and made it a reality.

I'd be remiss if I didn't offer a shout-out to the NorCal chapter of Sisters in Crime, the SinC Guppies, and my coconspirators at Chicks on the Case: Lisa Q. Mathews, Kellye Garrett, and Ellen Byron, who provided much needed moral support as we juggled book launches, platform building, and writing second books together.

I'd also like to thank Jeff Fowler, who was always there when I needed a plot twist; Eva Guralnick, who dropped everything to proofread my first chapters for submission; and my wonderful husband, Tim Bauer, who read this novel more times than really seems fair and cheered me on the entire time.

TERROR IN

Taffeta

CHAPTER 1

The sea-foam green bridesmaids' dresses had been a mistake. Not for the obvious reason—that sea-foam green bridesmaids' dresses are almost always a mistake—but because they added a sickly tinge to Nicole Abernathy's three very hungover bridesmaids.

I'd warned them not to overindulge the night before the wedding, begged them to have their bachelorette party back home instead of waiting until they got to San Miguel de Allende, but no one listens to the wedding planner when it's time to start drinking.

"Kelsey, I don't feel so hot," Nicole said, as I helped her step into her wedding dress.

"I'm not surprised," I said. "You've barely eaten all week."

"I've barely eaten all month," she said, studying herself in the mirror. "But at least the dress fits."

I laughed. Nicole couldn't have been any more than a size 6, and the forgiving corset dress she'd chosen would have fit even if she'd binged on cupcakes all month. "What are you talking about? It looks amazing on you. Always has. Promise me you'll eat something at the reception?"

"I should be hungry, but the thought of food right now . . . ugh." Nicole clutched her stomach and shook her head. "I should have listened to you and had the bachelorette party back in San Francisco."

"That's okay," I said with as chipper a smile as I could muster. "Being sick on your wedding day is good luck."

"Really?" Nicole's big brown eyes searched mine.

"Sure," I lied. "Now hold still."

I felt bad for her, and I tried to be extra gentle as I tightened the satin ribbons that crisscrossed the back of her dress.

"Owww," Nicole whined.

Okay, so I wasn't gentle enough.

"Sorry. Warn me if you're going to pass out or something."

"No, that's okay." Nicole took a deep breath. "Pull tighter."

After two or three more tugs, I tied off the ribbons and tucked them down into the dress, leaving behind a tidy herringbone pattern.

I spun her around for a final inspection. Her freshly highlighted honey-blond hair was pulled into a perfectly executed chignon, and the makeup artist not only had made her look downright dewy but had hidden all evidence of the dark circles under her eyes.

"Well, you might not feel well, but you look amazing."

As Nicole turned to admire herself, Zoe Abernathy ducked between the bride and the full-length mirror.

"Hey," Nicole said. "Move it, lady."

Zoe laughed as she checked herself in the mirror. "Maid-of-honor privileges. Or sister privileges. Or, I don't know, hungover-person privileges." She tried to smooth her short, messy hair, but her surfer-girl layers could not be repressed. "Did I mention I'm never drinking again?"

"Only about thirty times," said Dana Poole, a testy redhead who'd been hogging the other mirror while she applied the finishing touches to her makeup. The girl had been peevish all week, and the hangover wasn't exactly bringing out her best qualities.

"Well, I'm gonna say it thirty more times, so get used to it."

"I don't even want to hear it," Dana said, pointing her mascara wand accusingly at the bride's sister. "It's your own fault, you know."

"What do you mean?" Zoe said, batting her eyelashes innocently. "Nicole wanted a bachelorette party. And you can't have a bachelorette party without a cocktail or three."

"Yeah, but we're not in college anymore. We could have done without that last round of shots."

Zoe shrugged. "It seemed like a good idea at the time."

Dana scowled as she screwed the cap back on her mascara and tossed it into her makeup bag. "Well, next time, keep your good ideas to yourself."

"C'mon, Dana," said the bride, taking a playful tone with her cranky friend. "You have to admit it was pretty fun."

Dana shrugged. "I guess so. Kelsey, will you get us some sparkling water? San Pellegrino, preferably."

Wait—was she really demanding that I drop what I was doing and go find refreshments? "Sorry, I've kind of got my hands full here, but there's some flat water over there in the cooler."

"Whatever," she sighed.

Dana had been a late addition to the wedding party, having originally turned down the invitation to Nicole's destination wedding altogether. But after Dana found a last-minute plane ticket to Mexico, Nicole said *of course* it wasn't too late to join the bridal party.

I'd spent way too much time the previous week hunting down an extra bridesmaid dress and having it FedExed to the villa we'd rented to house the bridal party for the week. Plus, we'd had to promote one of the guests to groomsman, because the bride's mother thought an uneven number of attendants would be "tacky."

Of course, no one would ever know how hard I'd worked to pull it all off. I was the magical fairy who made things happen, and if magical fairies do their job right, everyone has a great time and the bride has a perfect day.

At least, that's how it's supposed to work.

Instead, Dana had been huffing around all morning, complaining about one thing after another. "Why do we have to get ready in this cramped little room?" *It's a two-hundred-year-old chapel, and it wasn't built for your convenience.* "Why don't my shoes match the other bridesmaids'?" *You're lucky to have shoes at all on such short notice.* "Why aren't there any vegan options on the menu?" *Um, because . . . shut up, that's why.*

I'd managed to bite my tongue for Nicole's sake, but Dana was being a total bridesmaid-zilla.

From somewhere behind me, the third bridesmaid let out a moan. She'd been so quiet all week and had caused so little trouble, I was blanking on her name. What was it again? Kristen? Kirsten? Christy? Whatever it was, she put her head down on top of her folded arms and declared that she was dying.

"Okay, Pepto-Bismol all around," I said, heading to my emergency kit. Wedding planners have to be prepared for anything—especially *destination* wedding planners. You can't just run to the nearest drugstore in a foreign country and assume you'll find what you need. I always made sure I had double-sided tape to hold errant straps in place, clear fingernail polish to fix runs in pantyhose, and anti-nausea medication for getting girls down the aisle after a night of drinking.

"Bottoms up," I said as I passed out the tiny plastic dose cups. With a little luck and two tablespoons of the thick, pink syrup, they'd be able to get through the service.

Nicole scrunched up her face, looking as if she'd just knocked back another tequila shot.

"Sorry, Nicole." I took the empty cup from her. "It'll all be over soon."

Poor Nicole. I felt terrible for her, being sick on her wedding day. I genuinely liked the bride, and had ever since we'd met a year earlier, back in San Francisco.

The mother of the bride, Mrs. Abernathy, had dragged the young couple into my office against their will, thinking I'd be the perfect person to put together the exquisite wine country wedding she'd always assumed her daughter would have. I knew immediately that she wanted it to be elegant. A strikingly chic woman, she was perfectly put together, from her sleek bobbed hairstyle down to her high-heeled Ferragamos.

But when I mentioned that I'd planned weddings from Napa to Mexico to Europe, Nicole's face brightened and her fiancé, Vince Moreno, looked up from his iPhone for the first time since he'd gotten there.

"Mexico?" Nicole asked, as Vince's face broke into a grin.

"Napa!" her mom corrected, with a slightly sharper than necessary nudge and an "Isn't that what you meant to say" look in her eyes.

Mrs. Abernathy hadn't realized that Mexico was on the table—neither had I, frankly, until that moment—or she probably wouldn't have brought her daughter to me.

"Mexico would be so romantic!" Nicole squealed, exchanging excited looks with her fiancé and her sister, Zoe.

Zoe nodded enthusiastically. "And fun, too! Remember that time we went to Playa del Carmen?"

I pulled a fat binder from a shelf behind my desk and flipped through some photos. "You could get married on a Mexican beach, or you could go for a colonial town like San Miguel de Allende. It's really beautiful, very European."

They looked through some glamour shots of the romantic, colonial town with cobblestone streets, and I showed them a thick notebook full of vendors I could personally recommend in San Miguel.

"Oh, these flowers look so . . . professional!" Mrs. Abernathy said. "Do they have, you know, *electricity*?" She whispered the last word to make sure she wasn't offending anyone.

"They have just about everything you could possibly need." *It's Mexico, not Burundi,* I wanted to add but didn't. "And what we can't get there, we can have brought in," I reassured her.

"That sounds good to me!" Nicole said. "Vince? What do you think?"

"As long as you're there, I don't care where we go," he said, giving his intended a spontaneous peck on the cheek. "But Mexico does sound pretty awesome."

Despite Mrs. Abernathy's initial misgivings, everything looked amazing now that the day had actually arrived. I'd peeked out earlier and seen the guests nodding their approval as they filled the wooden pews, taking in the charming, centuries-old church. The flowers were perfect, the groomsmen were all in place, and the tequila donkey was waiting patiently outside to lead the processional to the reception at the Instituto Allende.

Mrs. Abernathy didn't actually know about the tequila donkey yet, but the groomsmen had enlisted me to help pull off the surprise. She wasn't going to like it—having a burro laden with bottles of tequila being part of the proceedings—but since it was technically a gift for the newlyweds, she didn't get veto power. Personally, I couldn't wait to see her reaction; I'd told the wedding photographer, Brody Marx, who also happened to be a close personal friend of mine, to make sure not to miss the moment, under the threat of death.

But first, we had to get through the ceremony. Luckily, the Pepto-Bismol had started doing its job and the bridal party was beginning to perk up a bit.

"You ready?" I asked Nicole.

"Ready," she replied.

I guided her and the three bridesmaids toward the arched doorways at the back of the chapel, where Mr. Abernathy stood waiting for his daughter.

He smiled proudly and kissed her on the cheek. "You look beautiful, sweetheart."

"Kelsey," Dana said, interrupting the moment. "I have to use the bathroom."

"I'm sorry, Dana, but can't it wait until after the service?" I'd already given the nod to one of the groomsmen to seat Mrs. Abernathy, and the quartet was waiting for my cue to start the processional.

"I don't think it can," Dana said as she tossed me her bouquet and bolted down the hall.

I'd told them all to use the facilities before they got into their Spanx. Why hadn't she listened?

Zoe stared after the bridesmaid, incredulous. "That girl—"

The thought was interrupted by the slam of the bathroom door and the muffled sound of someone being sick coming from down the hall.

Okay, so she really *couldn't* have waited.

"Should one of us go check on her?" asked the third bridesmaid, whom I'd decided was definitely named Kristen.

"That's okay, Claire," Nicole said. (*Claire! That was it!*) "They can't start without me, right?"

"That's right," I said, as I tried to distract her with some unnecessary, last-minute adjustments to her veil.

Dana returned a minute or two later, her face blotchy red and droplets of water spattered across her shoes. No matter—all eyes would be on the bride.

Okay, *whew.* Now that we had everyone accounted for, the wedding could finally begin. I fluffed Nicole's gown around her, adjusted her veil one last time, and handed her the luscious bouquet of orchids and roses we'd picked out.

She was perfect.

"Okay," I said, "let's do this." I opened the chapel door, gave the nod to the musicians, and ducked back out. The sound of trumpets pierced the quiet of the church; then a violin, a guitar, and a *vihuela* joined in, signaling the start of the bridal procession.

Dana glanced back toward the bathroom, but I spun her around and gave her a little shove toward the center aisle. She tottered at first, then fell into the slow rhythm of the processional march.

Claire came next, followed by Zoe, both smiling gamely for the throng of guests who twisted in their seats, eager to catch a glimpse of the girl in the white dress.

"Okay, Nicole," I said, "remember to keep your bouquet low so you don't cover up that gorgeous gown, and don't forget to breathe."

She smiled and nodded, took her father's arm, and stepped into the chapel, entering to a collective murmur of admiration.

Vince stood waiting near the altar, looking absolutely smitten. I could see why Nicole had fallen for him. Dark hair, dark eyes, muscular build—he could have a bright future as a tuxedo model if the whole media rep thing didn't work out.

After Nicole's father had gotten her halfway down the aisle, I collapsed in the back pew and kicked off my strappy sandals. Everything was out of my hands, at least for the next fifteen minutes.

I pulled my hair up off my neck and fanned myself with a wedding program, wishing I could have a do-over with the hair-stylist. She'd generously offered to style my chestnut mop into an elegant updo—although I was pretty sure it had been at Mrs. Abernathy's urging—but I'd known it wouldn't last twenty minutes with all the running around I had to do, and I'd told her not to bother.

Whew. It was nice to have this little break in the chaos.

As Father Villarreal spoke about the bonds of marriage, I went through my mental checklist of reception to-dos. Food? Check. I had stopped by earlier and seen the caterer busily preparing the hors d'oeuvres. Music? Ready to go. The couple had opted for a DJ, and he was all set up. Flowers? We'd practically smothered the courtyard of the former-convent-turned-art-school with roses, lilies, and other colorful blossoms. I couldn't wait for Nicole and Vince to see the finished product.

I relaxed a bit and listened to Father Villarreal's deep, mellifluous voice. What a find he'd been. I'd never worked with him before—he was a last-minute replacement priest who agreed to fill in—but he brought just the right amount of gravitas to the proceedings. I allowed my mind to wander as he spoke. I hadn't talked to my assistant, Laurel, since the day before, and I made a mental note to call her later to make sure everything was going okay back at the office.

"If anyone sees any reason why these two should not be wed," Father Villarreal said, "let them speak now or forever hold their peace."

I stifled a laugh. No one used that line in wedding ceremonies anymore. I looked around to see if there were any objections, other than my own to his antiquated question.

My break came to an end all too soon. Father Villarreal pronounced them husband and wife and told Vince he could kiss the bride. I stretched my legs and wiggled my toes. Time to put my shoes back on. As I bent down to fish them out from under the pew, I heard a gasp.

Uh-oh. Gasps are never good news.

I shot out of my seat in time to see Dana lurch forward, holding her stomach. She looked like—no. Really? She looked like she was going to barf again, right there on the altar.

Dana tried to steady herself by grabbing a tall bouquet of orchids, but to no avail. She pulled the vase down with her, causing a loud crash as they both hit the stone floor.

"No, no, no, no, no," I whispered. "This cannot be happening."

I signaled to the mariachi quartet to start playing again as I rushed to the front of the church, ready to do whatever I could to minimize the damage.

By the time I reached the front, Zoe and Nicole were crouched down next to Dana.

"Come on, get *up*," Zoe demanded, shaking the bridesmaid's limp body.

"It's okay," I whispered. "Go back to your spots."

A panicky feeling rose up in my chest. Dana must have been sicker than I'd realized. I had to think fast. Addressing the congregation, I announced in my most confident voice, "She's fine, everyone." I fanned her with a wedding program, which I hoped would make her magically spring back to her feet. "She just fainted."

Reading the pleading look in my eyes, Father Villarreal raised his hands, and his voice boomed across the sanctuary: "I now present to you Mr. and Mrs. Moreno."

On cue, the mariachis began playing the recessional, prompting Vince and Nicole to begin their uncertain walk back down the aisle, followed by two pairs of attendants. The remaining usher stood awkwardly, unsure what his role was now that he was devoid of anyone to ush. I shooed him down the aisle as I mouthed, "Go! Go!"

The guests filed out, glancing back to see me hovering over Dana while trying my best to look upbeat. Once they were all safely outside, I felt Dana's wrist. I couldn't find anything, but then again, I wasn't an experienced pulse taker.

This could not be happening. I frantically felt up and down her forearm, but all I could feel was my own heart thudding in my chest.

"Dana, come on, wake up," I said, shaking her slightly. She didn't move.

I lifted one of her eyelids, not sure what I was looking for, and was greeted with an empty gaze.

Father Villarreal returned from closing the church doors with a questioning look on his face. *"Enferma?"*

Stunned, I shook my head as I sank down onto the floor.

"No, I—I think she's dead."

CHAPTER 2

*W*hen it comes to weddings, there are emergencies, and then there are emergencies. Having a trio show up when you were expecting a quartet? Unfortunate, but salvageable. Finding out the bakery accidentally sent a Styrofoam dummy cake to the reception? Pretty disappointing, but still not an emergency. Wedding dress catching fire? Okay, I suppose that would be an emergency—but still nothing compared to what I was dealing with now.

Because this was more than just an emergency. This was without a doubt the worst thing I'd ever had happen at a wedding. I mean, I'd thought through some pretty dire scenarios and figured out what I'd do—like if the bride got cold feet and bolted in the middle of the ceremony—but I could never have anticipated a tragedy like this.

Father Villarreal had called the paramedics, and they'd arrived quickly. They worked at trying to revive Dana, but after several minutes of performing CPR, one of them looked up at Father Villarreal and shook his head, the universal sign for "I'm sorry, there's nothing we can do."

I stood there frozen as Father Villarreal knelt over Dana's lifeless body. He made the sign of the cross, then whispered a prayer in Spanish.

The room was silent as the paramedics packed away their equipment.

"What happened?" I whispered.

Father Villarreal spoke to the paramedics, then turned back to me. "They don't know. Is there a family member we should contact?"

I wrapped my arms around myself and shuddered. "I'm not sure. I'll have to ask Nicole."

Nicole. She didn't know yet, and I was going to have to tell her. I dreaded having to ruin the party with this awful news, but there was no way around it. I watched numbly as the paramedics strapped Dana onto the stretcher and wheeled her down the aisle.

After they left, I retreated to the back of the church and collected my belongings as well as a few things the bridesmaids had left behind. I was loaded up like a packhorse and already way too exhausted to think, but the guests would be arriving at the reception, and I needed to break the bad news.

By the time I got to the Instituto Allende, the party was in full swing. Nicole and Vince were posing for family photos with the Morenos, including Vince's parents, his sister, and two rambunctious toddlers who couldn't stop squirming long enough for Brody to get a shot. Not wanting to interrupt, I waited patiently for them to finish so I could talk to the bride and groom.

"*There* you are," said Mrs. Abernathy, swooping in out of

nowhere and steering me away from the crowd. "Now, I've made a few last-minute changes to the seating arrangements and—"

"Mrs. Abernathy," I interrupted. "That's not important. I—"

"*Well*," she huffed. "I would think you'd want to make sure your guest of honor is happy." I had a feeling she meant herself rather than Nicole.

"Jeanette, *listen* to me." That did the trick. Mrs. Abernathy looked as shocked as if I'd tossed a glass of sangria onto her meticulously tailored mother-of-the-bride dress—a champagne-colored designer gown that, by the way, would have looked perfectly at home at a society gala.

"Mrs. Abernathy, I've got some bad news."

"Is it about the caterers? I *knew* they weren't up for the job."

"No." I jumped in before she could build up another head of steam. "It's about Dana."

"Oh, *her*. Listen, darling, there's simply not room at the head table, and she was a last-minute addition. Surely she'll understand."

"Mrs. Abernathy, she's not going to be sitting at the head table."

"That's right. I've got a nice little spot for her right over—"

"She's not going to be sitting at *any* table. Dana's dead."

"Dead? Why, whatever for?"

I stared at her while the message sunk in.

"You mean *dead* dead?"

I nodded.

"Oh, dear. That's unfortunate," she said, rubbing the bridge of her nose while she processed the information. "Well, okay, that means there's an extra space at table twelve."

Was she serious? A bridesmaid was dead and all she cared about was the seating chart?

"I'm sorry, Kelsey, not to be callous, but I haven't seen the girl in ten years. And standing here yapping about it isn't going to make her any more alive, is it? We've got hungry guests!"

There it was, then. She'd spent quite a chunk of money on this event, and she wasn't going to let the small matter of a death put a damper on things.

"Okay, well, do you want to tell Nicole, or should I?" *Please say you'll do it, please say you'll do it.*

She stared at me, puzzled. "I don't see any reason either of us should tell her, at least not right this minute."

"We have to tell her!" I exclaimed. "I mean, don't we?" I didn't want to do it any more than she did, but it seemed wrong to withhold the information.

"It will just ruin her night. Besides, that girl will still be dead tomorrow, right? And it's not like they were best friends or anything. You need to just let it be." And with that, she turned back to her guests, beaming, and began air-kissing a stream of well-wishers who had come over to offer their congratulations.

I looked around for Brody. He'd know what to do.

Brody Marx was an amazing wedding photographer and one of my best friends in San Francisco. We'd worked together for several years, and I always tried to get him hired when I could. Not that it was difficult. Good, reliable photographers are hard to come by, and you really don't want to try to track down photos in another country after you've flown back home to your own. Most brides agreed that it was worth the small extra expense to fly him in, and it was always nice to have a familiar face among all the chaos.

Thanks to his height—he's just north of six feet tall—I was able to pick him out easily in the crowd. He spotted me as I made my way over to him, and his face broke out into a big, broad grin. "Kelsey! There you are. Hey, is Dana feeling better? We wanted to get some group shots."

"Can I talk to you?" I whispered.

"Sure," he said, holding up a just-one-minute finger to Nicole and Vince.

I pulled him through a nearby archway into a quiet corridor.

"Brody, Dana isn't sick. She's dead!"

"What?" He stared into my eyes to make sure I wasn't joking.

"I thought she'd fainted, but she never got back up."

"That's terrible! What are you going to do?"

"Mrs. Abernathy said I'm not supposed to tell Nicole, but I have to tell her, right?"

"Hmmm," he said. "What would Emily Post do?"

"I don't know!" I snapped. "I skipped that chapter."

He opened his mouth to speak, then closed it again, sensing correctly that whatever he was about to say should be kept to himself.

"Sorry," I said. "You know how I get when I'm stressed. Oh, man, look at her."

Across the room, Nicole and Vince chatted with some guests. Vince said something and she threw her head back and laughed. The radiant bride. It's a cliché for a reason.

Brody shook his head. "She looks so happy."

"I know," I said. "I hate the thought of taking that away from her."

"Well, Mrs. Abernathy told you not to say anything, and she's the one paying the bills for this shindig. I say keep your mouth shut. You can always blame her later."

I nodded in agreement. It wasn't the best plan. But it would have to do.

I hadn't had a bite to eat all night long, so I headed toward the kitchen to see if I could wrangle some leftovers out of the caterer, whose snapper Veracruz had been the talk of the evening.

"Ah, Miss Kelsey!" he exclaimed as I walked into the kitchen. "How did you enjoy dinner?"

"It looked amazing, but it's been crazy out there and I didn't get a bite. Can you help a girl out?"

"For you, *señorita*? Of course. Let me see what I can put together."

As he buzzed around the kitchen, clanging lids and scavenging for leftovers, I peeked out to gauge how much longer we should wait before we cut the cake. Surely no one would notice if I disappeared for ten minutes. I needed a moment alone so I could figure out what to do.

"Here you are," he said, handing me a steaming plate that he'd warmed up for me. "There's plenty left, so come see me if you're still hungry."

"Thanks—I owe you one," I said gratefully, taking the food and heading back into the courtyard.

The bridesmaids, having gotten a few cocktails in them, were getting boisterous. "Kelsey, come dance with us!" Zoe yelled as she kicked off her shoes and ditched them under a chair.

"Yeah," Claire chimed in. She shimmied her way over to me and tried to drag me onto the dance floor. "C'mon!"

"I have to check on the cake," I replied, plastering a convincing smile onto my face. "I'll join you in just a bit!"

"Okay," Zoe said, "but as soon as you're done, get your butt back over here!"

I smiled and waved, sure she'd forget I existed as soon as I was out of sight. The girls danced away, and I made a U-turn toward the stairs to the second floor. I needed to get some food in me and I needed time to think, but before I could make it to the walkway, one of the groomsmen intercepted me.

"Kelsey," he said. "Can I talk to you?"

"Sure, Trevor—give me a few minutes and I'll be right back," I said, trying to breeze past him before he stopped my momentum.

"No, it's important." He grabbed my arm, coming dangerously

close to upending my dinner plate. Didn't he know not to stand in the way of a woman with blood sugar issues? My stomach growled at him menacingly.

"Okay, what's up?"

"I wanted to ask you about Dana."

My stomach dropped. "Oh, um, yeah?"

"How is she?"

"Oh, are you two friends?" I said, trying to keep my facial expression neutral. Okay, so I was stalling, but I hadn't seen the two of them even speak a word to each other all weekend. Then again, it wasn't unusual for groomsmen to inquire about the other members of the wedding party. Hooking up with bridesmaids was part of their unwritten duty.

"We've met," he said noncommittally.

Well, of course they'd met, but how well did he know her? Was he going to push me for answers?

"I'm not sure where she is right now," I said, which was very true.

"Is she okay?" he prodded. "She didn't look too good."

"Too much heat." I waved my hand casually. "Happens all the time."

"But I haven't seen her since the ceremony. How was she feeling when you left? Is she coming back to the party?"

My vague-but-truthful comments weren't satisfying him. I quickly weighed which would send me to hell faster: lying or letting Nicole find out from someone else that she was short a bridesmaid.

Deciding to go the lying route, I plastered a smile on my face. "She's absolutely fine. She's just had a lot of excitement. She's back at the villa. In fact, I'm taking her this plate so she can eat something. So if you'll excuse me . . ."

Trevor stared after me as I darted away. I'd tried to sound

convincing, but I'm no Meryl Streep. At least I hadn't cracked under the pressure.

Away from the crowd at last, I scarfed down a few bites and tried to formulate a plan. I needed to tell Nicole before she found out on her own, but when? How? This was *so* not part of my job description.

I still didn't have a plan, but having something to digest improved my mood dramatically. I steeled myself for a moment before I reentered the fray. Everyone looked like they were having fun; at least I had that going for me. Brody spotted me across the courtyard and worked his way through the guests. "Rough night, huh?" he asked.

"I'll say. I've never lost a bridesmaid before." I stared off, lost in thought. "Although I did lose a flower girl once."

Brody stared at me, aghast. "You did? That's horrible!"

"What? Oh, no, it wasn't like that. We found her in the garden, poking at a ladybug. Totally ruined the dress, though."

"Oh, thank God."

We watched the happy guests gathered in the courtyard, oblivious to Dana's absence. "I really should get back out there, but I don't know how much longer I can keep up this fake smiling."

"Don't beat yourself up," Brody said. "You're doing the best you can under the circumstances."

"I know." I shook my head. "But I have to get it together. I've been hiding from Nicole all night because I'm afraid she'll see right through me, but avoiding the bride is kind of a wedding-planner no-no."

"Hang in there," he said, wrapping an arm around my shoulders and squeezing. "We've only got a couple more hours."

"Thanks. Now get out of here. Don't you have to go get a picture of the dad with his empty pockets turned inside out or something?"

"Ouch!" he replied. "That hurts."

"And that," I said, giving him a quick kiss on the cheek, "is my cue to have them cut the cake!"

As I headed over toward Nicole, I passed Zoe and Claire chatting amiably with the best man, Ryan McGuire, at one of the eight-top rounds.

"Sorry to interrupt, but it's time to cut the cake."

"Okay," Zoe said, grabbing her drink from the table and slurping up the last of it. "I don't suppose Dana is going to grace us with her presence?"

I shook my head, smile frozen in place to keep my face from betraying anything.

Zoe rolled her eyes. "I can't believe she's being such a drama queen. I knew she'd mess things up for Nicole."

"Please don't be mad at Dana," I said, thinking how bad Zoe would feel when she found out the real reason for Dana's absence.

"Well, good riddance," said Zoe. Claire nodded in agreement.

Ouch. "Okay, well, let's go finish things up and I'm sure tomorrow—"

"We're six minutes past cake-cutting time." Mrs. Abernathy appeared out of nowhere, a particular talent of hers that I'd only just realized. "If we're going to be delayed, Kelsey, I certainly hope it's not because you're partying with the bridesmaids."

"I'm not partying with anyone," I said. "I'm working."

"Well, that couldn't possibly be true, or we wouldn't be six minutes past cake-cutting time. I'm sorry: seven minutes."

Oh, why had I given her the schedule?

"No, yes, of course," I said, pushing Zoe and Claire in front of me, partly to point them toward the cake but mostly to put them between me and the mother of the bride.

"Oh, for heaven's sake," Mrs. Abernathy said, glancing down at the bridesmaids' bare feet. "Girls, put your shoes on. This is a wedding, not a hoedown."

Two minutes later—making us nine minutes late, which I considered a victory overall—Nicole and Vince pulled off their cake-cutting duties admirably, neither one smushing fondant into the other's face. Not that they would have dared, as Mrs. Abernathy had warned them more than a few times that it was uncouth.

As the servers passed around the wedding cake, Nicole pulled me aside.

"Hey, Kelsey, where's Dana? Is she okay?"

That was it. I couldn't take it anymore. The statute of limitations on mother-of-the-bride threats had just run out.

"Nicole, can we talk for a second?"

"Sure," she said, looking concerned. We tried to duck out unnoticed, but an overly cheery voice interrupted our trajectory.

"There you are!" exclaimed Mrs. Abernathy.

"We've been here all along, Mom."

"Isn't this cake to *die* for?" she said, taking Nicole by the arm.

Okay, seriously? She was going to go there?

"Mom, Kelsey and I are going to step outside for a second—"

"Nonsense, darling! Your guests are starting to leave, and we simply must do the sparklers before everyone's gone."

"But, Mom, I asked Kelsey about Dana and—"

"Oh, yes, dear, Dana is sleeping. She even asked us to bring her a plate earlier, isn't that right, Kelsey?"

The evil eye Mrs. Abernathy gave me as she patted her daughter on the cheek had me rooted to the spot.

Oblivious to any tension, Mr. Abernathy approached, beaming at his daughter. "There are my two girls! Great job, Kelsey. What are you ladies gabbing about?"

"Nothing, darling," Mrs. Abernathy cooed at her husband. "Nothing at all."

CHAPTER 3

When my cell phone started sounding wake-up marimbas the next morning, I chucked it across the room. But when the church bells of La Parroquia started clanging every fifteen minutes, there was nothing I could do but pull a pillow over my head.

I hadn't slept more than two hours all night because I couldn't stop replaying the events of the evening in my mind. I burrowed down into the covers, but an insistent knock on my bedroom door sent me hurtling out of bed.

"You in there?"

Thank God. It was only Brody. I padded across the chilly, Saltillo-tile floor and opened the door to find him greeting me with an extra-large mug of *café con leche.*

"Caffeine!" I cried, seizing the cardboard cup. "My dear old friend."

"Me or the caffeine?" Brody asked.

"Well, I meant the coffee, but as the person who came bearing it, you're now officially my favorite."

"I thought you might need it," he said, rolling his suitcase into my room and dropping his camera bag on my bed.

"You thought right." I took a long swig. "You already checked out of your hotel?"

"Yep," he said. "Mrs. Abernathy had asked me to come by and shoot a few more photos at the farewell brunch this morning. Of course, that was before the whole . . . you know. Dana thing. So I'm not sure if it's still on, but I figured I'd better get on over here early just in case."

"I don't think they had time to cancel brunch. None of the guests know what happened." I took the lid off my cup so I could get to the caffeine faster than the little hole in the lid would allow. "Who else is up?"

"Nicole just came out of her room. If you hurry, you might get a chance to talk to her alone."

Not a bad plan. People would be arriving in just a couple of hours, and I wanted to make sure Nicole was okay and find out how she'd taken the news of Dana's sudden departure. After throwing on a sundress and twisting my hair up in a clip, I got the go-ahead from Brody—who deemed me "presentable, but barely"—and headed downstairs.

I found Nicole at the breakfast table with her new husband and her mom. The three of them had gathered for some coffee and pastries to hold them over till brunch. Nicole wasn't waiting for brunch to make up for all the months of dieting, though; she was digging into a plate of eggs with gusto.

"Kelsey!" she exclaimed. "We were just talking about you. Thank you so much. You did an amazing job last night. Dad had to catch an early flight out, but he told us to be sure to thank you." Her disposition was strangely sunny.

"Yeah," said Vince. "My family had to take off, too, but they said to tell you thanks for everything."

"Good morning," I said, smiling uncomfortably. I paused for a moment, not sure how to proceed. "How'd you sleep?"

"We slept *great*," she said, bumping Vince's shoulder playfully with her own. "Hey, have you checked on Dana this morning? I knocked on her door, but nobody answered."

Shocked, I turned to look at Mrs. Abernathy. Hadn't she told Nicole? Feigning ignorance, Mrs. Abernathy sipped her coffee and waited for me to answer.

Gritting my teeth, I pulled up a chair and sat down. It was time to end this. "Nicole, Vince, I have some bad news."

Nicole sat up straight. "Bad news?"

"What is it?" Vince asked. "What happened?"

"Something terrible. There's no easy way to say this, but Dana didn't just faint. She passed away."

"She passed what?" Nicole asked, not comprehending what I'd said.

"Away. She passed on."

"I don't understand."

"She died, dear," Mrs. Abernathy said.

"But that's not possible!" Nicole looked at me and then at her mother, trying to make sense of what we were telling her. "Are you sure she didn't just sleep in this morning?"

"No," I said. "It happened last night."

"What?! When? After you took her a plate?"

"There was no plate. I'm sorry, Nicole."

Nicole shook her head forcefully, her eyes welling with tears. "No!"

"Are you sure?" Vince asked, knitting his eyebrows in concern. "I mean, what happened?"

"I don't know. After she passed out at the church, she didn't wake up again. I'm so sorry. I'll see what I can find out from the coroner's office."

Nicole's tears began to flow in earnest as the truth sank in. "Why didn't anyone tell us?"

Well, now, there was a good question. I looked at Mrs. Abernathy for support. *A little help here?*

"Yes, Kelsey, why didn't you tell us?" Mrs. Abernathy demanded, but not as sternly as if she'd meant it.

Count to ten before you speak, I warned myself. Was she kidding me? I couldn't call her on her little deception, but what was I supposed to say? "I—I mean, well, we didn't think . . ."

"I suppose you didn't want to ruin the evening for Nicole," Mrs. Abernathy continued. "I guess I can understand that. But still. How dreadful."

But still? *But still?* Not only had she not told her daughter, she'd blamed the whole thing on me.

Nicole leapt up from the table and ran from the room. After an awkward pause, Vince drained his coffee cup, then stood. "I'm going to go make sure she's okay," he said, gesturing across the courtyard.

As his footsteps receded in the distance, Mrs. Abernathy sighed. "Well, that went well, don't you think?"

I turned and gave her a tight smile. "So . . . I guess you decided to let me do the honors?"

"Well, you are the wedding planner. Isn't that part of your job?"

My job? She had to be kidding me. Coordinating bridal parties. Sourcing tent rentals. Picking the perfect venue. *Those* were parts of my job. Making sure that everything goes off without a hitch and that everyone lives happily freaking after, that was my job. Breaking it to the bride that a member of the wedding party was dead? No, that had never come up before.

I stared at her, dumbfounded.

"You're responsible for problem solving, Kelsey. Don't forget that your contract clearly stipulates that you will handle the regular list of duties plus any dreadful, unforeseen situations that might arise in connection to the wedding."

Damn, it did say something like that, although I was pretty sure she was paraphrasing; I would never use the word "dreadful" in a contract.

"So what should I tell Fernando about brunch?" I asked. The villa came with a house staff, and the chef was already hard at work on the preparations. "Should I try to cancel it?"

"Oh, why create extra work for yourself, dear? Besides, I hear he's planning on making us his famous *huevos rancheros*. They're supposed to be just *divine!*"

"Okay, then, I'm going to go start packing. Don't forget that the driver is picking us up at four."

"Yes, you'd better hurry, because we're going to need you to pack up Dana's things, too."

"We *are?*"

"Well, certainly! You don't think I'm going to do it, do you? And surely you don't want poor Nicole to have to do it. That leaves you, of course. It's not as if Charles and I aren't paying you enough."

I was starting to think that no amount of money was enough. Unfortunately, after six years of working out of my apartment in San Francisco, I had finally signed a lease on a sunny corner space in a renovated Victorian in Pacific Heights, and my increased financial responsibility meant that I could no longer afford to tell a client to stick it.

"Of course, Mrs. Abernathy. Anything else?"

"That is all. Oh, actually—could you be a dear and get me a refill on this coffee?"

Back in my room, I found Brody leaning over my vanity, spreading minty-green goo onto his face. "I see you found out my beauty secret," I said.

"Oh, hey, this stuff is supposed to reduce pores, right? How fun! It tingles!"

"Brody, that woman . . ."

"Let me guess: Mrs. A?"

"Who else? She didn't tell Nicole. She left it for me to handle. And now I have to go pack up Dana's belongings, as if I didn't have ten thousand things to do before we leave."

Brody peered into the mirror, trying to spread the facial masque evenly over his one-day scruff. "You can put me to work."

"Really?" With his help, I might actually be ready to leave on time. "Oh, Brody, you're a lifesaver."

"I know. Hey, look," he said, fishing a cucumber from his glass of cucumber-lemon water and putting it over one eye. "I look like a pirate—at a spa!"

Yet another reason to love the man. He was always able to make me laugh.

I looked around the room. Not only did I have my personal belongings to pack, but my room had become the unofficial warehouse of all wedding-related items. I grabbed a tape gun and a box and handed both to Brody. "Okay, let's get my room packed first, then we'll go pack Dana's."

"Aye, aye, Captain. Hey, did you call your new boyfriend?"

"Who, Evan? He's not my new boyfriend. He's an old . . . friend."

"Whatever, Miss Picky. Did you call him? He seemed pretty

into you." A private pilot, Evan had flown me and Brody to San Miguel from Mexico City, saving us from the bus, and Brody had instantly picked up on our history—especially after Evan asked me to go to dinner with him while I was in town.

"Nope, never had time," I replied, folding up some pants and tucking them neatly into my suitcase.

"What? Why not?" Brody sounded disappointed. He wanted me to find a great guy to settle down with as much as he wanted to find one himself.

"C'mon, Brody, Evan and I would never work. For one thing, he lives in another country."

Evan and I had gone out a few years earlier, back when he lived in San Francisco. But after just a few dates, he'd announced that he'd quit his job as an airline pilot to pursue his dream of moving to Mexico, and our burgeoning romance had been cut short. We'd stayed in touch, and I'd even added him to my resources file. Knowing someone with his own plane came in handy when I had guests who needed shuttling around Mexico.

"Kelsey, has it ever occurred to you that that attitude is why it's 'always the wedding planner, never the bride'?"

I picked up a box and scowled. "Less talking, more packing!"

"Jeez, excuse me for caring about your personal life."

"I'm sorry, but it's just hard to take you seriously with that green stuff on your face. Now go rinse off and let's get out of here!"

He retreated into the bathroom, then came back a few minutes later. "Do my pores look smaller?" he asked.

"Microscopic," I said. "Now, you take that pile over there, and I'll take this pile over here. Anything that's not clothes, shoes, or makeup needs to be boxed up so we can ship it back home."

He scooped up a bag filled with custom-embroidered napkins. "What about these?"

"Well, they're not shoes or clothing, so what do you think?"

"In the box?"

"Yep, in the box they go."

Brody stuffed the napkins into the box and began rummaging through the things on the dresser. Approximately twenty seconds passed before he interrupted again. "What about this guest book?"

"Focus, Brody, or no more beauty products for you."

"Okay, okay, in the box." Ten seconds elapsed. "But what about—"

"Brody," I moaned, "if it's not mine, pack it."

"But I don't know whether it's yours or not."

I looked at the exquisitely wrapped package he was holding up in the air. "Actually, no. Sorry, that's for Nicole."

"Can we open it?" he asked, shaking it next to his head and listening for clues as to what might be inside.

"No, I told you, it's for Nicole."

"What'd you get her? Is it silverware?"

"It's not from me, silly. I found it in the rectory and brought it back with me last night."

"Who's it from?" he asked, turning it over and examining the bottom of the box.

"I don't know," I said. "Throw it here."

Brody tossed me the box, and I carefully removed the gift card from its tiny ecru envelope. " 'With love, from Dana.' "

An awkward moment passed as we stared at the gift. "Well, that sucks," Brody said at last. "You going to give it to her?"

"Yeah, but not right now. It'll only upset her more," I said, shoving the package into a nearby tote bag.

After we finished packing, Brody and I headed down the breezeway toward Dana's room.

"Why do we have to pack her stuff anyway?" Brody asked. "It's not like she's going to need it."

"True, but I'm sure her family will want it back. Besides, the rental agency will expect us to clear everything out before we leave."

We paused outside the last door on the left. I stared at the knob for a second. This felt wrong.

"What's the matter, are you chicken?" Brody asked.

"No, it's creepy, that's all."

"Oh, come on." Brody reached past me and grabbed the wrought-iron doorknob. "I'll do it."

The heavy door swung open. The room was a total mess.

"Jeez," Brody said. "How embarrassing for her."

Her clothes were all over the floor, belongings strewn everywhere. As we stared at the mess with our mouths agape, something occurred to me. This wasn't just a failure to tidy up while on vacation. Someone had been looking for something. And considering the enthusiasm with which they'd gutted the chair cushions and dumped the contents of the dresser drawers, they'd been none too happy.

We backed out of the room, pulling the heavy door closed behind us, and I looked at Brody, who for once was speechless.

"I think we'd better call the police."

CHAPTER 4

*a*s a wedding planner, you never know what you might be called upon to do. One day you're an A/V specialist; the next day you're a dove wrangler. My list of services was now growing to include "sneak police officers past unsuspecting brunch guests."

Luckily, Officers Antonio Ortiz and Frank Nolasco hadn't eaten breakfast yet, so the promise of *huevos rancheros* was enough to divert them discreetly through the kitchen. That was about all my bribe got me, though. They took their plates and dismissed me with a single word in Spanish. I didn't recognize it, but I was pretty sure it meant "scram," based on the accompanying hand motion.

After snapping some photos of the guests downstairs, Brody was free to join me in pacing the corridor outside Dana's room. What was going on in there? I was dying of curiosity, but the officers had closed the door firmly behind them. Though I tried to peek through the curtains, I didn't see anything except Officer Ortiz's scowling face before he came over and pulled them shut.

"What do you think is going on in there?" I asked.

"Calm down," Brody said. "They're just doing their job."

"I know, but finding out what happened is *my* job."

"Oh, come on, this is way outside the wedding planner's jurisdiction."

"No, I'm serious! Mrs. Abernathy has made it clear that dealing with this . . . situation is my responsibility. And I'm supposed to have us all out of here by four o'clock!"

Brody checked his watch and made a face. "We're going to be cutting it close."

"That's what I'm saying! We have to get out of here."

"I'm sure everything's going to be fine. They'll finish up, and then we can be on our way."

I tried again to peek, but the curtains were shut tight. What was taking them so long? "Brody, something is seriously messed up here."

"Yeah, you may be right."

"I mean, a twenty-nine-year-old girl doesn't ransack her own room, then drop dead from natural causes."

We leaned against the stucco wall in silence while I pondered everything that had happened. This couldn't be a coincidence; none of the other rooms had been touched. My hopes that Dana's death had been a tragic accident or the inevitable result of some obscure genetic defect had begun to seem fairly improbable—especially now that there were two uniformed officers involved.

I stood up. "Are you thinking what I'm thinking?"

Brody's face brightened a little. "Breakfast?"

"What? No, murder."

"I'd prefer breakfast," he sighed. "But yeah, this looks pretty bad."

"This is terrible! No one's ever going to hire me again."

"That's not true. No one could possibly think this is your fault."

"I know, but nobody wants to hire a wedding planner who can't even keep her wedding party alive."

"There's absolutely nothing you could have done to prevent this. What you *can* do is what you do best: deal with the family. Does Nicole even know what's going on?"

She didn't. None of them did. Frankly, I'd been avoiding them. As helpless as I felt, Brody was right: I did need to tell them what had happened.

After letting the officers know where to find me and sending Brody back to my room, I headed for the newlyweds' suite, where I found Nicole, Vince, and Zoe. The fact that Mrs. Abernathy was off somewhere saying good-bye to the last of her brunch guests settled the butterflies in my stomach at least a little. Nicole and I seldom had a chance to talk without her mom hovering nearby.

"Any news?" Nicole asked. Her eyes were red and puffy, and I could tell she'd been crying. "This is just horrible."

"Nicole, can we sit down for a minute?" I asked. "I need to talk to you about Dana. Can you think of any reason anyone might have gone into her room?"

"What do you mean, like she had someone staying with her?" Nicole said. Zoe and Vince exchanged uneasy glances.

"No, I mean more like breaking and entering."

"What? No! Why?"

"Well, the police are here investigating a break-in. Someone ransacked the place."

"Why would they do that?" Zoe asked.

"Beats me," I said. "That's what they're trying to find out. From the looks of it, someone wanted to find something."

"Are you saying this is connected to her death?"

"I honestly don't know. But it does look suspicious. Can you think of any reason anyone might want to kill her?"

"No!" said Nicole. "No one would want to kill Dana. She was so sweet. I mean, you met her. Can you imagine anyone not liking her?" She was searching my eyes for some sort of agreement, but I just bobbed my head in a not-quite-nod. I myself had wanted to kill her a little bit, and I'd only known her a week.

"Everyone loved Dana. Right, Vince?" She looked to her new husband for support.

"Um, yeah," he enthused, shuffling his feet while playing with the fringe on a throw pillow. Zoe had turned her attention to a small statue in a nook near the bed, deeply engrossed in its craftsmanship, no doubt.

"Oh, God, this is all my fault," Nicole said.

"What do you mean?" Zoe asked. "How is this your fault?"

"I'm the one who brought her here. If it weren't for me, none of this would have happened!"

"Nicole," I said, "this isn't anyone's fault. Well, it may be someone's fault, but it certainly isn't yours. Or mine. Let's be very clear about that."

Zoe set down the statue. "If it's anyone's fault, it's—"

"It's no one's fault," said Vince brusquely, interrupting a sentence I kind of wanted to hear the end of.

Right as I opened my mouth to ask Zoe what she meant, Mrs. Abernathy swooped into the room without so much as knocking. *So much for privacy,* I thought, forcing a smile onto my face.

"Mom, someone went through Dana's room!" Nicole said.

"It figures, with all the hoodlums I've seen loitering around the plaza. Why I allowed you to drag us to Mexico, I'll never know." She hadn't directed the comment at me, but I was pretty sure she wouldn't have phrased it that way if she'd been talking to Nicole.

"Mrs. Abernathy, this wasn't a break-in. Someone was looking for something. They destroyed Dana's room."

"How common," Mrs. Abernathy said, waving a perfectly manicured hand in the air. "Well, there goes our deposit."

How was it that Mrs. Abernathy was so skilled at missing the point? I didn't know how the girls put up with her. The woman should come with her own warning label.

"Okay, then," I said. "So that's what I know. I need to go tie up a few loose ends so we can get out of here. I'll be sure and tell you if the police find anything. In the meantime, if you can give me contact information for Dana's next of kin, I'll make sure the proper arrangements are made for her things."

Nicole's eyes were wide. "But what about . . . ?" The question hung there for a minute, unfinished.

"What about what?" I asked.

"Yes, spit it out, dear," added Mrs. Abernathy.

"Her . . . you know. Her body." Nicole's voice was barely audible. "Does she have to get buried here?"

"Don't be silly, darling. Kelsey will fly back with the body."

I would? No thanks.

"I don't know how these things work," Nicole said. "I've never known anyone who's died before. Well, one of my grandmothers died, but she was really old. She had dentures."

"Look, Nicole, it's really sweet of you to be so concerned, but don't you worry about it. What happens with the, the—with Dana is up to her family." *And no one else,* I wanted to add. "They'll take care of it. Now let's get you guys all packed up. The limo will be here at four, and Evan will be waiting at the airport to fly us to Mexico City."

From there, the bride and groom would be off to the Riviera Maya for their honeymoon. I'd fly back home and find a bride to work with who was an orphan or maybe had two dads, and Mrs. Abernathy could go back to whatever hell she came from.

"Okay," said Nicole.

"Great," I replied, heading toward the door, anxious to finish packing.

Ever the gentleman, Vince stood to see me out. "Thanks for everything, Kelsey. You really did do a great job planning our wedding."

"It was my pleasure," I said, and I even kind of meant it for a second or two, until Mrs. Abernathy chimed in: "Next time maybe you can keep a better eye on things. But I suppose the flowers turned out nice."

As I reached for the door, a sudden pounding on the other side of it made me jump back a couple of feet.

"Policía," I heard from outside the door. Oh, thank goodness. They were done, which meant I could finish packing Dana's things and get us out by four.

"Well, don't just stand there," said Mrs. Abernathy. "Let them in."

I opened the door for Ortiz and Nolasco.

"Hello, officers. Are you all done?"

"Who's in charge here?" asked Ortiz. I hadn't noticed before how intimidatingly tall he was. It didn't help that he was hovering over me with a scowl on his face.

I started to point to Mrs. Abernathy, but she cut me off.

"She is," she said, pointing a finger back at me.

"Oh, um, well—I'm just the wedding planner. Is the room all clear? Can I go finish packing it up now?"

"No, the room is sealed. You cannot go in."

I sighed. I hated to leave the mess for someone else, but I didn't have a choice. "Okay. I'll tell the leasing company. I'm sure they'll figure something out." I grabbed a pen and paper off the desk and scribbled my cell phone number. "Here's my contact info. If there's anything we can do to help—"

"I'm going to need a list of everyone who was staying here last night," Ortiz said, flipping open a notepad and poising his pen above it.

"You don't think *we* had anything to do with this, do you?" Mrs. Abernathy asked indignantly.

Ortiz ignored her. "The names, please?" It was more of a command than a question.

No one jumped in, and the two officers were staring at me expectantly. "Oh, sure. There was me, Kelsey McKenna. Then the bride and groom here, Nicole and Vince." I paused between names so he could write them down. "Nicole's sister, Zoe. Mr. and Mrs. Abernathy . . ."

Ortiz looked around the room. "Mr. Abernathy? Where is he?"

"I believe he had to fly out early this morning," I said, looking at Mrs. Abernathy for confirmation.

"That's correct," she said. "He had to be in Mexico City by nine A.M. to catch a flight home. Business calls!"

"There was also another bridesmaid, Claire Johnson, and Ryan McGuire, the best man, but they headed back this morning, too."

Ortiz and Nolasco exchanged exasperated looks. I could have told them that wrangling a wedding party is like herding cats.

"Okay, we're going to need their full names and phone numbers. In the meantime, don't anyone else leave until we can clear this up. We're going to need to talk to everyone who was staying here," said Officer Ortiz.

I checked my watch. "Sure, we've got a little time. We don't leave for another two hours."

His head jerked up from the notebook he'd been scribbling

in. "I'm sorry, but I'm going to have to ask that none of you leave town."

There was a stunned silence as the words sank in. Mrs. Abernathy was the first to speak: "You don't understand: we don't live here. *No live-o here-o.*"

Ortiz glared at Mrs. Abernathy's improvised Spanish. "I understand perfectly, but I must insist."

"Surely there's something you can do," I said, feeling the panic mounting in my voice. "Checkout time is four o'clock, and we have a private plane chartered to take us home."

Officer Ortiz looked unmoved. "A young woman is dead, and we have a lot of questions. I'm afraid we can't allow you to leave."

"Well, surely we get some say in the matter," said Mrs. Abernathy. "I mean, you can't *make* us stay here."

"The way I see it, *señora*," said Officer Ortiz, "either you can cooperate with us now and do what we ask—"

"Or *what?*" Mrs. Abernathy challenged, eyes flashing.

"Or I can assume you are guilty and arrest you for the murder of Dana Poole."

CHAPTER 5

S o let's recap," said Brody. I had texted him to meet me back in my room so I could update him on the situation. "You voluntarily called the police about a robbery and now you're a suspect in a murder? That doesn't make any sense!"

"Right? What kind of murderer calls the police and says, 'Hey, why don't you drop by later and see what else I've been up to?' "

"What did they say?"

"I already told you: they said we can't leave."

"I mean specifically. Did they say *you* can't leave?"

"Yep."

"Did they say *I* can't leave?"

"No, they don't even know you exist, but I'm stuck here, at least for the next few hours."

"Can they even do that?" Brody asked. "Can they really make you stay?"

"They haven't charged us with anything, but we should probably try to stick around long enough for them to talk to us all so they can see we didn't have anything to do with this."

There was a knock at the door. It was Officer Ortiz, who had come to fetch me for questioning. I followed him to the dining room, which he had commandeered as an impromptu interrogation room.

"So you're the . . . wedding planner?" he asked, flipping through his notepad.

"That's right," I said, nodding helpfully.

"How long have you known the deceased?"

"Just a few days. She was a late addition to the wedding party."

He jotted down notes while I talked. "Do you know anyone who would want to harm her?"

Pretty much everyone, I wanted to say but didn't. What I actually said—and which was very diplomatic of me, I might add— was, "Well, Nicole loved her. Beyond that, the rest of us didn't really know her all that well."

"Mmm-hmm," he said. "Did she have any enemies?"

"Probably," I said before I could catch myself. "I mean, who doesn't these days?"

He looked up from his notepad, his face inscrutable. "What about the sister, Zoe? How did they get along?"

"About like the rest of us." I was intentionally vague, not wanting to implicate anyone. "Why?"

"I'm trying to establish who might have had a reason to want to kill her." He peered at me intently, trying to gauge my reaction.

"Kill her? Do you really think it was murder?" I'd hoped he'd been bluffing earlier, throwing around the *M* word to get our attention, but he certainly didn't seem to be bluffing now.

He tapped his pen impatiently on the table. "Miss McKenna,

did you witness anything out of the ordinary between Zoe and the victim?"

My mind flashed back to several catty exchanges I'd heard over the past few days, but it was all typical bridesmaid stuff.

"No, I'm sorry. Zoe and Dana weren't best friends, but believe me, there wasn't anything between them that I haven't already seen at a thousand other weddings." Whatever he was trying to get at, I was pretty sure there was no way Zoe had had anything to do with it—whatever *it* was.

Officer Ortiz insisted I walk him through the whole week, from the welcome party to the rehearsal dinner to the group outings, as well as give him a detailed description of the wedding and reception. I checked my watch impatiently. If he didn't wrap it up soon, Evan wouldn't be able to get us to Mexico City in time for our flight home.

"I don't suppose you can tell me what the cause of death was?" I asked. Maybe if I knew what happened I could convince him to let us leave.

"No."

"Is it because you don't know, or you can't tell me?" I asked.

He looked up from his notebook and gave me a cold stare. That was all the answer I was going to get.

"But it wasn't natural causes?" I smiled at him, hoping to soften him up, but still no answer. "If you tell me what's going on, maybe I can help you."

That got his attention. He leaned forward menacingly. His bulky frame was built for intimidation. "If you have any information, I would recommend sharing it."

"No, I don't know anything. I just want to be able to help." I tossed my hair a little for good measure. "If I knew exactly what it was we were investigating . . ."

I won't lie: I was trying to work some of my feminine wiles.

"Thank you, Miss McKenna," he replied brusquely. "I believe we're done here."

So much for wiles.

You'd think with all the questions he had, he'd be open to answering a few of mine, but apparently it doesn't work that way in Mexico.

Okay, fine, it doesn't work that way anywhere, but it was worth a try.

He snapped his notebook shut. "You're free to go."

"About that . . . free to go back to my room, or free to go back to San Francisco?"

"Neither. You can't go back to your room until we've had a chance to search it. And we're going to need you to stick around for a few days."

"What? You've got to be kidding me!" I felt my face flushing.

"Don't make me arrest you, Miss McKenna."

"No, no, I won't. I mean, I'll try not to. You have my full cooperation." My dreams of escaping our Saltillo-tiled prison were slipping away.

"Good. Then you won't mind staying in town a couple more days while we investigate."

Damn. If only I'd taken an early flight like the others. "You realize some of the wedding party is already gone."

"I'm a detective, Miss McKenna."

"Right. So I guess I'll just, you know, hang out."

Ortiz nodded, glad I was finally starting to see things his way. "That would be best."

I swung by my room and cracked the door open, but Nolasco yelled something at me in Spanish and I closed it again. He was busy going through my things. The perv.

I went down to the courtyard, where I found Brody waiting.

I plopped into the chair next to his before filling him in on my own personal Spanish inquisition.

"Anyway, I have to hang tight for now, but you can still make it home tonight if you hurry," I said.

"I don't know," he said tentatively. He was clearly worried about me.

"No, it's fine. It's just so . . ." I waved my hand, at a loss for words.

"Ridiculous? Unfair? Completely sucky?"

"All of the above. Anyway, go on. Save yourself."

"Are you sure?" Brody asked.

"Yes. Absolutely. Well, no. But yeah, go. Seriously. I'll just . . ."

There really wasn't any good way to finish that sentence. My eyes welled up with tears of frustration.

"Listen," said Brody, leaning forward and squeezing my shoulder. "You booked me on a full-fare ticket, remember?"

"Yeah?"

"So it doesn't make any difference if I go back today or tomorrow or next week, even."

I laughed, wiping the tears out of my eyes. "Next week? God, I hope it doesn't come to that."

"You know what I mean. I don't have anywhere I have to be. That's the beauty of being self-employed. I can catch up on work stuff here as easily as anywhere else."

"You mean it?" I felt about a hundred pounds lighter already.

"I've already checked out of my hotel, though, so it would be great if I could move into one of these empty rooms."

"Oh, Brody!" I flung my arms around him. "You're amazing. I have to call the rental agency to see if we can stay, but we'll figure something out. Consider me your own private travel agent. And when you find Mr. Right, I'll plan your wedding for free."

"Well, that kind of goes without saying."

Calling the rental company proved easy enough. The next guests weren't arriving until Friday, which gave us a few extra days to figure everything out. It was ours—for a price, of course, but I wasn't the one paying the bills, so what did I care?

"Feel free to charge us double for the inconvenience," I generously offered the rental agent.

"No es necesario, señora," he replied. "It's no trouble at all."

"Oh, I insist."

Next on my list was Evan, who was already at the airport, waiting for us to arrive.

"Hi, you on your way?" he asked. "We need to leave, like, now if we're going to make it to Mexico City in time for your flight."

"We have a situation," I said. "We can't leave yet."

"What? Why not?"

"Because it would land us in a Mexican prison," I replied. "We kind of lost a bridesmaid while we were here."

"How do you lose a bridesmaid?"

"Well, not lost like 'look under the bed' lost. You remember Dana? The late arrival you picked up the other night?"

"Yeah?"

"She's dead."

"What? What happened?"

"We don't know yet. They're looking into it."

"That's horrible! Is there anything I can do?"

"I hope so. I'm not sure when we're going to be able to leave. Is there any way we can reschedule?"

"Of course. My calendar's pretty flexible this week. I have some flights to make, but that's the beauty of being your own boss."

"Thank you, Evan. I really owe you one." I relaxed a little.

"I do have one condition."

"We'll pay you double—it's no problem." I was starting to

enjoy running up a tab for Mrs. Abernathy. They could afford it. Perhaps I'd insist on luxury gift baskets for the house staff to make up for the inconvenience of dead bodies and histrionic guests.

"You're going out with me tonight."

"Evan—"

"No excuses. You can't possibly be booked up since you weren't even supposed to be here."

"I don't think I'd be very good company."

"What are you going to do, sit home and stew? You need some distraction."

"No way. You're a pilot. They'd probably arrest me for trying to leave the country."

"I have some friends down at the police department. What if I clear it with them first? Would that make you feel better?"

"Evan . . ."

"Kelsey."

"Okay, fine." At least it would give me an excuse to get away from my clients for a bit. Besides, Brody would be thrilled.

"I'll pick you up at seven."

"Okay, see you then."

Brody looked at me expectantly as I hung up the phone. "Well? What did he say?"

"That I'm going out with him tonight, apparently."

"What? Get out! That's great."

"I thought you'd approve."

"Of course I approve! Can I come with you?"

"Brody!"

"What? I want to make sure you two play nice. Then I'll leave when it's time for you to have sex."

"We're not having sex. We're just having dinner."

"Which is oftentimes a precursor to sex. I know you probably don't remember how these things work . . ."

"Fine, come along with us. What do I care? I'm being held date-hostage anyway."

"I'm just kidding. You kids have fun." He ducked behind a chair just in time to deflect the bottle of water I threw at him.

CHAPTER 6

*D*espite my protestations, there really weren't any good, solid reasons not to go out with Evan. Well, okay, there was the fact that he lived in another country and there was absolutely zero chance of it going anywhere, but who says all dates have to end in a destination wedding?

People always assume that when you're a wedding planner you want to get married really badly, when actually, nothing could be further from the truth. It's like if you worked at an ice cream shop. For the first month, you'd eat ice cream every day and think, *Wow, I'm super lucky; I can have ice cream whenever I want.* Then you'd start gaining weight *and* getting bored with the ice cream. You'd start to eat it less often, and after a few months, you'd find that you preferred salty snacks.

It's like that with weddings. You see enough of them, see what they do to people, and it dulls your appetite for weddings altogether. All those flowers and pretty dresses and lovey-dovey stuff? For me, it's just business.

I guess I'm a pretty terrible spokesman for my company.

Anyway, I'd finally agreed to go out with Evan, expecting nothing more than an evening away from the villa and maybe a nice glass of wine. He picked me up at seven, and we strolled toward the center of town.

"So how are you liking it here?" I asked.

"Can't complain," he said. "Everybody's pretty laid back, food's great . . . except now that San Miguel keeps making all those 'Top Places to Travel' lists, everyone wants to come visit me."

"Hard to blame them. It really is beautiful down here," I said as we walked through the town plaza, known to everybody as the *jardín*. On nights like tonight, with the weather mild and tourist season in full swing, as many as three or four mariachi bands strolled the *jardín* to field the constant stream of requests, like a chaotic battle of the bands where everyone plays at the same time.

We paused for a moment to sit on one of the park benches facing La Parroquia, a three-hundred-year-old church whose spires could be seen from almost anywhere in town. Even if you couldn't see the church, you could usually hear it: it marked the passage of time by chiming every fifteen minutes and clanging enthusiastically every hour on the hour.

I knew we'd stopped so I could appreciate the imposing building's Gothic architecture, but I took the opportunity to sneak a peek at my date. Mexico clearly agreed with him. He'd traded in his clean-shaven pilot look for a three-day scruff and grown his thick, brown hair out to his collar. Had it always been this wavy? It had never been long enough for me to tell.

He caught me studying him and smiled. "I'm glad I was able to lure you away for the evening."

I nodded. "I'll be honest: it's good to get out for a while.

Mrs. Abernathy's in a total snit about not being able to leave, and everyone else is pretty stunned by Dana's death. The mood over there is pretty intense."

"I'll bet," he said, taking my hand. "I'm sure they need some time to process everything that's happened."

"Yeah, that's for sure. Anyway, the chef was cooking them something special tonight to try to cheer them up, so I know they're in good hands. And I could use some downtime, too. It was nice of them to invite me to stay there with them, but it's hard not to feel like I'm always on the clock."

"Well, then it's a good thing you agreed to my demands," he said, squeezing my hand playfully. "You hungry?"

"I'm starving, actually. All I've eaten today is what I was able to scavenge off the brunch buffet." We'd passed several restaurants that I'd been meaning to try, including a Thai place that I was more than a little curious about. Not that Mexico wasn't allowed to deviate from Mexican food, but I was intrigued by the idea of slurping down pad thai and tom yum in a town known more for *barbacoa* and *albóndigas*. Besides, it was usually packed.

"Good," Evan said, taking my hand. "I'm having my chef prepare us something."

I looked at him in surprise. "Your chef? You have a chef?"

"Well, a part-time chef. He's amazing."

"That must be nice. It's also very crafty of you."

"How do you mean?" Evan asked.

"None of that awkward 'Do you want to come back to my place?' business after dinner."

Evan blushed just a little. "When you put it that way, I *am* awfully clever. Besides, Raúl makes the best sautéed sea scallops in the whole state of Guanajuato."

"Sold," I said, my stomach growling in a way that made it impossible to feign disinterest. "You had me at 'sautéed.'"

I was excited to get to see Evan's house. Throughout the historic center of town, the residences are all hidden behind tall adobe walls that come right up to the sidewalk, and it's impossible to tell what's behind them without an invitation. Behind the heavy wooden doors could be an opulent villa or a modest *casita,* a luscious garden or a tiled courtyard, each one a secret waiting to be revealed.

As Evan turned the key in his front gate, I couldn't wait to see what would be on the other side. It was no villa, but it *was* straight out of a design magazine, with beautiful antique furniture, colorful folk art, and a garden-like courtyard lit by tin *luminarias.* Sure, your money goes further in Mexico, even in pricey San Miguel, but he had to be making some serious cash as a private pilot.

It felt good to be hidden away for an Abernathy-free evening. A table was already set for two in the courtyard, and as we sat down, a middle-aged man appeared with a pitcher of sangria and two chilled glasses, right on cue.

"Thank you, Raúl," said Evan.

House staff. Nice.

Evan gently clinked his glass against mine. "Here's to our fourth date, five years later."

"Better late than never." I smiled, taking a sip of my fruit-laden beverage.

"Maybe you'll stick around long enough for a fifth date," Evan said.

"No offense, but God I hope not."

Evan looked a little hurt. "At least wait till you taste the ceviche before you make any hasty decisions."

No wonder I'm such a hit with the fellas.

"I'm sorry. This is wonderful, and I'm glad I came. I'm just anxious to get back to San Francisco. Speaking of, sorry for canceling on you today."

"It's no problem. I ended up booking a charter to Mexico City at the last minute, so it's all the same to me. Besides, it gives us a chance to catch up."

And catch up we did.

Raúl brought us a seemingly never-ending parade of *antojitos,* leading up to the grand finale, his famous scallops, which were every bit as fabulous as I'd been led to believe. It would have been easy to lose track of time altogether, were it not for the church bells ringing in the distance.

"So, any word on when you're flying back?"

"No, the police are still investigating Dana's death, and we've been instructed to stay put. I guess with the break-in, they're assuming something suspicious happened, but there's no way any of us had anything to do with it."

"I don't know, though," Evan said, sipping his drink. "Don't you think it sounds a little suspicious?"

"How do you figure?"

"Did your room get broken into?"

"No."

"Did anyone else's room get broken into?

"No."

"Just the dead girl's?"

"Well. Yeah."

"And you can't think of one reason the police would be suspicious?"

"Look, Evan, I can see how it looks bad, but I know these people. They're annoying as can be, but they're not murderers." I fished some fruit out of my sangria and munched on it distractedly. "Couldn't it be a coincidence? I mean, we don't even know the cause of death. The stupid police wouldn't tell me anything."

"The nerve."

"I know, right? I even tried flirting with one of them, and he was completely nonresponsive."

"That I find hard to believe," he said, leaning across the table and kissing me softly on the mouth.

Swoon. Okay, just because he was the most charming man I'd encountered in, oh, five years, didn't mean I was going to chuck it all and move to Mexico, but for one heated moment, I pondered what it would be like to be a kept woman. Nah, I'd be bored with nothing to do but order around the part-time house staff. Besides, I was booked solid for the next year and a half. But damn, he made it tempting. It would be nice to be taken care of for once, rather than doing all the caretaking. Not to mention the handholding, decision-making, *t*-crossing and *i*-dotting.

"I admit it looks suspicious, but I'm sure everything will be fine. They'll figure out that none of us has anything to do with this mess, and we can all go back to our lives."

"I have selfish reasons for hoping they drag it out," Evan said, "but I'll see what I can find out from my friends at the station."

Handsome *and* handy to have around. My kind of man.

After dinner—and, to be fair, more kissing—we walked to the *jardín* to listen to the mariachis for a bit. After a group of tourists finished nodding their heads enthusiastically to "El Jarabe Tapatío"—also known as "The Mexican Hat Dance," also known as "the only Mexican song some people can name when approached by a mariachi"—Evan pressed some pesos into the bandleader's hand and whispered something in his ear. They began to play a romantic ballad as Evan slipped his arm around my waist and pulled me close. We danced for a few minutes while passersby smiled appreciatively. I could tell what they were thinking: *Just two young people in love.*

As the song finished, an older woman patted me on the arm

and said something in Spanish. My Spanish wasn't good enough to catch what she'd said, but the twinkle in her eye made me blush.

The date had been a good one, I had to admit. San Miguel was one of the most romantic towns in Mexico, maybe even North America, but I'd never really been able to enjoy it properly before now.

We got to the gate of the villa, and Evan kissed me again as the bells of La Parroquia chimed midnight in the distance.

"You know," he said, leaning in for a kiss, "one of the benefits of dating a pilot is that distance isn't really an issue." Just as our lips were about to touch, the heavy wooden door to the villa suddenly swung open.

"Kelsey!" Nicole cried, oblivious to the moment she had interrupted.

"What?! Oh! Hi. Nicole. We were just—I was just—you remember Evan?"

"Hi, Evan. Kelsey, where have you been?" She threw her arms around me and managed to get out a wobbly "Thank God you're here" before completely bursting into tears.

Maybe it was a mistake to have left her here with her mother. There's no telling what Mrs. Abernathy had said to put her in this state. I knew it had to be stressful for the young couple, being cooped up when they should have been off somewhere consummating their marriage. From the looks of it, Mrs. Abernathy had badgered the poor girl to the breaking point.

"What's up?" I asked, self-consciously wiping at my mouth in case my lipstick was smeared.

Nicole had yet to regain her composure, and my eyes met Evan's over Nicole's shoulder.

"Sorry," I mouthed silently, to which Evan shrugged good-naturedly. I was eager to finish my good-night kiss in private, but that seemed unlikely, especially when Mrs. Abernathy joined us on the sidewalk.

"Kelsey, you mustn't leave without telling us. We've been looking for you for hours. Now come inside, girls, so we can stop making spectacles of ourselves for all of San Miguel."

I felt peevish. I wasn't on the clock. "Evan and I were just catching up."

"Catch up on your own time," said Mrs. Abernathy. "Zoe has been arrested."

CHAPTER 7

*A*fter being snatched from Evan's arms, I bid him a hasty good night and followed the Abernathys into our walled compound. Fernando, the chef who had kept us well fed throughout our stay at the villa, had thoughtfully laid out a midnight snack to fuel our middle-of-the-night summit, and the family filled me in on the events of the evening. It was starting to feel increasingly like a hostage situation, except with really good snacks.

It was hard to follow what had happened, since everyone was trying to talk at once. Their garbled cross talk came out sounding something like: "Kelsey Zoe police tonight Nicole interrogated because Dana and Zoe was accused and handcuffs jail . . . do something!"

I couldn't follow any given sentence, but all the words were there. Zoe was in jail, which was very, very bad.

"That's terrible!" I said when the hubbub had finally died down long enough for me to speak. "I can't believe they think she did this. What I don't understand—and if you can talk one at a time, that would be super helpful—is why?"

Unsurprisingly, Mrs. Abernathy was the first to jump in. "They wouldn't tell us! Can you imagine?"

Actually, I found it pretty easy to imagine, but Mrs. Abernathy wasn't used to dealing with people who didn't have to do her bidding.

Mrs. Abernathy, Nicole, and Vince all stared at me, waiting for my response, but I was at a loss for words. On what grounds could they have possibly arrested Zoe? "Did they tell you *anything*?"

Nicole shook her head. "It all happened so quickly. The policemen—those two who were here earlier—came by while we were having dinner. They said Zoe had to go down to the station with them. We told them there had to be some mistake, but they wouldn't listen."

Mrs. Abernathy nodded in agreement with her daughter's description of the events. "It was like they were entirely unconcerned with our feelings."

I leaned over the table and put my head in my hands, rubbing my eyes, trying desperately to come up with some response. I wanted to go to bed so badly. Why had I let Mrs. Abernathy bully me into staying at the villa instead of in my own private hotel room? And how had Brody managed not to get roped into all of this? He was probably hiding in his room, the traitor.

"I've called the consulate," Mrs. Abernathy continued, "but no one will be in till ten o'clock tomorrow morning."

"Do you need me to get you the name of a lawyer?"

"We *have* a lawyer, Kelsey." Silly me. Of course they had a lawyer. He was probably part of the house staff.

"Getting him on the phone—now, that's a different story. But as soon as he calls me back, I'm going to get him on the next plane down here."

"Well, great, sounds like you've got it all under control," I said. I felt terrible that Zoe had to spend the night in jail, but I was glad she was in capable hands.

Mrs. Abernathy looked incredulous. "Kelsey, we need your help!"

"Me? What can I do?"

"Get Zoe out of jail, for starters!"

I glanced over at Nicole and Vince for support, but Nicole just looked at me expectantly while Vince stared at the floor. What superpowers did these people think I possessed? "How am I supposed to do that, exactly?"

"You're the wedding planner!" said Mrs. Abernathy. "I'm sure you'll think of something!"

Was she *serious*?

"Mrs. Abernathy, I can't do anything! If she were trapped in a wedding cake, I might be able to get her out, but this is outside of my jurisdiction!"

"But you know these people. You work down here. Surely there's something you can do, someone you can talk to. The thought of my baby in a Mexican prison . . ."

Sure. I could probably just sashay into the station and explain that there'd been a huge mistake. I'm sure they'd let her out on my say-so. This midnight ambush coupled with the sangria was making it hard to think.

"Mrs. Abernathy, I'm sorry. I really don't know what to tell you right now. This is a lot to process, and I'm sure we'll all feel better after a good night's sleep."

Nicole and Vince looked like they were exhausted, too, and nodded with glassy-eyed stares.

Mrs. Abernathy sighed and slumped in her chair. "Oh, all right. There's probably nothing we can do at this time of night anyway."

Finally—she'd finally said something reasonable.

"But first thing in the morning I want you to march down to that police station and tell them they've made a terrible mistake. And be sure to remind them that she's an American!"

So much for reasonable.

I wasn't sure what magical power she thought I could wield over the police, but the woman was clearly used to getting her way. She didn't see me as the wedding planner—she saw me as staff, and she assumed I would do her bidding.

"Look, Mrs. Abernathy, I don't think—"

"I'm not paying you to think! Just fix this. Now, I'll see you in the morning." And with that she stood, kissed her other daughter good night, and vanished down the hall.

Whoever had painted the ceiling of my bedroom had done an impeccable job. Top-notch, really. I knew, because I'd been staring at it for most of the night. I cocked one bleary eye open to check the time on the digital clock across the room. The glowing numbers read 4:18 A.M. I had the same feeling of sleepless despair that I'd experienced at 1:23, 2:47, and 3:05.

I'd returned to my room around one o'clock and crawled into bed, hoping the next morning I'd wake up with a clear head and a brilliant plan. But to do that, I'd have to get a good night's sleep—and to do *that* I'd actually have to *fall* asleep.

What was I going to do about Zoe? I didn't want her to sit in jail, but it really was beyond my particular skill set. Too bad Brody wasn't awake. He always had good advice. Well, okay, maybe not

good advice, but he'd let me talk until I figured it out for myself.
I was tempted to wake him up, but that would be mean.

Five minutes passed. Waking someone up at four-thirty in the
morning *was* mean, right?

Or was it just mildly inconsiderate?

I decided I could live with mildly inconsiderate in the face of
an international crisis, so I threw on some yoga pants under my
sleep tee and tiptoed down the hall to his room.

He didn't immediately answer my knock, and I started to feel
silly standing outside in my hastily assembled attire. I knocked
again. Nothing. What if I ran into someone out here? It wasn't
likely, but it would sure be embarrassing. I tried the door. It was
unlocked, so I stepped inside the dark room.

"Brody? You in here?" I whispered.

"Who's there?" he demanded, fumbling at his bedside lamp.

"It's me, Kelsey." I padded across the room toward the sound
of his voice.

He clicked the light on and glared at me. "What the hell?"

"You shouldn't leave your door unlocked," I said. "Anyone
could come in."

"So I see. What are you doing? What time is it?"

"Scooch over," I said, climbing into bed next to him. "We
have to talk."

"You could have at least brought me some coffee," he said,
yawning as he spoke.

"What? Don't be silly. It's the middle of the night. Anyway,
did you hear about Zoe?" Somehow he'd managed to miss the
whole drama, having weaseled his way out of joining the family
for dinner, so I recounted my earlier conversation with Mrs. Abernathy, throwing in occasional nudges to keep him awake. "Brody,
are you listening? This is important!"

Brody sat up and rubbed his eyes.

"Sorry, I just had the weirdest dream that a crazy woman broke into my room and woke me up at four in the morning. Oh, and look: here you are!"

"Okay, I'm sorry I had to wake you up, but this is important. You wanna go get coffee?"

"No, I want to go back to sleep."

"Yeah, me too. Anyway, Mrs. Abernathy expects me to march into the police station in a few hours and, I don't know, slip Zoe a file in a cake or sweet-talk the police into letting her go."

"I'm sure you'll do great at that," he said, burrowing farther into his bedding. "Good night."

"Brody!" I pulled away the pillow he had strategically put over his head to drown me out. "C'mon, how am I going to get the police to listen to me if I can't even get *you* to listen to me?"

"Okay, okay," he said, sitting up and yawning. "I'm listening. Now, what's your problem?"

"Mrs. Abernathy thinks it's my job to fix this, but I don't know the first thing about getting someone out of jail."

He sighed as he leaned up on one elbow. "Did it ever occur to you that you're going to have a lot better luck getting through to the police than Mrs. Abernathy would?"

"True. But what am I going to say to them? Zoe looks great in taffeta? She carried those flowers like a champ?"

"I don't know, but at least you can say you tried."

"But then what? Mrs. Abernathy isn't going to be content with 'I tried.' And I don't have time to stick around until this gets sorted out. I have to get back to San Francisco. The Richardson wedding is in two weeks, and I've still got a ton of work to do."

"Then we'll have to go with Plan B."

"Plan B? We have a Plan B? What is it?"

"I don't know. You wedding planners always have a Plan B, don't you?"

I sank back into the spare pillow. Dang it. I was Plan B. I at least had to try.

"Okay, I guess I'll sleep on it and maybe in the morning I'll know what to say."

"Soundslieaplahn," he replied, his face smushed back down in the pillow.

"Brody?" He shook his head and buried his face deeper in the poly-down mix. "Brody, can I stay in here with you?"

I took his snoring as a yes.

I got myself to the police station relatively early, which I considered an impressive feat on three hours' sleep. The jovial officer I talked to was a lot nicer than the detectives who'd questioned us at the villa. He nodded politely as I fumbled my way through an explanation of who I was and why I was there, then told me to "just speak English," rather than commit any more atrocities on the Spanish language. After I finished my impassioned appeal for Zoe's innocence, he asked me to wait.

This is going better than I thought! Maybe I actually got through to him! I tapped my feet on the gray linoleum floor and squinted up at the fluorescent lights overhead. *I'm sure they'll realize they've got the wrong person and we'll all have a good laugh at this and Mrs. Abernathy will give me a bonus for being awesome.*

My fantasy was shattered as the two double doors at the end of the hall swung open and Officer Ortiz strode through. He glared at me as he approached, and I tried to make myself invisible.

"*Hola,*" I said meekly.

"Come with me," he replied, not sounding even a little bit welcoming.

I followed him to a small, windowless room with a worn wooden table and a couple of beat-up chairs. Was I about to be interrogated? I looked up at the ceiling to check for a security camera as Officer Ortiz pulled up a chair and flipped open his note pad.

"First of all," he began, pointing his stubby finger at me, "it's important that you understand that I'm the lead on this case. If you have any information, you need to come directly to me."

"Got it," I replied. "Sorry."

"So what is it you wanted to tell me?" Ortiz looked at me expectantly. If he thought I was here to hand over evidence, he was mistaken.

"Just that you've got the wrong girl!" I said. "Zoe didn't do this. She couldn't have."

He narrowed his eyes at me. "Miss McKenna, how long have you known Zoe Abernathy?"

"Oh, I've known her for months!" I answered. The words didn't sound as impressive out loud as they had inside my head.

"And are you aware of her past relationship with the deceased?"

"What? No. I mean, kind of." I didn't think they'd had a relationship, other than both being connected to Nicole.

"Would you say she and the victim were friends?"

I froze. "Friends? They weren't *friend* friends, but they were friendly enough, I guess."

He scribbled in his notepad thoughtfully. *What is he writing in there?* This wasn't going well. I had to make sure he didn't have the wrong idea.

"Look, Officer Ortiz, Zoe is innocent, okay? Whatever you heard about them arguing at the wedding, it's unrelated."

"So they did argue at the wedding?" More jotting. *Great.*

"Well, sure, but it was no big deal. I see bridesmaids fight all the time, and it never leads to murder. Just drunken bickering and awkward group photos."

He peered at me intently. Something I'd said had gotten his attention. "Tell me more about these photos. Are we talking blackmail?"

"What? No! I was talking about wedding photos. That's all, I swear." My lame attempt to lighten the mood with humor had not translated well.

"Mmm-hmm." He squinted at me as if trying to decide whether to ask more questions about the pictures. "Did Zoe have access to the victim's food or drink before the wedding?"

"Access? I'm not sure I under— Ohhhh, you mean, like, to poison it? Is that what you think happened?" It made sense. Dana had died at the wedding and there wasn't any blood, nor was there any sign of trauma.

Officer Ortiz stared at me. "I'm the one asking the questions."

"Right. Gotcha." I didn't say so, but I took his answer as a yes.

I weighed my words carefully. If he thought Zoe had poisoned Dana, I needed to quit while I was ahead. I knew the girls had all gone out the night before the wedding, but I hadn't been there, and I certainly didn't want to get Zoe into any more trouble than she was already in. "I don't know what Zoe did or didn't have access to. I'm sorry."

He snapped his notepad shut. "Okay. If you decide you *do* have anything useful to tell me, you know where to find me. Thank you for your time, Miss McKenna."

"Thank you for your time"? As if I had come there to help him? What I'd come there for was to convince him that he had the wrong girl, but he hadn't listened to a word I'd said.

He led me back to the front office, me fuming silently and him ignoring me. After dropping me at the entrance, he retreated behind the swinging doors. I stared after him, silently cursing my luck. I hadn't helped at all. If anything, I'd just made it worse.

As long as I was there, I decided to see if they'd let me speak to Zoe. After leaving me to wait half an hour on a seriously uncomfortable metal bench, a guard ushered me back to the visiting room. The decor was sparse—no surprise there. Just a smattering of beat-up tables and chairs occupied by anxious-looking prisoners conferring with lawyers and family members. The guard pointed me over to where Zoe sat. She seemed just as anxious as the others but looked seriously out of place in the harsh surroundings. I was happy to see they hadn't put her in an orange jumpsuit yet, although she was wearing handcuffs.

"Kelsey!" she exclaimed. "Thank God you're here!" The dark circles under her eyes accentuated her "just spent the night in jail" look.

"Hi, Zoe," I said, pulling up a chair across from her. The legs screeched loudly across the concrete floor, causing the guard to scowl at me. "Are you okay? I'm so sorry about all this. Is your mom here?"

"You just missed her. She was going to go yell at the guards because I haven't gotten breakfast yet," she said, rolling her eyes.

"Don't worry," I said, reaching across the table to squeeze her hand. "I'm sure they'll realize it's all a big mistake."

The guard cleared his throat and tilted his chin in my general direction. Taking the hint, I released Zoe's hand and made sure all my limbs were on my side of the table.

Zoe's bloodshot eyes searched mine for any glimmer of hope. "Kelsey, you've got to get me out of here!"

"I wish I could. I tried. They didn't listen to me. In fact—well, never mind. Are you doing okay? Is there anything I can bring you?"

"I don't know. I'm scared. Really scared." She tried propping her head on one hand before realizing there was no comfortable way to pull that pose off wearing handcuffs, then dejectedly put both hands in her lap.

"I know. I'm sorry."

Zoe shook her head helplessly. "This is so unfair! Sure, I hated Dana, but I didn't want her dead!"

"I know, Zoe. This is just a misunderstanding. I'm sure your mom and dad will have you out in no time."

"Have you *met* my mom? She won't exactly help my case. She's just going to piss the police off more!"

I shrugged, not sure what to say. She might have had a point there.

"In the meantime, Dad's dealing with some work crisis," she continued, her eyes welling up with tears, "and I don't know when he's coming back."

"I'm sure he'll be back as soon as he can get here," I reassured her.

She swiped at her cheek and stared up at the ceiling, avoiding eye contact. "I know. He said he'd come back as soon as he can, but his company lost a big account, and he's fighting for his job. He was barely able to get away for the wedding." She blew out a deep breath.

"I wish I could help, but I don't know what to do!"

Her eyes welled with tears, but she held my gaze. "I just feel so alone!" She managed to choke the words out before breaking down altogether.

I quickly weighed my options. One, stay and help her—but how exactly was I going to do that? Two, fly back home and wish her the best of luck in all her future freedom-related endeavors. The first was disastrous for me, but the second didn't feel very

good, either. Could I really leave her here in a Mexican jail and
blithely return to my life back home? I couldn't imagine how miserable I'd feel if it were me sitting there in that cell.

There had to be something I could do. Right? As long as I got
back by next weekend, I could still pull off the Richardson wedding with my assistant, Laurel, doing most of the legwork. She'd
been begging me to give her more responsibilities, so I was sure
she'd jump at the chance.

Besides, I thought, an idea forming, maybe I *could* be of some
help.

The San Miguel police thought they had something on Zoe,
but I had something they didn't: a guest list that contained seventy-
eight potential suspects.

CHAPTER 8

S o," I said, plunking a fat binder down on the wooden table in the dining room, causing the chunky goblets of the hibiscus tea Fernando had brought us to jump a little. "I wanted to go through the seating plan and see what you can tell me about the guests."

Nicole's eyes grew big. "You don't think one of my guests had something to do with the murder, do you?"

"Maybe, maybe not, but it's a good place to start. Odds are, it was someone she knew."

Mrs. Abernathy sighed and rubbed her temples. "You think I'd let a murderer on the guest list? I approved every last person myself." That was true. She'd vetted the guest list with the gusto of a seasoned politician. "But if it was one of the guests, it'd have to be one of his," she said, jerking her thumb toward the groom.

A vein in Vince's temple throbbed as he pretended to be

engrossed with the condensation on his glass. He was exercising remarkable control over his emotions. "I can assure you it is no one from my side of the family," he said.

"I can't imagine that anyone we know could have done this," said Nicole, glancing warily at Vince and stroking his arm in a conciliatory fashion, a move I'd seen over and over again during all joint planning sessions that included her mom.

"But you're also sure Zoe didn't do it, aren't you?" I said.

"Of course I am!"

"Then let's get to work. We might not come up with anything, but we have to try."

I unclipped the sturdy rings and removed the seating chart, then pushed the rings closed with an efficient snap.

"Now," I began, "let's start with who actually knew Dana before this weekend."

"Well, there's all of us, of course," Nicole said.

"Right," I said, taking out my red pen and circling our names—even mine, although I was pretty sure I'd end up eliminating myself as a suspect.

"No one from table seven," she continued, as I crossed them out one by one. "Or table three."

"What about your Uncle Roy?" asked Vince. "He'd never met Dana before, but he sure did follow her around a lot the last few days."

"That's Uncle Roy. He's just . . . friendly."

Lecherous was more like it, but he probably wasn't homicidal. "Okay, a question mark next to Uncle Roy."

In a few minutes, we narrowed it down to fourteen people who'd had past encounters with the fallen bridesmaid.

"Okay, let's start with the head table. What about Claire? What was her relationship with Dana?" The other bridesmaid wasn't particularly suspicious, but the process of elimination is, after all, a process.

"We were all friends in college. Actually, Claire and Dana were friends first, and Dana introduced us. We all shared a house together one summer."

"House?" snorted Mrs. Abernathy. "That dump?"

"And did they get along?" I asked, ignoring Mrs. Abernathy's commentary.

"Sure, we did everything together. Until Dana started dating Trevor."

My ears perked up. "Trevor? As in Trevor"—I scanned the seating chart to find the usher's last name—"Reckholtz?"

"Yes, Dana and Trevor hooked up our senior year. Claire was a little jealous, I guess, because she'd had a crush on him, but they got past it eventually."

I put a check mark next to Claire's name. I didn't really think she had it in her to kill someone, but "love triangle" way beats "wouldn't flirt back with uncle" in the rock-paper-scissors of murder motives.

"Tell me more about Dana's relationship with Trevor," I prodded.

"Oh, well, you know," Nicole said, stalling. "It ended."

"Ha!" chortled Mrs. Abernathy. "I'll say it did."

"It ended *badly*," Vince amended.

"That's putting it mildly," said Mrs. Abernathy. "Now that I think about it, with all she put him through, I wouldn't blame him one bit!"

"What do you mean?"

Nicole looked hesitantly at Vince, who sighed and nodded at Nicole's unasked question. "Go ahead and tell her," he said. "It's not like we have to protect her reputation. At least not anymore."

Protect Dana's reputation? This was going to be good.

"I don't know," Nicole said. "I don't want to get Trevor in trouble."

"Oh, for heaven's sake," said Mrs. Abernathy. "You might as well tell her! I think he looks good for it, myself."

"Looks good for it?" I had to bite my tongue to keep myself from reacting to Mrs. Abernathy talking like a TV homicide detective. Next she'd start referring to him as the "perp" and Dana as the "vic."

Nicole sighed. "They'd been dating for about a year, and things were going really well, but then Dana got pregnant."

"Pretended to get pregnant," Vince interjected.

"We don't know that," said Nicole. "She said she was pregnant, and I believed her. Anyway, she wanted to get married. He kind of freaked, but eventually he agreed to do it."

"Key word being 'agreed' to," said Vince. "He never would have even considered it if it weren't for the baby."

"Anyway, we were all busy trying to throw a wedding together in a month, because she wanted to do it before she started to show. But then Trevor started acting really weird. He said she didn't seem all that pregnant, but what would he know?"

"She never had morning sickness, and she didn't even have one of those, what do you call it? Baby lumps?" said Vince.

"Bump," continued Nicole. "But every woman carries her pregnancy different."

"That's right," said Mrs. Abernathy, "and Dana was carrying hers in her head."

"Anyway," continued Nicole, "we were going shopping for bridesmaids' dresses, and Dana had a doctor's appointment later that afternoon. Trevor texted her, 'I'm coming with you.' And she was all, 'You want to shop for bridesmaids' dresses?' and he was all, 'No, I'm coming with you to the doctor.'

"She said she didn't want him to come, but he made a big deal about it. At some point, she stopped texting back and turned off her phone. By then, we were at the bridal shop anyway. But then Trevor showed up and they had a big fight. He said if there was a baby in there, he wanted proof. They were yelling at each other right there in front of that nice dress lady and all the bridesmaids. It was pretty awful."

"Wow, I can imagine. So what ended up happening?"

"He broke up with her," said Vince. "There was no baby."

"There *was* a baby," insisted Nicole. "After he left, she told us she'd had a miscarriage, but she hadn't told him because she was afraid he'd call off the wedding."

"Of course he'd have called off the wedding. That was the only reason he was marrying her," said Vince. "There was never any baby."

"But the miscarriage—"

"Oh, honey, don't be naïve," said Mrs. Abernathy. "You know what I call a five-month-pregnant bride-to-be with no baby bump who suddenly loses the baby when her fiancé gets suspicious?"

Nicole shook her head.

"A manipulative little tramp, that's what."

"Okay, good, that's very helpful," I said, trying to break the tension. I put an asterisk next to Trevor's name. "What was his date's name?" I asked, checking the seating chart. "Oh, here it is. Naomi."

"He hadn't been dating Naomi very long," volunteered Vince. "But he knew Dana had been invited, so I think he wanted to make sure she knew he wasn't available. At least not to her."

"Do we know anything about this Naomi person?" asked Mrs. Abernathy.

"Not really," said Nicole. "She was just a plus-one. Seemed nice, though."

"Whoever she is," said Mrs. Abernathy, "I'm sure she's a significant improvement over Dana."

"Yeah, especially with Dana being dead and all," I said before I could catch myself. Oops. "Sorry, Nicole."

"So, what now?" asked Mrs. Abernathy. "Do we take a vote or something?"

"I definitely think we should talk to Trevor," I said. "He sure was asking a lot of questions about Dana at the reception." I flipped to the tab in the binder marked "Travel Info" and scanned down to Trevor's name. "And luckily, he hasn't left town yet."

"Do you want me to talk to him?" asked Vince. "I've known him the longest. He might be more likely to open up to me."

"I don't know," said Nicole, looking up at her husband. "You can't come right out and accuse your friend of murder."

"Besides, you shouldn't have to do that," said Mrs. Abernathy. "You're on your honeymoon!"

Some honeymoon, I thought. The couple hadn't even shared so much as a meal alone since the wedding.

Feeling sorry for Vince, I jumped in to volunteer. "Why don't I go? I'll come up with some reason to drop by and see if I can get him to talk. If I can't get anything out of him, you can always follow up later."

"Okay, it's settled then," said Mrs. Abernathy. "Kelsey will handle it."

"But what if he didn't do it?" asked Nicole. "Who else do we have?"

I checked the seating chart to see where we'd ended up. "Well, there's Claire, Uncle Roy, Trevor, and I guess his date, Naomi. There's the San Francisco crowd, but most of them don't have any motive."

"Don't forget the four of us," said Nicole.

"Oh, darling, don't be ridiculous," said Mrs. Abernathy.

I went ahead and added our names to the final list, just to be fair, eliciting a scowl from Mrs. Abernathy.

The door to the dining room swung open and Brody sauntered in, carrying a plate of food he'd managed to finagle from Fernando. "Hey, guys. What's going on?"

"Suspect list," said Mrs. Abernathy. "Watch out or she'll put you on it, too."

CHAPTER 9

*I*t's funny what constitutes an emergency in some people's minds. While I was trying to decide how to approach a groomsman about the murder of a bridesmaid, I got a call from one of my clients who was having a full-blown panic attack over her "ruined" wedding programs.

Tamara Richardson's wedding was two weeks away, and the bride-to-be had opened the box for a sneak peek and discovered a misprint on page 3. I wished I could explain the relative gravity of having a bridesmaid sitting in a Mexican prison versus the last stanza missing from her favorite love poem, but that would have required getting a word in edgewise.

"Yes, Tamara, I'll try to—"

"Uh-huh."

"I'm sure they didn't mean—"

"Of course."

"No, I don't think Rumi would—"

"Okay."

"I agree, I think they can—"

"All right. I'll take care of it."

Brody laughed at my one-sided conversation as I covered the receiver and mouthed the word "sorry" to him.

"Whew," I said, hanging up the phone and sinking back into my chair. I was used to multitasking, but this was ridiculous. "Real detectives have no idea how easy they have it. All they have to do is question suspects and frisk people occasionally. I'd like to see them try to juggle a few brides while they're at it."

"They'd crack under the pressure," said Brody.

Nodding in agreement, I grabbed his fork and attacked what was left on his plate, realizing I hadn't eaten anything in way too long. You'd think I'd be too stressed to eat, but I usually have quite the opposite reaction.

"Help yourself," he said, a little bit of sarcasm creeping into his voice.

"What? You were done."

"No, I wasn't. Some people pause in between bites to chew their food. You should try it sometime."

"Too bad. You shouldn't have set your fork down."

He slid the plate toward me, dodging my fork as I aimed for the tamale. "Fine," he said. "You owe me a street taco."

Smart man. You should never argue with a hungry girl holding a pointy metal implement.

"By the way," he said, "when you're done eating my lunch, you should call Evan. Not to add to your to-do list, but he stopped by earlier when you were visiting Zoe in the pokey."

Oh, yeah—Evan. I hadn't had time to think about it, but I did kind of owe him a call after last night's *datus interruptus*.

"Thanks for the message," I said, reaching for the phone. "Now, please hold all my calls for the rest of the day. I have a wedding to plan and a murder to investigate."

Brody got up from the table, scooped up his empty plate, and gave me a wave. "I'll be in my room if you need me."

I licked the remaining chile sauce off my fingers before dialing Evan's number, but he caught me crunching on a stray piece of jicama when he answered.

"*Bueno?*"

I swallowed quickly. "Evan, hi! It's me."

"Hi, yourself!" he answered. "That was quite a date last night. I would've loved to have seen how it ended."

My stomach felt kind of funny, and my ears blushed a little.

"Yeah, sorry about that. We had a family emergency."

"So I heard. Everything okay?"

"Not really, but thanks for asking. Looks like I'll be sticking around for a few days."

"That's great news!" he said. I was glad he thought so. I had so many reasons to hurry back, but at least getting to spend some time with Evan was a little bit of a silver lining.

"So when can I see you?" he asked.

"Unfortunately, I'm going to be busy trying to get Zoe out of jail, but hopefully I can find a little downtime."

"Anything I can do to help?" Evan asked.

Help? I hadn't really thought about Evan being able to help me with anything other than my dismal love life and short-hop flights, but come to think of it, having someone local on my side would be nothing short of amazing.

"Do you mean it?"

"Sure. All the quicker to get you all to myself."

"Then you're hired! Um, let's see . . . did you say you knew someone at the police station?"

"Yes, I have some connections."

"They don't seem to want to talk to me much." I didn't mention that Officer Ortiz would probably arrest me if I tried again.

"Want me to see what I can find out?" he said.

That's what I love. A man who doesn't make me beg. "That would be the absolute best thing ever—or at least the best thing that I have any reasonable hope of actually happening. I'd really appreciate it, Evan."

"Don't mention it. Dinner later?"

"Absolutely," I said. "And I'm buying."

Next on my list? Figuring out where Trevor was staying. He and Naomi had found their own accommodations at the last minute. I figured the two of them just wanted some privacy, especially with Mrs. Abernathy's not-too-subtle comments about unmarried people sharing a room, but now that I knew his history with Dana, I understood why he'd given up his place at the villa.

Luckily, I'd been the one to point them to a rental agency run by one of my contacts, so one phone call later, I had an address in hand and was headed out to see what I could find.

Funny, the receptionist hadn't even hesitated to give me the address. What if I were a killer?

Which led me to a startling realization: *What if Trevor were a killer?*

He had a motive, but I couldn't really see him murdering someone, especially not with Naomi around. Face it: you don't bring a date when you're plotting revenge. Then again, maybe it wasn't planned. Maybe they'd gotten into an argument when Naomi was off somewhere shopping for local handicrafts. Maybe things had gotten out of hand and he hadn't meant to do it.

Wait, the officers seemed to think she'd been poisoned. How do you accidentally poison someone in a fit of rage? Okay, so it hadn't been an accident. And it could have been Trevor. I didn't know what I was walking into, and I had to be careful.

Their rental was only a few blocks away, so by the time I figured all that out I was already at their gate. I put my hand on the heavy brass knocker, then pulled it back quickly. What was I doing here? If he had killed Dana, he could kill me, too. Although, to be fair, he had absolutely no motive to kill me. Besides, Naomi would probably be there, and nothing would happen with her around. I decided to call Brody for backup, just in case, so I pulled my phone out of my bag. He wasn't doing anything important, and besides—

"Kelsey?" I hadn't noticed the door swinging open while I was searching for cell reception, but suddenly Trevor was standing in front of me.

"Um, *hola*!" I said, trying to sound casual.

Trevor didn't look very happy about the surprise visit. "What are you doing here?" You'd think I'd have gotten a warmer reception after helping him out with the tequila donkey.

I stalled. "I was wondering if I could talk to you for a minute."

"I was just heading out."

"Oh, it will only take a minute. I wanted to ask you about . . . your tux." I didn't want to blurt out the real reason for my visit. At least not until I'd had a chance to assess the situation.

"My tux? What about it?"

"Yes, I'm taking Vince's back, so I thought I'd return yours, too, and save you the trip." That was plausible enough.

"Um, okay, I guess. Thanks." He opened the door and motioned for me to follow him inside.

"Don't mention it. That's what I do. I'm a helper. It's my job— helping people. So, where's Naomi?"

Trevor froze for a second. "She's not here."

"That's cool. I mean, I'm sure she's . . . doing something. And why shouldn't she be? I mean, you're on vacation. She probably—"

"Wait here," he said, cutting off my rambling, which was actually sort of a relief. "I'll go get the tux."

A real detective probably would have found an excuse to follow him inside the house to look for clues, but not me. I was happy to be left standing in the courtyard. At least the gate leading back out to the street was open, so I could run for it if necessary. But I was going to have to get him talking if I wanted to leave with some information and not just an errand involving rental clothing.

A moment later he returned, garment bag in hand. Trying to look casual, I pretended to be engrossed in a potted geranium plant, picking off some of the dead blossoms. "Oh! That was fast."

"Thanks for taking this back," he said.

"Don't mention it. I'm just trying to stay busy and help the Abernathys out however I can. Everyone's really upset about the whole Dana thing."

"I'm sure." His expression was unreadable, but there was a frosty undertone to his voice.

"In fact, I guess I should express my condolences. To you, I mean. I know you two were close once."

"I guess." He shifted uneasily from one foot to the other.

"I'm sure it must have come as quite a shock to you." *Unless, of course, you were responsible?*

"Yes, it was," he said, after a long pause. "Do you know what happened?"

"No, we're still waiting to find out."

He blew out a sigh and fixed his eyes someplace over my left shoulder, avoiding eye contact. "The night of the wedding, you made it sound like everything was okay, but Vince said she never left the church."

That was true; I had lied to him the night of the wedding. If he was innocent, that would explain the chill I was feeling in the warm Mexican air.

"I know," I said, "and I'm sorry. I couldn't tell anyone because Mrs. Abernathy—well, you know."

"Ah, Mrs. Abernathy." He shook his head, his face softening ever so slightly.

"Yeah, she's a piece of work. She wouldn't even let me tell Nicole because she didn't want to ruin her night. Can you imagine?"

"I can, actually."

"And if I couldn't tell Nicole, I couldn't tell anyone else. So, I'm sorry. I lied."

"I get it. Mrs. Abernathy's not a woman you want to cross." He pulled out a chair from the patio table and motioned for me to take a seat.

Although we were having a bonding moment, I still chose the chair closest to the gate. I couldn't let my guard down with nothing more to defend myself with than some dead geranium blooms and Mexican partywear.

"So how long had it been since you'd seen Dana? Before this weekend, I mean."

"Not since—well, I guess you know we used to date."

"I'm sure that must have been awkward, especially with Naomi here."

He laughed bitterly. "Yeah, it was a mess. Hard to avoid her when we're in the same wedding party. Even when Naomi and I would go off on our own, we'd run into her. It's not that big a town."

"You two had a pretty nasty breakup, from what I hear."

Trevor looked surprised, and surprisingly defensive. "Who'd you hear that from? Were people talking about us?"

"No, it was nothing like that," I quickly corrected. "Mrs. Abernathy told me so I could keep you guys separated."

"I wouldn't have even come if I'd have known Dana was going to be here."

"And no one would have blamed you, after what she did."

"So you know the whole story?"

"Yeah, Mrs. Abernathy filled me in on all the gory details." I worked hard to keep my tone breezy. "You must have been awfully mad at Dana for what she put you through."

He sat quietly for a second, his jaw muscles tensing. "Of course I was angry. She lied to me. Not just once, but for months and months. She made me look like an idiot."

The poor guy. Everyone goes through a bad breakup eventually. I'd been through a spectacularly horrible one myself. But when a guy gets involved with a psycho like Dana, it's way worse. I'd known girls like her, and they could make a person start questioning his own sanity. If he had killed her, it was a crime of passion.

"Trevor, I understand. I know crazy, and that girl was batshit." Realizing how callous that sounded, I quickly added, "God rest her soul."

"That she was." His attention was focused on a bit of paint peeling off the table, which he was hastening along with his thumbnail.

I pushed forward. "I was curious, though . . . you asked me about her at the reception."

He looked at me suspiciously. "Yeah? What about it?"

I shrugged. "What were you trying to find out?"

"What do you mean? I was just wondering if she was okay." He tried to sound nonchalant, but I wasn't buying it.

"It's just, I would have thought you'd want to stay far away from her."

"I did!" His voice rose. He was getting irritated. This was where the cops always got people to crack, at least on TV. "If you want the truth," he said, "I had planned on leaving the reception early, but I was actually having a pretty good time and I was hoping she had bailed on the party so I could stay."

That actually seemed pretty plausible. Still, I wasn't sure. After all, he seemed to have more motive than anyone.

"Trevor, I know you were angry with her. After what she did to you, you had every right to be. But I have to ask: Did you do anything to hurt her?"

He suddenly sat up, his eyes flashing in anger. "What? No! I can't believe you'd even ask me that!"

"I'd understand if you did. I wanted to strangle her myself, and I'm just the wedding planner. Maybe you two got in a fight and it got out of hand? Is that what happened? Because if it is, you have to go to the police. It'll be so much better for you if you go talk to them now."

He shook his head vigorously. "We got into a fight, but I didn't kill her, if that's what you're trying to imply."

"I'm not trying to imply anything. I'm just trying to find out what happened."

"Nothing happened," he said, enunciating each word. "We did get into an argument the night of the rehearsal dinner, but Naomi was with me the whole time."

I weighed my words carefully. I wanted to believe him, but there was only one way to be sure. "I'm sure Naomi will be able to verify all of this?"

Trevor's face darkened. "I told you, Naomi's not here right now." He got up from the table and thrust the garment bag into my hand.

"When will she be back?"

No answer.

"Trevor, look, I believe you," I said, following him to the gate, "but we have to find out what happened, and it would be really helpful if I knew for sure that Naomi was with you the whole time."

He narrowed his eyes at me. "Do I need to get a lawyer?"

It didn't take a seasoned police officer to figure out that this interview was winding up, so I tried to end on a light note. I attempted an airy laugh, but it came out as a nervous cackle. "Of course not! I'm just trying to help the Abernathys understand what happened."

He walked to the gate and swung it open in what was not a subtle hint.

"Can I just talk to Naomi?" I persisted. "I can come back"—I checked my watch—"whenever. You tell me."

He opened the gate wider and waited for me to use it. "I'm afraid not." His words had a definite air of finality.

"Okay, well, can you have her call me, or . . . ?"

He stared at me intently. "Naomi is gone." There was that frost again.

"You mean . . . ?" I hugged the garment bag closer to myself as if it offered some sort of protection.

"She's gone home."

"But you were supposed to fly back together. I've got your flight information in my binder."

"Sorry, I don't know what to tell you. We got into a fight and she left."

Kind of like you and Dana got into a fight?

A tingle went all the way up my spine and back down again as I stepped through the gate and onto the sidewalk.

"Thank you for returning my tux, and give the Abernathys my regards," Trevor said. Right before closing the gate firmly in my face.

CHAPTER 10

*H*e did *what*?" Brody asked, squinting in the late afternoon sun. When I'd returned from the villa, I'd found my friend lounging by the pool in my absence, enjoying an icy drink Fernando had concocted for him.

"I'm telling you, he shut the gate right in my face. Is there alcohol in that?" I asked, pointing at his beverage.

He nodded. "You want a sip?"

"No, that's okay." I stared longingly at the glass. "Is it passion fruit?"

"Oh, for heaven's sake, just take it."

"Well, if you're not going to finish it," I said hastily, grabbing the glass.

"So anyway," he continued, "what does your gut tell you?"

"That we need another round." I scrambled to my feet, noisily vacuuming up the remnants at the bottom of the glass with the straw. Before I could even take two steps toward the kitchen, Fernando appeared out of nowhere.

"*Buenas tardes*, Kelsey. Can I get you something to drink?" he asked.

"Wow, that's service. Can I have one of these . . . whatever this was?"

"Of course," Fernando said, taking the empty glass from me.

"Better make it two," said Brody.

"Better make it a pitcher," I added.

Brody got up from his lounge chair and waded into the shallow end of the pool. "You know, when you asked me to stay, I thought I was being selfless. But this doesn't suck at all."

I walked to the edge of the pool, dipped a toe in, then lowered myself onto the ornate tiles, dangling my feet in the tepid water. "I'm glad at least one of us is getting a chance to enjoy it," I said, stirring my feet around idly.

"Grab your suit," Brody said, gesturing toward our rooms. "A swim will help you clear your mind."

"That's okay. I'm having dinner with Evan later, so I don't want to get my hair wet."

"You're missing out," he said, floating lazily on his back. "So what do you think? Is Trevor our man?"

"I don't know," I said. "Honestly, I felt bad for the guy, but the whole Naomi thing was just so weird. One minute he was opening up to me, but then he clammed up when I asked to talk to her."

Brody paddled over to me and hung off the edge of the pool, kicking his feet behind him. "So do you think she really left?"

"Either that or he really doesn't want me talking to her. But you should have heard the tone in his voice. When I pressed him on it, he sounded almost . . . menacing."

"Sounds like he's got something to hide."

"Well, right now he's hiding his date. And I really want to talk to her."

"What about calling her? Do you have her cell?"

"I tried that, but it went to voice mail."

I jumped at a sudden noise behind me, but it was only Fernando, returning with our afternoon refreshments. God bless him, he'd even thrown in some chips and guacamole.

"Thank you, Fernando," I said. "You're a lifesaver."

"You're most welcome. I hope you enjoy it. It's a family recipe," he added, gently unloading his tray onto the table. "May I ask . . . We have other guests arriving on Friday. Do you know how long you'll be staying?"

I laughed and rubbed the bridge of my nose. "That's a good question, Fernando. I wish I knew."

After having my way with the chips and guac, I wasn't exactly ravenous for dinner, so when Evan came by to get me, I suggested we take a walk and enjoy the sunset before heading off to eat.

"You want a sunset?" Evan asked, offering me his arm. "Right this way."

Knowing that cobblestones and heels don't mix, I'd left anything even vaguely resembling date shoes back in San Francisco. It was a good thing I had, because our evening stroll involved a vigorous climb up a steep hill that left me fairly winded and wanting to shower all over again.

Oh, but the view.

From El Mirador, the lookout point at the top of the hill, we could see the rooftops of San Miguel de Allende stretching before us. The historic center lay at our feet, with the spires of La Parroquia dramatically punctuating the landscape. The soft light bathed the reds, oranges, and yellows of the adobes and their tiled roofs in a glow that was matched only by the riot of colors streaking across the sky.

For a few dizzy moments, I leaned back against Evan, pondering what exactly would be so wrong about relocating my business to Mexico. He nuzzled my hair as we stood in silence. I was falling in love. With San Miguel, that is, although Evan was seriously scoring some points.

The sun finally dipped below the horizon, breaking the spell.

I sighed, drunk on the view, and maybe a little bit on that passion-fruit thingy Fernando had made me. "Okay, let's get down to business."

Evan looked surprised. "Right here? In the park? All right, although it's a little public for my tastes." He laughed and pulled me in for a kiss. "Or we could go back to my place."

Flirting. I'd kind of forgotten how much fun it could be. "I'm talking about that *other* business," I said, blushing at least a little. "Did you get in touch with your friend at the police station?"

"Oh, that. Yeah, I went by today and talked to him. He wasn't able to tell me a lot since he's not actually in homicide, but he was able to find out a little bit about the case."

"So?" I asked eagerly. I loved the prospect of having an inside source. "What did he say?"

Evan took both my hands in his. "Well, for one thing, they aren't looking at any other suspects right now."

"Are you kidding me?" I said, pulling away abruptly. "They have to keep looking! Zoe didn't do it. They're not even trying to investigate other possibilities?"

Evan shrugged. "He said they thought they had the right person."

I put my hands on my hips. "Why? Based on what?"

"When they searched Zoe's room, they found something."

I rolled my eyes. "Oh, come on. What could they have possibly found? A deadly bridesmaid's bouquet? An incriminating amount of eyeliner? They don't even know what Dana died from."

Evan crossed his arms in front of his chest. "Actually, they think they do."

I braced myself, knowing I wasn't going to like whatever was coming next.

"They found what looked like poison in her room. The lab's going to run a tox screen to see if it could be the cause of death."

"But that's not possible!" Evan went to put his arms around me, but I was in no mood to be hugged. I wriggled out of his would-be embrace, my mind spinning with this new information. "What kind of poison?"

Evan held his hands up in the air. "He didn't know. Does it even matter?"

"Yes! I mean, how do they know if it even *is* poison? It's not like they tasted it!" Okay, so not exactly a great rationale, but it was all I had at the moment.

"Kelsey, they're the police. If they think it's poison, it's probably poison."

I stormed off down the hill. The brilliantly colored sky had started to turn dark, the clouds nothing but black wisps.

"Kelsey, wait!" Evan called after me, but I was too agitated to slow down and listen to him. He caught up and grabbed my elbow, whirling me around to face him.

He took me by the shoulders and looked me in the eye. "Kelsey, listen to me. I know you believe your friend. But I have to ask you, how well do you know this girl?"

I shrugged. "Not best-friends-since-first-grade well, but well enough to know she isn't a killer."

"You've known her for, what? A year? Six months?"

"Something like that," I said, my righteous indignation starting to falter.

"And you've spent how many hours together during that time?"

"More than you'd think. These weddings don't plan themselves, Evan."

"Come on, Kelsey, she isn't even your client. So you sat through a couple of dress fittings together. That doesn't mean you know the girl."

"True, but . . ."

But what? My convictions were getting harder and harder to cling to in the face of actual evidence. "I don't know. I guess we'll have to wait for the autopsy. Maybe it will exonerate her."

"Sure," he said diplomatically. "Maybe it will." He pulled me in close and kissed me on the forehead.

Damn it. I'd already let this whole situation throw my work life into chaos, and now it was putting a serious damper on what could have been a gloriously romantic evening. I vowed not to allow my impromptu murder investigation to infringe on my evening any more than it already had.

I sighed. I felt bad for berating my inside source, especially since he was also my dinner date.

"You hungry?" I asked.

"Starving," Evan replied, cupping my face in his hands before pushing me up against a wall and kissing me deeply. The adobe was still warm from the sun, which was only partially to blame for the sudden flush I felt spread over my whole body. I officially declared myself off duty for the night as I wrapped my arms around his neck and kissed back.

Dinner would have to wait.

CHAPTER 11

The next morning I woke up just before dawn. I was a little disoriented at first, which you get used to when you travel a lot, but instead of the usual "What country am I in?" moment, I had an "Okay, seriously, where am I?" moment. I quickly assembled the clues: the striped bedspread confirmed that this was not my room at the villa. My dress draped over a chair told me I hadn't made it home last night. And the snoring coming from the next room provided the final piece of the puzzle. *Evan.* Mystery solved.

It had gotten late, so I'd stayed over in his guest bedroom. It had seemed like a good idea at the time, but now that it was morning, I wished I'd gotten myself tucked into my own bed to avoid suspicion.

Maybe if I hurried, I could make it back to the villa before everyone woke up and save myself the raised eyebrows. I crawled quietly out from under the covers and quickly got dressed in last night's clothes—once again thankful I hadn't been wearing super-obvious high heels.

Cómo se dice "walk of shame" *en español?*

The streets were deserted at that hour, and the sun wasn't even fully up as I slipped through the gates of the villa, praying I could make it back to my room without being noticed. I carried my flats in my hand and padded softly across the courtyard, which was mercifully quiet. Whew. Thank goodness no one was up. I could relax.

"Late night?" The voice cut through the silence, making me freeze in my tracks.

Busted.

"Good morning, Mrs. Abernathy," I called across the courtyard. "I couldn't sleep and went out to search for coffee."

"I'm sure Fernando could have made you some."

"I didn't want to bother him so early. See you at breakfast!"

As I darted down the hallway, I could have sworn I heard a *tsk*.

I took a long, hot shower, replaying the events of the night before in my head. I'd definitely needed a distraction from everything that had happened, and more importantly, I'd needed a reminder of what it was like to have a personal life. Even though I was surrounded by romance on a more or less everyday basis, I seldom had time for dating back home, so it felt good to indulge in an evening out.

I wanted to go tell Brody all about it, but that would have to wait. Now that I'd had a shower, I had to strategize my wardrobe: change into fresh clothes, which would confirm to Mrs. Abernathy that I'd spent the night out? Or put on my dress from the night before and act like it was perfectly normal to show a little cleavage at breakfast?

Either way, I lose, I thought, as I pulled on a pair of khakis and a cotton top. *Might as well be comfortable.*

I still had some time before breakfast, so I spent a while returning e-mails and writing up a proposal for a bride who wanted a
Disney-themed wedding. I padded the cost to the point where I
might as well have put "all the money in the world" for the total,
because that's how much it would take for me to want the job. Prin-
cesses are a definite job hazard, and experience has taught me that
they're just not worth it. Then I sent my assistant, Laurel, a lengthy
to-do list that included last-minute tasks for Tamara Richardson's
upcoming nuptials, as well as booking tickets for a site visit to
Hawaii next month.

It felt good to be back in wedding-planner mode. I needed to
remember that this was temporary and my life would be returning to normal soon. Although I was enjoying my time with Evan,
I really couldn't wait to be back in the land of champagne and
happy endings and away from this world of poison and uncer-
tainty.

After I caught up on my e-mails, I went down to the breakfast
room, where I found Mrs. Abernathy, the newlyweds, and Brody
already gathered around the table. When I saw Fernando heading toward me with a pot of steaming hot coffee, the words
"Yes, please" were no sooner out of my mouth than Mrs. Abernathy arched an eyebrow at me and smiled. "More coffee? Why,
dear, you're going to be all a-jitter if you keep this up. Are you
sure you wouldn't prefer decaf?"

I blanched at the thought of skipping my morning brew just to
save face, but Brody jumped to my defense. "Kelsey's frequent-
flier points are nothing next to her Starbucks rewards card. She
drinks at least five cups a day."

Bless him, looking out for my caffeine intake like that. He might
have exaggerated the quantity, but if I don't have at least sixteen
ounces by about eleven A.M., I start feeling like someone shoved
a fork into my right eyeball.

Fernando filled my cup, and Mrs. Abernathy moved on to a different subject. "I see you changed clothes," she said.

Well, damn it. I poured some cream and ripped open a packet of sweetener. "I think it's supposed to rain later," I mumbled.

"It's probably best you changed. I told Zoe you'd be by to visit her this morning, and you don't want to cause a scandal down at the station."

Nicole and Vince stared at Mrs. Abernathy, confused. "Did we miss something?" Nicole asked.

"Nothing at all, dear," she replied as Fernando returned with a tray of food. "Oh, goody—waffles!"

Properly fueled, I was more than happy to bid *adios* to Mrs. Abernathy and head to the police station to see Zoe. I'd endured enough of Mrs. Abernathy's veiled comments for one morning. What business was it of hers if I wanted to spend the night somewhere else? I was a grown woman, not a promiscuous teenager. Besides, it wasn't like I was on the clock twenty-four hours a day. I wasn't even on the clock at all, was I? Mrs. Abernathy wasn't paying me for this extra-credit assignment, although she seemed to think I should be grateful she was covering my expenses for the extra days at the villa. Kind of like a paid vacation, right? Ha.

"Kelsey, you came!" Zoe looked happy to see me as she was escorted into the visitation room, although "happy" was a relative term under the circumstances. The harsh lighting did nothing to enhance her wan complexion.

"Hi, Zoe, how you holding up?"

"Oh, okay. As well as you'd expect," she said, pulling her plastic chair up to the worn wooden table. I could tell from her dejected expression that she was just being brave.

"I can't even imagine what you're going through," I said.

"I won't lie. It pretty much sucks. I think my bunk might have bedbugs," she said, scratching absently at her shackled arms.

"Ugh, that's terrible."

"And so far all they've fed me is rice and beans."

"Oh, man, I should've smuggled you in a *chalupa* or something. I'll see if they'll let me bring in food."

"It's not so bad," Zoe said, "but I'd love it if you could bring me some bottled water. I'm terrified to drink out of the water fountains."

"I don't blame you," I said. I'd warned everyone to stay away from the tap water; our American digestive systems are no match for the local water supply. "I'll make sure we get you some. But in the meantime, I want you to know that we're doing everything we can to get you out of here."

"I appreciate it, Kelsey."

"Your mom tried calling the consulate, but she hasn't gotten in touch with them yet. Hopefully they'll call her back today."

"What can they do for me, exactly?"

"I'm not really sure. I don't think they can get you out of jail, but at least they can make sure you have drinking water that won't kill you. They can help you find a lawyer, but I'm pretty sure your dad's already got someone."

"I know he keeps a couple on staff, but they mostly deal with all the corporate stuff."

"In the meantime," I said, "your mom's kind of drafted me to try to figure out what happened. I'm not sure I'm the best person for the job, but I'll do what I can until they can get some lawyers down here."

"You have no idea how much I appreciate you helping. I can't believe you're doing all this for me. You must have other weddings to get to."

I shrugged. "No worries. Laurel's handling things for me back in San Francisco. But I do have a couple of questions for you."

"Sure, anything," she said.

"Zoe, do you know why you're in here?"

"No! I have no idea. I didn't really care for Dana, but that doesn't seem like any reason to arrest me." She ran her finger absentmindedly over the word *pendejo* that was carved into the wooden table. "Don't they need some sort of proof?"

I sighed. "That's what I wanted to talk to you about."

"What do you mean?"

"You remember when they searched your room?"

"Of course. They searched everyone's room."

"Yeah, well, yours was the only one where they found anything."

"What?" Zoe looked pale. "There was nothing to find!" If she was acting, she was good at it.

"My friend talked to another detective on the squad, and he said they'd found poison in your room."

"Poison? Like *poison* poison?" The blank stare on her face dissolved into a look of horror. "Oh, God. That explains all the questions they've been asking me, like what sorts of illegal substances I had brought with me, what I'd bought since I'd gotten here. . . . I thought they thought I was on drugs!"

"Is there anything you can think of? Maybe something that could be *used* as a poison? A can of Raid or something?"

"I don't even use moisturizer with parabens in it. I don't have anything that would be toxic to anyone, bugs included."

"Well, they found something. We'll have to wait and see what it is—then we'll try to figure out how it got there."

Zoe stared at the table between us, deep in speculation. "Kelsey, if she was poisoned . . . I wonder if Fernando could have had something to do with it?"

"The chef at the villa? Why?"

"The day before the wedding, I saw them fighting. I was too

far away to hear what they were saying, but he looked pretty mad. I didn't think that much of it at the time. I just figured Dana was being Dana. But what if there was more to it than that?"

I thought about it for a second, then shook my head. "I can't imagine Fernando killing anyone."

"Um, hello? As opposed to me?"

Oops.

"I'm sorry, Zoe. That's why I suck at this! I can't imagine anyone killing anyone for any reason ever." I needed to start thinking less like a wedding planner and more like a hardened detective.

"He would have had access to Dana's food," Zoe said. "If she was poisoned, it would have been easy for him to pull off."

"True. And he also would have had access to your room to plant the poison later." It wasn't much to go on, but it made as much sense as anything else.

"Can you see what you can find out?"

"Of course. I'll do whatever it takes to get you out of here."

I promised to visit again as soon as I knew more, then headed back to the house to talk to Fernando. I had to figure out how to broach the topic carefully, though. Accusing the chef of murder can make things pretty awkward come dinnertime.

Entering the courtyard, I found Nicole, Vince, and Mrs. Abernathy sitting in the middle of a modest pile of wedding presents, expensive wrapping paper littering the ground.

"Oh, Kelsey, good thing you're here. You should be logging these gifts," said Mrs. Abernathy.

Well, sure, in between questioning suspects and counseling your daughter, I'll get right on that.

"Oh," I said. "I didn't realize we were doing this right now."

You'd think opening presents would have been the last thing on their minds.

Mrs. Abernathy snatched a piece of discarded wrapping paper

off the ground and handed it to me. "We have to get thank-you notes in the mail. We're not *animals*."

Nicole tossed aside a gigantic white bow as she ripped into some silver paper. "I'm sorry, Kelsey. I know this seems kind of . . . insensitive. I had to do something to get my mind off of everything."

Vince rubbed his hand over her back, trying to soothe his new wife. Poor guy was supposed to be on his honeymoon right now.

I softened a little. This had been hard on Nicole, losing a friend and having her sister thrown in jail. If this gave her some comfort, who was I to say no?

Besides, I didn't mind stalling while I decided what to say to Fernando.

"Let me go get the gift log so we can do this properly," I said, heading toward my room.

I'd grabbed the notebook from the back of my closet when I suddenly remembered the gift I'd retrieved at the church.

Crappity crap crap.

I wasn't sure what to do. Take it to her? Give it to her later? Leave it behind as a tip for the maid? I flopped on the bed, at a loss. Of course Nicole would want it. But this was terrible timing. It wasn't going to get any better, though, short of Dana coming back to life and handing it to the couple herself, and that wasn't going to happen. No, this was the time. If I didn't give it to her now, it would be even harder to explain later.

I brought the impeccably wrapped present with me and sat down next to Nicole.

"Here," I said gently. "This was from Dana. I found it at the church after the ceremony. She must have been meaning to give it to you afterward."

There was a stunned silence as Nicole held the box in her hand. Even Mrs. Abernathy was at an unprecedented loss for words.

Nicole handed the present to Vince, who set it on the table in front of him. Everyone stared at it like it was a bomb that was about to go off.

It was Mrs. Abernathy who finally spoke: "Aren't you going to open it, dear?"

Nicole buried her face in her hands, shaking her head.

Vince pushed the package away. "We don't have to do it now, Nicole. It can wait."

"Sorry," I said. "But I knew you'd want to have it."

"She was a good friend," Nicole said, sniffling loudly.

"She was, and she loved you very much," I said. I didn't know whether it was true, but it seemed like the right thing to say, like if I were a character in a movie and Dana were a cherished friend.

Nicole wiped her eyes and picked the box up off the table. "This is the last gift I'll ever receive from her. I have to know what it is."

She slowly began to unravel the bow, drawing out the moment.

"Come on, Nicole," said Mrs. Abernathy. "Let's not be *dramatic*."

"Mom, please." Nicole's hands were shaking, and she handed the box back to Vince. "You do it," she said. "I don't think I can."

Vince pulled the paper off. "You sure?"

Nicole nodded.

"Okay, here goes." Vince opened the flap and stared inside. No one spoke.

He looked back and forth between the box, his wife, and me.

"Well, what is it?" asked Mrs. Abernathy.

"I'm not sure," he replied.

"Vince?" Nicole whispered.

He turned the box upside down and dumped the contents out on the table.

The last gift Dana would ever give Nicole turned out to be a DVD, some 128GB memory sticks, and a hard drive. And I definitely didn't remember that being on the registry.

CHAPTER 12

*W*hat do you get the couple who has everything? Data, apparently. At least it was beautifully wrapped data.

"So," I began, since everyone else had been rendered speechless. "Were you hoping to increase your digital storage capacity, or . . . ?"

Nicole looked at Vince, question marks in her eyes. He looked shocked in return.

"Really," Mrs. Abernathy said, rolling her eyes, "would a place setting have been too much to ask?"

"Nicole," I said, "do you know what—I mean why—I mean, what *is* this stuff?"

"I have no idea!" she replied, as bewildered as I was. "Are you sure it was meant for us?"

"Dana brought it to the church with her and it was wrapped

in wedding paper, so I just assumed. I mean, it's not like she had another wedding to go to right after."

"I can't imagine why she'd give us these," Vince said. "There must be some kind of mistake."

Yeah, asking Dana to be a bridesmaid was the mistake. The girl had been drama from the beginning, and the small matter of her death hadn't changed anything.

Vince scooped everything back into the box and closed the lid. "Well, thanks for this, I guess."

I'd never encountered a wedding present quite like that, and I didn't know what to make of it. I thought for a moment. "Could it be pictures, maybe? Like of the two of you? Something she wanted to share with you?"

"I don't think so, but who knows?" said Nicole. "Do you have your laptop so we can see what's on them?"

Of course I did. I don't go anywhere without my laptop; it's command central for my business. I sprinted to my room to get it and made it back in record time, slightly out of breath and dying of curiosity.

Nicole handed me one of the USB sticks, and I inserted it. A log-in window appeared on my screen. Encrypted. I should have known. We checked another just to be sure. Encrypted again. This was turning out to be one mysterious gift.

"Any guesses what the password would be?" I asked.

We tried birthdays, pets' names, even the combo of 1234 on the off chance she'd chosen the world's most common password. Then again, anyone who encrypts files isn't going to make it easy.

"Oh! Try 'artichoke,'" said Nicole.

"'Artichoke'?" I asked.

"Yes, it was her favorite vegetable."

Being the good sport I am, I humored her. Unsurprisingly, the password was not "artichoke."

"Huh. Okay, hand me one of those discs and let's see what's on them," I said, undeterred. I slipped the DVD into the drive. Finally, something that didn't demand a password. There were only a few files, and they had mysterious, unhelpful names. Two clicks later I was staring at a spreadsheet, Nicole and her family crowded over my shoulder.

"Weird," Nicole said.

"Yeah," Vince concurred.

"Soooooo, congratulations on your nuptials, here's a spreadsheet?" I asked.

"Is this what the young people are doing these days?" asked Mrs. Abernathy. "Thank God we don't have to write a thank-you note."

I scrolled through the numbers, not really knowing what I was looking at. "Does this mean anything to anybody?"

"Not at all," said Nicole.

It appeared to be financial information, but why, and for whom? It was clear this wasn't meant to be a gift. Dana had used the camouflage of gift wrap to hide something she didn't want anyone else to see. It sure wasn't her own personal checking information; the numbers were way too big.

I kept my thoughts to myself for the moment, although surely the others were wondering the same thing.

"Is there any information other than numbers?" Vince asked.

I scrolled to the bottom of the page and back up again for due diligence. Nothing. With not much more understanding than I had before, I ejected the disc and sat back in my chair.

"Well, looks like we'll never know," Vince said, taking the disc and returning it to the box.

"Actually, I have an idea," I said. "This would be a good job for my Information Technology department."

"You have an IT department?" Vince asked, surprised.

"Yes. His name is Brody."

In addition to being my favorite wedding photographer, Brody was my go-to guy whenever I needed a little extra tech support, and I felt certain he'd know what to do. I scampered to his room, data in hand, and thrust the box of discs and drives toward him. "Here, want a special project?"

He peered into the box and looked back up at me. "What, you want me to back up your hard drive on these?" he asked, one eyebrow raised quizzically.

"Nope, better. These files are encrypted. Work your magic!" I waved one hand dramatically over the box before shoving it into his hands.

He sat down at his desk and opened up his laptop. "Do you have the encryption keys?"

"Well, if I had those I wouldn't need you. Duh."

"Clearly. Look, I don't know if I can do much with these. You don't need me; you need a hacker."

"C'mon, Brody, who taught me how to repair permissions and, whatchamacallit . . . reboot in single-user mode? You did! Help me, Obi-Wan, you're my only hope!"

"What are these, anyway?" He inserted one of the drives and was greeted with a password request just like I had been.

"World's worst wedding gift."

"What?"

"Remember the box from Dana that I found at the church? This is what was inside."

"Ohhhhhh," he said, realizing the full implication of his assignment. "Wow. So this could help us figure out what happened."

"Exactly! Now you get it." I told him about the financial information, and he agreed that it sounded like a lead, especially considering the pains Dana had taken to hide it.

Brody looked thoughtful. "I guess we could try to guess what she used as a password. Maybe Nicole could help."

"I'll tell you right now, it's not 'artichoke.' "

"Huh?"

"Never mind. Can I leave these with you? I have to go talk to Fernando."

Mission Fernando had fallen to the bottom of my priority list, but I had promised Zoe I'd ask him about his altercation with Dana.

Brody stared at the screen, and I could almost hear the wheels turning in his head. "All right, but no promises."

It didn't take long to find Fernando, who was busy in the kitchen preparing our evening meal. When I walked through the door, he was chopping cilantro, and my sudden and unexpected arrival caused him to jump.

"Kelsey! *Buenas tardes.*"

"Sorry, Fernando, I didn't mean to startle you."

"It is nothing," he said, pushing the cilantro into a small mound with his knife. "Are you hungry?"

"Always," I said, smiling in spite of myself. Some "bad cop" I'd make.

"There are some tamales in the fridge. Help yourself."

I opened the double-wide stainless-steel refrigerator and only paused for a second before grabbing the dish. I'd be pretty easy to poison, I thought ruefully. Oh, well, the odds of him keeping poisoned tamales on hand for just such an occasion seemed slim, so I went ahead and forked a couple onto a plate, then popped them into the microwave.

"Thanks, Fernando, you're a lifesaver." When I was done heating the tamales, I pulled up a stool and watched him work, balancing my plate on one knee. "Fernando, can I ask you something?"

"Of course. As long as it is not my recipe for *chili con carne,* because I make that up as I go along."

I took another bite, stalling. "These are delicious, by the way." I swallowed and set my fork down. "You know Dana, the woman in the wedding party who died?"

"The one who is the reason you all stayed, right?"

"That's right."

Fernando nodded, dumping the carrots into the pot. "Very sad. I am sorry for your loss." He hardly missed a beat before moving on to some cilantro.

"Oh, it wasn't my loss," I was a little too quick to say. "But, you know, the Abernathys are pretty upset."

"Of course."

"I was wondering if you might be able to help us out. We're trying to figure out what happened."

"I am afraid I don't know anything that would help you. I never even talked to her, outside of serving her meals."

A bite of tamale had been en route to my mouth, but my fork froze in midair as I took in what he'd said. Never talked to her? But Zoe said she'd seen them arguing. Why was he lying? What was he trying to hide? I inched the fork back to my plate on the off chance that I was about to ingest deadly chicken-stuffed masa dough.

"You never talked to her? Not at all?"

He looked up from his cilantro-chopping duties and shrugged innocently.

Not that I'm a human polygraph machine, but I could tell he wasn't being forthright.

"That's weird. Zoe seemed to think you didn't like Dana much."

His face darkened as he continued to chop, putting a little more shoulder into the task than was necessary against the innocent herb. He could say what he wanted, but the vein in his temple was pulsing in time to his bladework. Finally he looked up at me. "It is not right to speak ill of the dead."

Normally I would agree, but I'd already made an exception for Dana more than a couple of times.

"Fernando?" I wanted to intercede before he pulverized our entire meal. "Fernando, what do you know?"

He set down his knife and put both hands on the edge of the counter, blowing out a long breath.

"That girl—she was no good. *La diabla*."

"Tell me what happened."

"One night after dinner, I came into the kitchen and I found her in here. She said she was still hungry and just wanted to make a snack. I told her guests aren't allowed in the kitchen, but she did not care. She said she could have me fired like *that*." He snapped his fingers to illustrate.

"Oh, jeez. I'm sorry, Fernando." I wished I'd been there to tell him not to listen to her. She didn't have any power over him, but there was no way he could have known that.

"I told her fine, I would make her some food, but then she decided to help herself to one of the bottles of champagne from the refrigerator. I said, 'No, no way, you can't have that. It is for the newlyweds.' "

"What did she say?"

"She said they would not miss it. I told her my employers keep a strict inventory, but she did not care. She just kept saying, 'Charge it to my room!' I told her it didn't work that way, that this was not a hotel." Fernando waved his arms to emphasize his point, knocking the knife to the floor with a clatter. "I begged her. I said, 'If a bottle goes missing, it will come out of my paycheck.' She said, 'Well, I guess that's your problem, isn't it?' " He had picked up the knife and was waving it in the air to punctuate his thoughts.

"That's super weird, and I really want to hear the rest of the story, but could you possibly put that knife down?"

"Oh, sorry." He dropped the knife back onto the cutting board, much to my relief, and wiped his hands on his apron.

"Thanks. Okay, go on."

"Anyway, I grabbed her arm to stop her, but she told me if I did not let go, she would scream. Then she got really angry. She said if I didn't back off, she really *would* have me fired. Then she left, and she took the champagne. I didn't know what to do. It was a very expensive bottle. More than I can afford." His eyes grew worried. "I cannot afford to lose this job. I have a family to feed."

What had Dana been thinking? Surely she must have understood what an awkward position that would put Fernando in, but she obviously hadn't cared. "So what did you do?" I asked.

"There was nothing I could do. We have one rule here: Make sure the guests are happy. And she told me if I said one word to anyone, she was going to make my life—what did she call it?—a living hell." He leaned back against the counter, folding his arms across his chest.

I could see a trend here. The more I learned about Dana, the more I realized that she'd made a lot of enemies. Including one pissed-off house chef who'd had both motive and opportunity. "Fernando, you have to see how this looks. Dana threatened you, then she turned up dead."

The cook's eyes grew wide. "You have to believe me. I did not hurt that girl. If I had killed her, I would have lost my job anyway, because I would be in jail, *verdad*?"

"I guess so . . ."

"I hope you believe that I did not do this thing." His eyes searched mine.

I nodded, not sure what to say. I didn't really believe he'd poisoned Dana, but I still didn't understand why he'd lied. "So why did you tell me you'd never talked to her?"

"I didn't want any more trouble."

Poor guy. "Well, don't worry, you're not in trouble. I'm just trying to find out what happened, because right now Zoe is sitting in jail and apparently I can't leave the country until she's free."

"You cannot leave? But why not? You are just the wedding planner, not the police."

"I'm glad someone sees that." I picked up my abandoned tamale and finished it off.

"These people you work for, they are very strange."

"You've got that right," I sighed. "I don't know how I got myself into this mess. Except that I feel really bad for Zoe. I visited her at the jail today, and she looked awful. I promised I'd help figure out who did this and get her out of there."

He gave me a sympathetic nod, then furrowed his brows as if working out a complex math problem. After a moment of silence, he spoke: "There is one thing you should know."

I put my fork down again. He had my attention. "Yes?"

"If I tell you something, will you promise not to tell anyone who told you?"

"Of course, Fernando."

"It is not my place. What my guests do, it is not my business. I am paid only to cook. Promise me, you don't tell anyone."

"I promise. What is it?"

"The night she came to me, I did try to go to her room. I wanted to talk to her, beg her not to get me fired."

"You *what*? Fernando, this is terrible! Why didn't you tell me before?" Either he was about to confess, or he was about to make it a whole lot harder for anyone to believe his version of the story.

"Wait!" he cried, holding up his hands. "I never made it to her room. As I was walking down the hall, I saw someone else by her door. He knocked, and she let him in."

"He? He who?"

"It is hard to be certain. But I think it was the—what is the word? *El novio*."

"Boyfriend? I don't think Dana had a boyfriend." Of course, it could have been someone she met in town, although jeez, even Dana didn't seem that easy. Maybe she had hooked up with someone from the wedding. It happened all the time. Whoever it was, I had to find him, because he would have had the opportunity to poison Dana.

He looked around to make sure we were still alone, then lowered his voice to a whisper. "No, not *her* boyfriend. The one who was getting married. Señor Moreno. Vince. He's the one who was in her room that night."

CHAPTER 13

*Y*ou could have knocked me over with a *churro*. Vince? In Dana's room? I've heard of grooms getting cold feet, drunk-dialing their exes, and engaging in all sorts of questionable behavior the night before the wedding, but Vince didn't seem like the type for such last-minute shenanigans. Besides, he knew Dana well enough to stay far away from her. Didn't he?

"Fernando, are you sure?"

"It was dark, so I cannot be positive, but it looked like him. Whoever it was, he was wearing an orange *guayabera* shirt."

I couldn't remember what Vince had been wearing that night, but I couldn't rule out orange. It was a good color on him.

"And what time was it?"

"I got finished cleaning up around eleven, but I was too upset to go to bed, so I opened a beer. Around eleven-thirty, I decided to go see if she was awake. That's when I spotted him in the corridor."

My head was swimming with this new information. What reason could Vince have possibly had for a late-night liaison? "And she let him in?"

"*Sí.*"

"You're sure of it?"

"Yes, he went in, and she closed the door behind him."

This was so not good. Even if Vince hadn't killed Dana, there couldn't have been any good reason for him going into her room in the middle of the night. Nicole would be devastated either way. I would have to handle this with extreme caution.

With promises not to divulge my source, I excused myself and headed straight for Brody's room. I found him right where I'd left him, working on his computer.

I flopped onto the bed and watched him peck away at the keyboard. "Any luck?"

"Hold on, I'm in the middle of . . ." He trailed off, engrossed in his task.

"You're never going to believe what I found out."

"Just . . . hold on. I'm trying to . . ." More keystrokes and a few murmured curse words.

"But, Brody—"

He shot me a look. "What part of 'hold on' don't you understand? You asked me to do this, now hold your horses."

I waited patiently for at least twenty seconds before interrupting again. "But this is important!"

"Seriously? You are such a toddler. Okay, fine. What is it that can't wait, other than you?"

I squirmed up into a sitting position. "Guess who Fernando saw going into Dana's room the night before she died."

"Oh, let me think. Benito Juárez."

Was I detecting a note of sarcasm?

"The former president of Mexico? No, he's dead, Brody."

"Ah, that's too bad. Then I give up. Who?"

I looked at him expectantly, eyebrows raised. "Who would be the last person you'd ever guess?"

"I already told you: Benito Juárez."

This would have been a lot more fun with a willing partici-pant. "I'll give you a clue: What if Benito Juárez had been getting married the next day?"

"Then that would have been very, very bad of Benito and very unfair to Mrs. Benito."

I nodded encouragingly. "You're getting warmer."

"Wait. You're not telling me . . . ?"

I nodded again, watching the expression on Brody's face change as the news sank in.

His eyes opened wide. "Get out! Vince was in Dana's room?"

"Yes! Or at least we think so. Fernando saw someone going into her room and he was pretty sure it was Vince."

He let out a long, slow whistle. "Wow. What are you going to do with *that*?"

"No idea. That's a pretty big accusation, and breaking up a new marriage is a major wedding-planner faux pas. But if it was him—"

"Then he'd have some pretty major explaining to do," Brody finished.

"It still doesn't mean he killed her," I said. "But if Vince spent the night before the wedding in Dana's room, Nicole might just kill *him*."

"So where does that leave us?" Brody asked.

I sighed and flopped back onto the bed. "Heck if I know. When I started this little extracurricular project, I didn't think I'd find anything. But the more I learn about Dana, the more the list of suspects grows. Oh, yeah, I guess technically I should include Fernando on that list," I said, before filling him in on the chef's story.

"Wow," Brody said. "So how many suspects do you have so far?"

"I don't know. Let's make a list." I grabbed a notebook and a pen off Brody's bedside table and started drawing a grid.

"There's Zoe," I said, scribbling her name in the left-hand column. "She disliked Dana, but just in a regular way, nothing special. Plus she says she didn't do it, and I believe her."

"Okay, next?"

"Next was Trevor. He definitely had the motive with the mental anguish Dana put him through, pretending to be pregnant and all. But he wouldn't have had much opportunity because he was here with a date."

"A date we haven't heard from since," Brody reminded me.

"Right! I've left her several messages, and she hasn't called back. I'm getting worried about her."

"Should we tell the police?" Brody asked.

"I don't really know what we'd tell them: Some girl was here but then she went home?"

"Yeah, that wouldn't work."

"All right, so Trevor is a maybe," I said. "Don't you have any highlighters I can use to color-code this?"

"Oh, let me check," Brody said, patting his pockets in an exaggerated way. "Sorry, I seem to be out."

"No worries," I said, ignoring him. "I'll fill it in later. Okay, so that brings us to Fernando. Dana snatched the champagne from his kitchen, threatened his job, and was constantly sending back her food, which might not be a motive, but it's super annoying."

Brody waited for me to finish jotting notes, then asked, "So what about Vince?"

I tapped my pen against the notepad in contemplation. "If

what Fernando said is true, Vince would make the list, at least as a possibility. But I'd better not write it down for now. He can't know that we know—especially since we don't really know."

"Oooh, what about Mrs. Abernathy?" Brody asked, a mischievous twinkle in his eye.

"As a suspect? Okay, I'll bite. Motive?"

"Being an evil cow!" He cackled gleefully.

"C'mon, Brody, you're going to need more than that."

"Okay, the vic failed to RSVP in a timely fashion."

"Better. Murder weapon?"

"A million cc's of Botox, administered straight into the right ventricle of her heart."

I laughed as I tore my burgeoning list of suspects out of his notebook. "You're a natural at this. I'll be sure and share your findings with the police next time I talk to them."

"All right," Brody said. "Off you go now. I've got some files to hack—just in case my 'murderous-mother-of-the-bride' theory doesn't pan out."

I stopped by my room long enough to ponder my next move. Napping sounded like a particularly attractive option, but first I needed to check my e-mail. Yikes. I had fourteen new messages to deal with—seven from my assistant, Laurel, with accompanying text messages on my phone:

> Need to talk about Richardson wedding. Call when you can.

> Hey, Kelsey, call me ASAP.

> WTF? Where R U???

As the urgency increased, so did her use of abbreviations.

Sigh. Time to pull it together.

I dialed Laurel, who picked up on the second ring.

"*There* you are!" she said, with a mix of exasperation and relief.

"Why, hello to you, too!" I had a split second of panic that I was in trouble before remembering that I was the boss.

"Guess who wants to make her grand entrance in a hot air balloon?"

"Oh, no. Tamara?"

Hot air balloon rides over the vineyards were a popular wine country attraction, so I didn't have to rack my brain to figure that one out.

"Of course it's Tamara. She saw it on some stupid Travel Channel show and now she has to have it for her wedding."

In deference to Laurel's foul mood, I resisted making a joke about the sky being the limit. "Well, that's not going to work. You can only do hot air balloon rides really early in the morning because it gets too hot."

"Yeah, you try telling her that. She didn't believe me, but maybe if you were here, you could talk some sense into her."

"Sounds like she's turning into a total Veruca." Veruca was the code word we'd come up with for demanding brides one night after watching *Charlie and the Chocolate Factory*.

"She is! Total Veruca. When I tried to tell her it wouldn't work, her response was, basically, 'But I want it.'"

"Don't worry, I'll talk to her."

"Well, better make it quick, because we have our final menu tasting tomorrow. I'm about ready to strangle her with her stupid twinkle lights, which, by the way, she thinks aren't quite the right color so I'm having to reorder."

"Please fight the urge to kill her," I said, rubbing my temples. "I've already got one murder on my hands."

"Well, you'd better get back here if you want to keep that number at one, because I'm ready to snap!" She really did sound even more stressed than me, if that was possible.

"Believe me," I said, "I would much rather be there with you than here dealing with all of this."

She paused for a second and blew out a breath. "I know. I'm sorry, I'm just venting. You're dealing with much worse things than I am."

"Don't worry. I totally get it. It's frustrating. But you'll get used to it after a while, and you'll learn to smile and nod and say, 'Let me look into that.' Even if they say they want a kangaroo for a ring bearer."

"Unless the wedding's in Australia. Then that makes perfect sense," she deadpanned.

"Of course," I said, laughing.

"Oh!" Laurel's voice brightened. "On a slightly more positive note, I've got something for you. It's actually kind of interesting. We got an inquiry through our website from a woman who lives there in San Miguel. She got your name from someone who was at the Abernathy wedding, and she was wondering if you're available."

"Wow," I said. "Does she know about the . . . you know?"

"She didn't say, but maybe you could go meet with her, as long as you're there. Even if you don't end up taking the job, it might be nice to go play wedding planner for a few hours. You know, take a break from crime fighting."

"Good point. What's her name?"

"Jacinda Rivera. She's actually from Texas—an artist, I think she said. But her family has a home in San Miguel, and she's thinking of having her wedding there."

"All right. Couldn't hurt. Send me her contact info, and I'll give her a call."

"Okay, sending now." I could hear her typing the e-mail over the line.

"Thanks for everything, Laurel. I couldn't do this without you."

"You're welcome. And you're right: I am pretty awesome."

"Believe me, I know." And I did. A million people wanted Laurel's job, but I couldn't imagine having someone better than her around. She was organized, easygoing, and creative. And basically running my business for me while freaking out only a little. "Don't worry, Laurel, this will all be over soon. I'll figure this out, and I'll be back home before you know it."

I sure hoped I wasn't lying.

CHAPTER 14

Thanks for coming over on such short notice," said Jacinda Rivera, leading me into her living room. When I'd called to set up a meeting with the bride-to-be, she'd been thrilled that I was available to meet in person and eager to get started right away. "Would you like some refreshments?" she asked, gesturing to a tea tray and plate of cookies she'd set out on the coffee table.

"What I'd like is to move in," I exclaimed, taking in the large, dramatic space stuffed with Mexican folk art, quirky antiques, and enough paintings on the walls to warrant their own museum exhibit. "This place is amazing."

"Thanks," she said, beaming. "It belongs to my parents, but they let me hang out here."

"Is that a Chagall?"

"One of his lesser works, but yes. Good eye."

I was struck by an enormous and colorful abstract that hung over the fireplace.

"That's one of mine," Jacinda said, gesturing at the extra-large canvas.

I did a double take. "Wow, it's beautiful."

"Thanks," she said, blushing. "There are plenty of terrible ones where that came from. I'm still learning, but being down here really inspires me."

The first time I meet with potential clients, I'm interviewing them as much as they're interviewing me, but I had no doubt that I would jump at the chance to plan Jacinda's wedding if asked. An artist? My mind was buzzing with the possibilities. I had a feeling her wedding would be amazing with me or without me, but I certainly hoped it was with. There'd been a time when I would have done it for free just to have the pictures for my portfolio, and it didn't hurt that I'd taken an instant liking to the willowy brunette.

"My fiancé and I live in Austin," she continued, "but this place has been in the family for decades. I come down here and paint sometimes when I need to get away."

It was ironic. Jacinda considered San Miguel a place to escape to, and here I was wanting to escape *from* it. Of course, having a house like this might make me see things differently. I would move in with her in a heartbeat if she asked, with wedding-planning services thrown in for free.

I did love San Miguel, and now that my relationship with Evan had been rekindled, the thought of living in the same town had flitted across my mind a couple of times. I wouldn't need to work much to afford to live here. Maybe I'd take up painting, too.

But what was I thinking? A couple of nice dates didn't warrant relocation and a change in profession.

Maybe it could just be my winter home.

I shook my head, banishing my spontaneous fantasy life. "So,"

I said, "have you picked a venue?" Maybe we could knock out some site visits while I was here. "The Instituto is gorgeous for a reception, and since it used to be a convent, there's actually a chapel right there on-site."

She nodded enthusiastically. "I agree. In fact, I dropped by the other day to check it out, and they were setting up for the wedding you did. It was beautiful."

I smiled sheepishly. "I swear I'm not trying to duplicate that wedding. I just love the idea of an artist getting married at the art institute."

"Of course!" She nodded. "I totally agree."

"Your event should be all about you, and we could really make it special. Nothing like the Abernathys'. I mean, not that theirs wasn't special, just that yours would be unique."

Jacinda picked up the teapot and filled two mugs, instantly releasing the fragrance of jasmine into the room. "I heard there was a little . . . incident."

I froze, not sure how to respond. What had she heard?

"One of the bridesmaids passed away?" she said, handing me a mug.

Oh, that.

"Yeah," I said, blowing on the hot liquid while trying to decide what to say. "That was unfortunate. Definitely not something we saw coming."

"I feel terrible for that poor bride. Do they know what happened?"

"Not yet." I decided to leave it at that. There was an awkward silence, during which I resisted the urge to give her unsolicited advice about picking bridesmaids who weren't so eminently murderable.

"I'm sorry," she said, breaking the tension. "It must have been horrible for you. Let's talk about happier things. Like cake!"

"Yes!" I said, relieved. "Cake is important."

"And dresses, and guest lists."

"And tequila donkeys!" I exclaimed, caught up in the moment.

She looked at me quizzically, apparently unaware of the tradition. "Tequila donkeys? Is that some sort of a—?"

"Okay, maybe not tequila donkeys," I quickly interjected. We'd tackle the subject of booze later. "Do you have an officiant yet?"

"We don't have a church here, so that's something we'll need to figure out."

"I've got the perfect guy," I said, happy to be able to put my new resource to use.

We talked for another half hour, during which we covered a lot of ground. We made plans to meet the next morning for some site visits, and I promised to take her to meet Father Villarreal. By the time I handed her my empty tea mug and gathered my things to go, I was feeling more optimistic than I had in days. I'd found an important clue, interviewed a suspect, and even worked in a potential client, all before dinnertime. I would have traded it all to sleep in my own bed, but for now, I'd take it.

When I got back to the villa, I found a note stuck to my bedroom door: "Where are you? I may have cracked the case. Love, Nancy Drew."

I hurried to his room to hear the latest development.

"I'm a genius," he said as he swung open the door.

"I've always suspected. What'd you find?"

"First, tell me I'm a genius."

"You're a genius. You wear nice shoes and you're kind to animals. Now spill it."

"I spent some more quality time on the computer." He tapped

the space bar to wake the laptop. "The first USB was encrypted. Totally unhackable."

"Duh. Why do you think I dumped it on you?"

"But this USB drive is only password-protected."

"That's still bad, right? I mean, if you don't have the password."

"For mere mortals, yes, but I booted it up in target mode. Now, yes, there was a firmware password, but since I was at root level—"

"Boring!" I interrupted. What kind of a geek did he take me for?

"No, but this is really good. I was in at the root-user level so I tried—"

"Will you please cut to the chase, nerd?"

"Fine. Let's just say that because I'm a genius, I was able to unlock some of the files, and guess what I found?"

"Naked pictures!" I squealed.

"Close. I found *this*." He opened up a document that had a lot of numbers.

I stared at the screen and then up at him. "How is that close to naked pictures?"

"Let's just say it was very *revealing*."

Groan. "Okay, how? All I see is a lot of numbers."

"I found out what this stuff is. It's financial data."

"Okay?" I was trying to stay interested, but he'd oversold the naked-pictures comparison.

"I found out whose it is. Does the name LionFish mean anything to you?"

I paused while I searched my memory. "Oh, you mean Lion-Fish, as in . . . ?" I was bluffing. "No, sorry, I have no idea."

"I didn't either, at first. But I did a little research, using the magic of the Internet. It's a start-up company. I did some digging, and guess what I found out? One of the founders is Ryan Mc-Guire."

I instantly recognized the name, and my heart sped up a little. "Ryan McGuire as in the best man Ryan McGuire?"

"Bingo. I can't even really tell what they do. Website is all blah, blah, blah, end-to-end-solutions blah."

"Why would Dana have his company's financial information?" I asked, perching myself on the edge of his desk. "She didn't work for them."

"I don't know, but apparently LionFish was in a lot of trouble," he said, gesturing to a bunch of numbers in red that kept getting ominously larger.

I watched as the figures scrolled by, wondering how Dana had come to have this information and what she'd intended to do with it. "Could she have been blackmailing someone?"

"That's kind of what I was wondering," Brody said.

"So what do we do with this? I would say we should go talk to him, but he flew out the day after the wedding."

"Take it to the police," Brody said. "They can look into it."

"Officer Ortiz?" I laughed. "All he'd do is stick it in a drawer. They're so convinced that Zoe is their killer that it's going to take a lot more than this to get their attention."

"Well, there are still more files. I'll see if I can find a bomb-shell in here somewhere."

Brody's discovery gave me new hope that we'd be on our way home soon. But either way, time was ticking on our stay at Casa de Muerte. Some group of happy vacationers was going to be arriving soon and wouldn't be expecting to find another family lounging in their courtyard. If they were lucky, no one in their party would die. They'd probably even be allowed to come and go as they pleased.

They didn't know how good they had it.

Frankly, I'd been in denial and hadn't really started looking, because if we moved to another rental house, that meant we weren't going home anytime soon. But if we did have to move, I didn't mind being the one making the reservations. That way, I could find Mrs. Abernathy a nice place somewhere far, far away from wherever Brody and I would be staying.

Which reminded me: when we left, we'd have to take everything with us. And that included Dana's stuff, which was still strewn about her room. I'd felt so helpless when I'd had to call and break the news to Dana's parents, I'd found myself promising them that I'd take care of things till they could get here. It was the only consolation I could give them, short of offering to plan her funeral—a task Mrs. Abernathy would certainly have volunteered me for, had she been within earshot.

I'd even been cleared by Officer Ortiz to box up her things. They hadn't found anything useful when they'd searched the room, and they didn't consider it a crime scene—or at least not *the* crime scene. The ransacking had to be connected to the murder, but since they had "solved" the latter, they weren't concerned with the former.

Figuring I had a little time to kill before dinner, I decided to go ahead and tackle the job. At least I'd get to cross one thing off my list.

Dana's room didn't look that different from how Brody and I had first found it the morning after the wedding, which is to say it looked like a disaster area. If only the detectives had taken a moment to tidy up as they went, it would have made my job a lot easier.

I dragged her luggage out from the closet and started filling it with her clothes. It felt strange to be going through her things, but I really didn't have a choice. I folded her clothes neatly, clean and dirty alike, and put them into the suitcase. Did they really want her personal belongings, too? I mean, of course her jewelry and her watch, but should I send along the leftover energy bars she hadn't gotten around to eating, or the in-flight magazine she'd crammed into her carry-on? What about her colorful collection of thong underwear? It wasn't my place to decide what they'd want and what they wouldn't; I decided to pack everything that didn't come with the room. Until I found a box of condoms in her bedside table. Those I would spare them from, I decided, as I tossed them in the trash.

As I filled her toiletry bag with her makeup, a small tube of lipstick fell off the table and onto the floor, rolling under the dresser. *Oh, skip it,* I thought as I packed up her tweezers and eye shadows.

Approximately twelve seconds later, my conscience got the best of me. Even though they'd never notice it was missing, I'd know. That's me. Attention to detail. Both a blessing and a curse.

I knelt down to peer under the heavy wooden furniture. The lipstick had rolled to the back wall, just out of reach. I grabbed a clothing hanger and used it to retrieve the small plastic cylinder, noting to myself that I would probably be pretty good at that claw game if I ever needed a small stuffed toy.

There was something else under there. I raked at it until I pulled it close enough to reach. Just her plane tickets. Probably too late for her family to get a refund for the unused portion, although it wouldn't hurt to try. I plopped down on the bed and opened up the envelope to find her return flight.

There wasn't one. At least not to the United States.

There was a receipt for her flight to Mexico, and she'd paid a lot for the last-minute ticket. But instead of a return flight home, she had booked a one-way ticket to Barbados.

Funny, Mrs. Poole hadn't mentioned that when I'd talked to her. Had she known that Dana wasn't flying back home? Weird.

It wasn't unheard of, piggybacking one trip onto another, but San Miguel to Barbados seemed like an odd itinerary. What had she been up to? I shrugged and set the ticket aside, in case Dana's mom wanted to try to get some money back from the airline.

As I finished up, my pocket buzzed with a text from Brody:

Where are you? It's time to go down to dinner.

I'd lost track of time, but the bells of La Parroquia confirmed my tardiness, so I dashed out a reply:

On my way. Wait for me?

I hurriedly zipped Dana's bags and did a final check under the bed and in the closet. I didn't want to miss out on one of our last remaining Fernando meals—especially after having smelled it simmering earlier in the day. One of the few things I would miss about this place, I thought, as I closed the door to Dana's room behind me.

CHAPTER 15

The family was already seated when Brody and I got down to the dining room, and the newlyweds looked fairly miserable as they listened to Mrs. Abernathy go on about how a cricket had been chirping all night either in or near her room.

"It positively *destroyed* my sleep," she said.

"Do you want to trade rooms, Mother?" Nicole asked.

"Oh, no, dear, I couldn't ask you to give up the bridal suite, now, could I?" The way she said "could I" sounded more like she was weighing her options than making a point: *Could I? I don't know, let me think. Maybe I could.*

Brody and I nodded our hellos as we sat down at the table.

"Oh, *there* you are, Kelsey," Mrs. Abernathy said. "I'm glad you decided you could spare an evening for us, given your busy social schedule." She smiled as she dabbed the corners of her lips delicately with her napkin. *All in good fun,* her casual tone said, but her eyebrows arched a little beyond what they'd been plucked to do.

I smiled gamely, refusing to take the bait. "Good evening, Mrs. Abernathy. Of course I'm here. There's no place I'd rather be."

Brody, who had just taken a sip from his water glass, almost did a spit take in reaction to my obvious lie.

Okay, perhaps I was laying it on a little thick. I could think of plenty of places I'd rather be—San Francisco, Evan's house, the dentist—but this was where I was stuck, so I might as well make the best of it.

"Our lawyers are arriving tomorrow, and I was hoping for an update," she continued. "Have you learned anything new since this morning?"

Fernando, who had been pouring drinks for everyone, froze in his tracks.

"I, um, well—we've been trying to break into those files," I said, looking at Brody pointedly and getting ready to kick him in the shins if he said anything to indicate that I hadn't been by his side the entire time. I was afraid to mention my meeting with Jacinda; heaven forbid I take an hour for myself. I also didn't want to tell Mrs. Abernathy that I'd questioned Fernando— especially not in front of Fernando—and I definitely didn't want to say anything about Dana's mystery guest. Especially if that mystery guest turned out to be Vince.

Brody nodded. "Yes. Um, she's been a big help. Will you excuse me? I forgot to wash my hands."

Okay, at least if he was going to crack under the pressure, he had the good sense to flee.

Fernando's look of panic passed when he realized I wasn't going to mention our conversation, and he resumed filling the glasses. Our eyes locked as he poured a glass of wine for Vince. *Not to worry, Fernando.* I planned to watch *el novio* carefully while I decided what to do with that little nugget of information.

Mrs. Abernathy was still staring at me expectantly. She clearly thought I should have done more than just watch Brody try to hack some files.

"I also packed up Dana's room," I said, hoping that would satisfy her curiosity as to my whereabouts.

"Well, it's about time," said Mrs. Abernathy. "I assumed you'd taken care of that days ago."

I ignored her comment as Brody slipped back into the chair beside me. "I was wondering," I asked Nicole and Vince, "do either of you know when Dana was planning on flying back to Denver? I only found a one-way ticket to Barbados."

Nicole's eyes grew wide. "Barbados? She didn't mention that."

Was it my imagination, or had Vince's expression shifted? In the dim light, it was hard to read his face, but there definitely seemed to be something going on there.

Mrs. Abernathy shrugged. "Lots of people vacation, Kelsey. I can't see how that's any business of yours."

"I was surprised, that's all. I assumed she'd be flying back to Denver."

"Well, she's flying back to Denver now, isn't she? Have you made arrangements for the body?"

"Mrs. Abernathy, I really don't think that's—" Her stare-down stopped my sentence in its tracks.

"You don't think it's what? Your job? You certainly don't think *I'm* going to do it, do you?" She stared at me, dumbfounded by my apparent stupidity.

"I just figured—"

An awkward silence ensued.

"Oh, for heaven's sake," said Mrs. Abernathy.

I felt my face flush. "I'm sure her family will want to make the arrangements." I was glad when Brody reached over and took my hand, because it was the only thing stopping me from stabbing her in the eyeball with my salad fork.

The silence was broken a moment later when the door to the kitchen swung open and Fernando reappeared, a steaming dish in his hands. *Perfect timing,* I thought. *That's a much better use of a fork.*

"Carne asada," he announced as the room filled with the fragrance of marinated steak.

I couldn't wait to dig into the dish I'd watched him preparing earlier in the day. It smelled even better than before, and my stomach gurgled its approval.

As the tortillas were passed around the table, one of the housemen entered and whispered something to Fernando, who glanced toward me. They continued their hushed exchange, and then Fernando nodded and came around to my side of the table. "Excuse me," he said, his voice discreetly low. "You have a visitor."

Mrs. Abernathy let out an exasperated sigh. "It's dinnertime, Fernando. Tell Kelsey's little friend we're eating. She can call him later."

"It's not Evan," I said, offended that she'd assume it was my fault. "He's flying right now."

"Then who is it?" Mrs. Abernathy demanded.

"It's a young man," said Fernando. "He asked for Kelsey specifically."

"Okay," I said, bewildered. "Did he say who he was?"

Fernando bowed his head slightly before replying. "Yes, madam. That girl, Dana?"

I nodded. I wasn't sure where this was going, but I was pretty sure I didn't want anything to do with it.

"It is her fiancé."

We all looked at each other, trying to identify the person at the table to whom this might make sense. I didn't know Dana had had a fiancé, and judging by the look on her face, Nicole didn't, either.

"He has flown in from the States," Fernando continued. "Shall I send him in?"

"Um, sure," I said, glancing around the table for approval. As much as I hated to disrupt dinner, this new development had gotten the better of my curiosity, and everyone else nodded in agreement.

"Of course, Fernando," said Mrs. Abernathy. "Send him in. The poor boy."

As soon as Fernando left the room, we all tried to cram an hour's worth of speculation into the ensuing two minutes. Why hadn't Dana told us she was engaged? Why hadn't she invited him to the wedding? And was she flying on to Barbados without him? How had he known where to find us? Was he heartbroken? Would there be tears? Would he—please, oh, please—be taking over the duties that had been dumped on me?

All whispering stopped as the door swung open a few moments later. A tall, skinny guy with messy brownish-blond hair stood in the doorway, looking teary-eyed, jet-lagged, and awkward as all hell.

"Hi, I'm Kirk. Kirk Larsen." His eyes darted around the room, not sure exactly whom he should be introducing himself to.

The moment might have been uncomfortable if it weren't for Mrs. Abernathy, who seamlessly switched into hostess mode. "Fernando, set another place, please. Kirk, you must be starving. Please, put your things down."

"Thanks," he said. He dropped a backpack on the floor next to his rolling suitcase and gratefully took the chair Fernando had pulled up to the table.

We all stared at him, not sure what to say.

"I'm Kelsey," I said. "We're so sorry for your loss." The introductions and condolences continued around the table.

"Dana told us such nice things about you," Nicole said. I cocked my head at her lie. Bless her heart. Nicole would do anything to make someone feel better.

"Thank you. I talked to Dana's mom Sunday night, and she told me what happened."

"Have you arranged for a place to stay?" I asked gently. What was one more guest?

"No, when I heard the news, I packed my things and came."

"Well, don't you worry one bit," said Mrs. Abernathy. "We've got plenty of room here, at least until Friday. You can stay with us."

"That's awfully nice of you," Kirk said. "But really, I don't mind finding a hotel."

"Don't be silly," Mrs. Abernathy said. "I insist."

His voice cracked with emotion. "Thank you. I don't even— thank you."

"Fernando," I said, "can you send a housekeeper to make up—oh, shoot."

"What is it?" asked Mrs. Abernathy.

"Well, the only room that's open is . . . was . . ." It was Dana's. I couldn't get the word out.

Mrs. Abernathy chimed in: "Kirk, is it okay if you stay in Dana's room? Kelsey's removed her belongings already."

"About that—her things are still in there." I cringed, waiting for the response. "I was going to finish after dinner."

Mrs. Abernathy looked disappointed in me, but she bit her tongue in the presence of our new houseguest.

"That's okay," Kirk said. "I'll finish packing her stuff. I was planning on doing that anyway. I promised Mrs. Poole I'd settle Dana's affairs."

Yes! I felt bad for Kirk, but I was happy to be absolved of

Dana duty. I'd let him deal with her belongings and the coroner's office; I had plenty to do just tending to Mrs. Abernathy.

"Well, it's settled, then," said Mrs. Abernathy. "Fernando, please tell the housekeeper to freshen up Dana's room."

"Very well," said Fernando, exiting back into the kitchen.

I felt excited about my newly lightened load for about twenty whole seconds before it hit me: *the condoms!* I didn't know what Dana had been doing with a fully stocked condom drawer and I didn't want to know, but I definitely didn't want to leave them there for Kirk to discover. I didn't really care about protecting her reputation, but I did care about protecting Kirk.

"Will you excuse me?" I asked. "I just want to make sure they . . ." I pointed toward the door, then dashed through it, making record time up to Dana's room. I retrieved the package from the garbage can, stuffed seven or eight foil squares into my various pants pockets, and wadded the empty box up into an unrecognizable ball that I hid in a planter of bougainvillea in the courtyard.

I slipped back into my seat as Kirk was finishing up a story. "So anyway, that's how we met."

"Had you set a date yet?" asked Nicole, clearly wondering why she hadn't been invited to be in the wedding party.

"It was all very sudden," Kirk said, "but we wanted to do it before the baby came."

Vince choked on the bite of steak he had taken, coughing furiously while Nicole patted him on the back.

A baby? *A baby?!* Poor Kirk. Dana had struck again, just like she had with Trevor. Brody and I focused our attention on our plates. Mrs. Abernathy simply stared, as expressionless as a Botox junkie. I hoped that for Kirk's sake no one would mention the Dana and Trevor saga. It was too late for it to matter.

Kirk looked alarmed at the reaction. "I'm sorry. Hadn't she told you? Maybe I shouldn't have said anything."

"Wow," I responded, just to have something to say. "I had no idea. Then again, I'm just the wedding planner. Why would she tell me, right?" I was hoping we could gloss over the facts of who knew what, because if Dana really *had* been pregnant, surely she would have told Nicole, and it was clear she hadn't said a word about it. Which could only lead me to one conclusion—one that was most likely shared by several members of our party.

"Well," Kirk said, "she might not have wanted to say anything till she was a little further along. We had just found out."

"I guess so," Nicole said. "She hadn't even started to show." The expression on her face hardened as she caught up to what the rest of us had already concluded.

"Well, we're doubly sorry for your loss, then," Mrs. Abernathy said, acting much kinder than I thought she was capable of being.

We made polite chitchat, asking Kirk about his flight and how long he planned to stay; then Fernando returned to let us know that Kirk's room was ready.

"You must be exhausted after your flight," I said, pushing my chair back. "C'mon, let's get you settled in."

While Kirk gathered his bags, I heard Mrs. Abernathy clearing her throat behind me. "I believe you dropped something," she said.

Lying on the floor next to my chair was a ribbon of condoms, which I quickly snatched up and stuffed back into my pocket under the scrutiny of Mrs. Abernathy's stare. Dammit. What was I going to say, "They were Dana's"? I sheepishly shrugged and tilted my head toward Kirk, hoping Mrs. Abernathy would pick up on the psychic messages I was sending her. She didn't. She just looked at me and shook her head.

"Really, Kelsey. What are we going to do with you?"

CHAPTER 16

The next morning, I woke early and grudgingly began searching for a new place to stay in San Miguel de Allende. After leaving a message with my favorite rental agency, I called a few of my old standbys, only to find that they were booked.

I did a cursory search from my laptop, running some dates through a couple of reservation sites. How many nights? Well, that was a big question mark, but I started with five, just to be safe. Nothing was available. I tried four days; still no luck. Three? Two? How could it be there was nothing available? I expanded my search parameters to include three-star hotels. Mrs. Abernathy wasn't going to like it one bit, but at least she wouldn't be sleeping in the bus station, using her Louis Vuitton luggage for a pillow. Still, nothing was coming up.

Finally, my contact at the rental agency called me back. Lydia had helped me out many times before, and I was optimistic that she'd be able to find something for us.

"This weekend?" she asked. "Oh, no. Kelsey, I hate to tell you this, but I've got nothing."

"Are you serious?" I asked, tapping my pen on the notepad that was waiting for me to jot phone numbers down on it. "Nothing at all?"

"I'm afraid not. This weekend is the San Miguel Chamber Music Festival, and everything's booked."

Mrs. Abernathy was going to kill me. I should have started calling sooner, but how was I supposed to know the chamber music festival was coming to town? It's not like the streets were filled with the sound of cellos warming up—although their ominous sound would have probably made a fitting accompaniment to all the drama.

"Okay," I sighed. "Call me if anything opens up." I hung up the phone.

After seriously lowering my standards, I found some rooms available at a two-star motel on the outskirts of town, and I went ahead and reserved them just in case. Picturing the look on Mrs. Abernathy's face when I helped her get checked in at the Casa Grande provided plenty of incentive for me to keep looking. Besides, considering Zoe's situation, no one in the family was going to want to stay at someplace called the Big House.

I sighed and slumped in my chair. Why couldn't we just stay here in the villa? Stupid vacationers with their stupid rental agreement.

At a loss as to what my next move would be, I decided to go visit Brody since I had some time to kill before my appointment with Jacinda. He opened the door, greeting me with "Oh, good, you're up," then yanked me inside before I even had a chance to say good morning. "I couldn't sleep last night after our surprise guest arrived, so I spent some more time with the files."

That got my attention. His eyes were dancing with excitement— not to mention a vaguely self-congratulatory look that could only mean good news.

"Wow, I was going to see if you wanted to go get croissants, but this is way better. Please tell me you found something."

"I found something. Dana had an entire dossier on LionFish."

"A dossier? What do you mean?"

He opened his laptop and pointed at a spreadsheet with lots of red numbers. "She had all this information on the company, like e-mails and financial records."

"Really? Why?"

"From what I could tell, the company was failing. Which in and of itself isn't all that remarkable, except for the investors."

"The investors?" I didn't know where he was going with this, but I perked up based on his tone alone.

"Apparently, it wasn't just Ryan's company that was at stake. He had gotten his friends involved, too. And guess who was a silent partner? His best friend, Vince Moreno."

"Wow, that's awkward."

"Only if Vince knew," Brody said. He raised his eyebrows expectantly, waiting for me to catch up.

I peered at the screen, then looked back at Brody as I started to piece it together. "What do you mean? Vince didn't know the company was in trouble?"

"Not according to these," he said, double-clicking a folder to reveal dozens of backed-up e-mail files. "Ryan had been keeping it a secret from everyone, but somehow Dana found out. Apparently, she had a few thousand dollars invested, and when she realized it was gone, she found a way to get it back."

"You don't mean . . ."

"She was blackmailing him."

"Seriously? Whoa . . ."

"Yeah. And he was paying her out of the company's funds—which only compounded their financial problems."

"Wow," I said, soaking it all in. "So if Dana was blackmailing him, that means he had a motive to kill her."

"That's the best motive we've heard so far," Brody said.

A thought occurred to me, propelling me off the bed. "Brody! The tickets!"

"Yeah? What about them?"

"Remember? Dana was flying on to Barbados. This explains why there was no return flight home."

Brody nodded in agreement. "Right! Because she wasn't going home."

I paced back and forth, excitedly putting all the pieces in place. "She was blackmailing Ryan, she came here to get the money, and she was going to disappear for a while. If you remember, she wasn't even going to come until a couple weeks ago. I bet the only reason she changed her mind was so she could get her hands on the money."

Brody let out a low whistle. "Wow, good work."

"Thanks, but it was mostly you," I said modestly.

His blue eyes twinkled mischievously. "Oh, yeah, sorry, I meant me. I'm awesome."

"In fact," I said, ignoring him, "it was probably Ryan who went to her room that night."

"So what now? Should we go talk to him?"

"We can't; he left town right after the wedding. But we could go talk to the police. I'm sure they can track him down."

Brody smiled and closed his laptop. "I think this calls for a breakfast cocktail, don't you?"

"Yes! Oh my God, I'm so relieved. This proves that he had a motive, and we know he had the opportunity—"

"Not to mention the devilish good looks."

"Brody!" I tossed a pillow at him, but it sailed right past. "He's a murderer. Don't tell me you find him attractive?"

"What? I'm only human. I notice things. Don't tell me you didn't."

"Whatever. I'm going to let your momentary lapse in judgment pass because you may have just freed us from this nightmare."

"So, can we go now?" Brody asked, looking at his watch.

"Shoot," I said. "I'm supposed to meet with Jacinda to talk about her wedding, but maybe we could get together afterward? I should be done by noon or so."

"I'll do you one better, if you want. I'll go to the police station and show them what we've found so they can get going on it."

"That'd be great!" I exclaimed. "Then maybe we can come home and start packing!"

"Don't get too excited. They probably won't release Zoe just because we bring them a new lead. But hopefully this will point them in the right direction, and maybe in a day or two . . ."

"Let's hope so. I'm coming up empty on places for us to stay, and if I don't figure out something soon, we're going to be commuting into San Miguel from Querétaro."

We said our good-byes, and I headed toward the *jardín,* stopping at a little café to order a coffee to go. Transitioning into work mode, I grabbed an extra for Jacinda. Why? Because I'm an awesome wedding planner who takes care of people, anticipating their every need, from officiants to caffeine. If the last few days hadn't proved that there was nothing I wouldn't do for my clients, I didn't know what would.

I arrived about ten minutes early, settling onto a park bench. The *jardín* looked different in the light of day, much more subdued than when Evan and I had taken our evening stroll. Which reminded me: I owed him a phone call. I hoped he'd be excited that I'd found a new lead, even though it meant I was one step closer to going home. We'd both known this was temporary, but it was too bad we wouldn't have more time to see where it might end up.

Nah, I thought, shrugging it off. It was too bad we didn't live in the same city, but I wasn't about to feel bad about going back to my own life. He was the one who had decided to move to Mexico. If he wanted to see me, he could literally hop on a plane almost anytime.

"Good morning," Jacinda said, interrupting my thoughts and holding up two paper cups of coffee. "Look what I brought you!"

"Ha!" I picked up the two cups I had secured earlier. "Great minds . . ."

"Looks like we've got caffeine to spare," she said jovially. "I brought *café con leche*. It's really good. They make it with cinnamon."

"Oooh, let's drink yours first, then. It sounds delicious." We both took long drags off our coffee. If we were going to be overstimulated, we'd be overstimulated together.

"I've been thinking about your venue," I said. "I don't know if you've seen the Escuela de Bellas Artes, but it has a similar feel to the Instituto."

"Oh, interesting," she said. "I've looked into taking classes there, but I've never actually been in the building, I'm ashamed to say."

"It's beautiful," I replied. "It was part of a church—a monastery, I think—and they turned it into an art school back in the 1930s. It has a courtyard that would be just perfect."

"Sounds great! Maybe we can go look at it later." She popped the plastic lid off her cup, releasing ribbons of steam, then swirled the creamy liquid around to let it cool. "So how does this work—with you, I mean? Do we do a contract, or . . . ?"

"Well, if this means I'm hired, then yes!"

"Of course! I'm sorry. I thought it was obvious," she laughed.

"Great. Then I'll write up a proposal, and we can go from there."

"I hope you'll accept these fancy coffee drinks as a down payment, at least until I can get you a check," she said. We clicked our paper cups together in a makeshift toast.

"Luckily for you," I said, "I am easily bribed." I stood up, a coffee cup in each hand, and gestured toward the church. "Shall we?"

The church was only a few minutes' walk, as are most things in the center of San Miguel. We entered the church vestibule, the large wooden doors snuffing out the cheery daylight behind us. It took a few seconds for my eyes to adjust to the dim lighting, the main source of which was coming through the dark, stained-glass windows. In the nave, I dipped my fingers in the holy water reflexively, making the sign of the cross. I wasn't Catholic, but I'd spent enough time in churches to be able to pass for any religion.

A middle-aged woman wearing a gray apron was dusting the pews, emptying the slots at the back of each one to make sure they contained only hymnals.

"Excuse me," I said. *"Con permiso. Dónde está Padre Villarreal, s'il vous plaît?"* She looked at me curiously. "Oh, sorry, I mean, *por favor.*" I knew a smattering of Spanish, but anytime I said more than a few words, I'd get confused and end up speaking French.

Still, she shook her head and kept polishing the dark, cherry-stained wood.

"Padre Villarreal, por favor?" The cleaning woman rattled off

something in Spanish as she walked toward the altar and disappeared into the sacristy. That's the trouble with attempting a foreign language: even if you know the question, it doesn't mean you'll understand the answer.

"That was weird," I said to Jacinda. Maybe I should have called ahead, but I hadn't thought our drop-in would be so oddly received. "Do you think I said something wrong?"

"Don't look at me. My dad only spoke English around the house, and my mom was from Waco. Based on two years of high school Spanish, though, it sounded okay to me."

Before we could decide on our next move, the door to the sacristy opened again and another woman emerged, walking slowly toward us. *"Buenos días,"* she said, looking tired and a little put out at having to deal with unexpected visitors.

"Buenos días," I said, extending my hand and giving her my best smile to try to win her over. Before she could launch into something I wouldn't be able to follow, I quickly added, *"Habla usted inglés?"*

"Sí, sí," she answered, nodding, much to my relief, though she didn't return my smile.

"Gracias. I'm looking for Father Villarreal. Is he in?"

"No, he is not," she said, folding her hands in front of herself.

"Oh, I'm sorry. We can come back later. Or make an appointment, if that's better."

"I'm afraid that won't be possible," she said, bowing her head slightly.

"Oh." I was disappointed and a little bit embarrassed at this small failure in planning. I really should have called first. "When do you expect him back?"

She fished in her pocket for a tissue as she let out a sniffle, and I noticed that her eyes were rimmed with red. Was she crying? I looked at Jacinda helplessly. What had I said?

"I'm sorry," I said, turning to go. "I seem to have caught you at a bad time."

The woman blew her nose and regained her composure. "No, I'm sorry," she said. "You must not have heard. Father Villarreal—he is dead."

CHAPTER 17

My mind was reeling and my stomach had gone all wobbly. I suddenly found myself shaking, and only partially because of the coffee. *Dead?* How could that be? We had just seen Father Villarreal a few days before, and he'd looked fit, healthy, and several decades away from needing a cemetery plot. "I'm so sorry," I said. "What happened?"

The woman pulled her navy blue cardigan tight around her, then fingered the small, gold cross she wore around her neck. "We're still waiting to hear." She eyed us suspiciously. "Did you know him?"

"Sort of," I said as I fumbled for words, trying to make sense of the news. "I mean, he performed a wedding for my friend, and we wanted to see if he was available to do another one." I gestured toward Jacinda, who was looking a little ashen.

"I'm afraid you're going to have to find someone else," the woman said, turning back toward the altar and walking away.

"Wait!" I needed to know what had happened, but I wasn't sure exactly how to ask. "It wasn't—I mean, it was natural causes, though, right?"

She stopped and turned back to me. "I'm not allowed to talk about it," she said, fixing me with a level stare that told me everything I needed to know. "The funeral is tomorrow morning, if you'd like to come pay your respects," she said as she walked away.

Jacinda took a couple of steps back, a distressed look on her face. She pointed toward the front doors. "I'm just gonna—"

I followed her outside, where we stood in silence for a moment, squinting into the sunlight, both of us unsure what to say. I hadn't known Father Villarreal for long, but I'd genuinely liked the man, and he had come through for us in a pinch. "Poor Father Villarreal," I said. "I can't believe this."

Jacinda nodded pensively.

One wedding, two deaths. I knew it must look bad. I had to get it together. Be professional. Not let the second death in less than a week throw me off my game.

I took a deep breath. "That's okay. I mean, it's tragic, poor man, but we can find someone else. In the meantime, do you want to go take a look at Bellas Artes?"

"I don't know, Kelsey. I know this sounds silly, because it's not like you killed the guy or anything, but bad luck seems to be following you around."

I wished I could say it sounded silly, but it didn't.

"Let me assure you that this is not at all how things usually happen."

"I know, I'm sure it's not. You seem great, and I'm sure you're really good at your job, but this is a lot to process."

"I understand," I said. And I did. I couldn't blame her. I didn't know if I would have hired me, either, under the circumstances. "You want to just talk later?"

"Sure," she said, her voice uncertain. "I'm sorry, I'm probably just being superstitious. I just—I don't know."

"Of course. Well . . ." I was at a loss for words. "Call me."

"Good-bye, Kelsey," she said before turning and walking away. At least she hadn't broken into a sprint. Maybe there was still hope.

I was disappointed, of course, but there was something much worse nudging at the back of my mind. *Murder.* Could Father Villarreal have been murdered? His death had obviously been unexpected. It could have been an accident, but then why would the woman at the church have been so secretive?

No, I refused to believe it. Father Villarreal could not have been murdered. Because if he had, then it couldn't have been a coincidence, and I wasn't willing to accept that the wedding I'd planned so perfectly had somehow led to two people's deaths.

Stunned, I texted Brody, then wandered back to the *jardín* to wait for him. I replayed the conversation in my head over and over again. Maybe there was some sort of mistake. Maybe he'd—I don't know, faked his own death. Like maybe he had some gambling debts he couldn't repay, or he was on the run from the Mexican Mafia.

When I'm in denial, I go all in.

Brody showed up a few minutes later. "Hey," he said as he shrugged off his messenger bag and set it beside me. "That didn't take long. I just got done at the police station, and then I got your text. I wouldn't say they were as impressed as we were by what we found, but they promised to look into it."

"Brody, sit down." I gestured at the bench next to me.

"Whoa, you look like hell! What happened? You were only gone for an hour."

I shot him a look before realizing I probably did look pretty shaken, then recounted what had happened at the church.

His eyes went wide with disbelief. "Dude," he said, not as a nickname but as a general observation about the suckiness of the situation. "Are you sure?"

"I didn't ask to see the body or anything, but the word 'dead' didn't really seem open to interpretation."

"Sorry, I can't even wrap my head around this. What happened?"

"I don't know! The woman I spoke to didn't offer up any details."

"I don't want to let my imagination go running away with me here, but two deaths . . . What are the odds that it was a coincidence?"

I buried my face in my hands. "I know. As much as I don't want to believe it, I thought the exact same thing. What if he was killed by the same person who killed Dana?"

We both slumped in our seats, staring at the ground in silence as we tried to make sense of this new piece of information.

A thought suddenly occurred to me, propelling me into an upright position. "On the bright side, Zoe wouldn't have had any motive to kill Father Villarreal. Surely the police will be able to see that."

"Hey, that's true," said Brody. "Plus, she might have already been in jail when it happened."

"That would certainly help our case," I said, chewing on my lip pensively. "I just wish we knew more. We could get Zoe out of jail, and I could convince Jacinda that my weddings aren't inherently lethal."

Brody and I abandoned our spots on the park bench and headed off to find the street taco lady who had a cart a few blocks away. I told him about Jacinda and how she'd practically fled after learning about Father Villarreal. We sat on the curb with our paper plates in our laps, speculating over *tacos de carnitas* about whether the police would release Zoe and what exactly the Abernathys' attorneys were doing to help.

After polishing off the *carnitas,* what I really wanted was a nap—isn't that what you're supposed to do after lunch?—but first I wanted to go by Evan's house and see if he was home. So much had happened since our last date, and I wanted to catch him up on all of it. I'd learned about Dana's blackmail scheme, found and probably lost a new client, met Dana's fiancé, Kirk, and gotten the evil eye from Mrs. Abernathy no less than eight times. All that and another death to report, too. I was nothing if not full of news.

Brody walked with me to Evan's house, but when Evan answered the door, Brody all but abandoned me, mumbling something about giving us our space before vanishing around the corner.

"This is a pleasant surprise," Evan said, pulling me in for a quick hello kiss. I hoped there would be more where that came from. We retired to the hammock in his courtyard, where I updated him on everything as we swung lazily back and forth.

"I heard about that," he said, when I told him what I'd learned about Father Villarreal. "When I was at the market earlier, I ran into one of my neighbors, and she goes to his church."

"Did she say what happened?"

"Not really. They found him at his house after he didn't show up for services on Sunday."

I sighed. "But no one knows the cause of death?"

"That's all she told me, sorry. But I'll let you know if I learn anything else."

I told him all the rest of my news. My right arm was going a little numb from being pinned under me, but it felt good to be pressed against the warmth of his chest.

"Wow," he said, rubbing one hand idly up and down my back. "You've been busy."

"Tell me about it. We're getting kicked out of the villa the day after tomorrow, and I have to find someplace we can all stay. Stupid chamber music."

He shifted and propped himself up on one elbow, red indentations crisscrossing his forearm where the hammock had pressed into his arm. "What about here?"

"Here? You don't have room for all of us."

"No, but I have room for you, and that's a start. Maybe even Brody, if he doesn't mind taking the foldout."

I chewed on my lip and thought about it. "Well, it would be nice to have a little distance from Mrs. Abernathy."

"C'mon," he said, giving me a quick kiss as if it settled the matter. "It'll be fun, like a slumber party."

"And it would mean two less beds to find."

"See? There you go. I won't take no for an answer."

"Okay, then. If you're sure . . ."

"I'm sure," he said. "And who knows? Maybe you'll like it so much here you'll never want to leave."

I craned my neck around to look at the clock. "Speaking of leaving, I should probably skedaddle. I have to fill the villa folks in on everything that's happened."

I hated to go, but there was still so much to do. At least I'd found a place for me and Brody to stay, but I was going to have to get creative or I'd have to show up with four or five extra people in tow. I wondered how Mrs. Abernathy would feel about sleeping in a hammock.

Back at the villa, I had Brody help me round everyone up for a family meeting. Mrs. Abernathy, Nicole, Vince, Brody, and even Kirk gathered around the patio.

"What is this about, Kelsey?" Mrs. Abernathy demanded, right as I was about to open my mouth.

"I've got good news and bad news. Well, and some other news that's somewhere in between."

"Let's start with the in between," said Mrs. Abernathy, "since I have no earthly idea what you're talking about."

I hadn't realized I'd been holding my breath until she said that. I wasn't ready to break the news about Father Villarreal, at least not yet. Not that the extra few minutes would make it any easier, but I was still struggling to find the right words. "As you may or may not be aware," I began, "we have to move out of here on Friday to make way for new guests."

"I'm sure they can find another place to stay," said Mrs. Abernathy, dismissing the new tenants with a wave of her hand.

"I wish it were that easy, but we're getting kicked out."

"Where are we supposed to go?" Mrs. Abernathy demanded.

"That's what I've been working on," I said. "It's been difficult finding accommodations, because everything is full up this weekend, but I do have some leads."

"I should hope so," said Mrs. Abernathy. "So what's the good news?"

I filled them in on the information we'd found on the USB drives and told them we'd visited the police. I kept an eye on Vince to see how he reacted to the news, but his face didn't betray anything one way or the other about whether he knew that LionFish was in trouble.

"That *is* good news," said Mrs. Abernathy. "When do you think Zoe will be released?"

"It's not that simple," I replied. "They aren't ready to let Zoe go, but at least they're looking into it, and that's something."

Mrs. Abernathy let out an exasperated little sigh. "Wait, you mean you weren't able to convince them to release her? I thought you said this was *good* news."

"Mom, Kelsey did everything she could," said Nicole. "These things take time."

Mrs. Abernathy looked unconvinced, but Kirk leaned forward and touched my arm in a gesture of appreciation. "I'm sure you did great, Kelsey. I appreciate everything you're doing to help find out what happened to Dana." I smiled and nodded in response. Poor Kirk. It was nice to have someone on my side. I made a note to ask him later if I could help him with anything.

Ignoring Kirk's speech, Mrs. Abernathy rolled her eyes. "If you call that good news, then I hate to hear what the bad news is."

"Oh, yeah. That. So, I went to the church today to see Father Villarreal."

"Why?" asked Vince. "Is he a suspect?"

"What? No, nothing like that. I was taking a woman named Jacinda Rivera to meet him. Anyway—"

"Who is this Jacinda woman and why have I never heard of her?" asked Mrs. Abernathy.

"It's not important. She's a new client. So we went—"

"A *what*?" asked Mrs. Abernathy.

Oh, boy.

"I met her the other day. She's planning a wedding and asked me to help."

"So *that's* what you're doing with your time?" Mrs. Abernathy shook her head. "I'd think we'd be keeping you busy enough that you wouldn't have to be looking for outside work."

"I am. I mean, you are!" Why had I even mentioned Jacinda? It was all Vince's fault.

"If you were a little more focused on this job, maybe you could have convinced the police to release Zoe. But I guess you were too busy planning this Jacinda woman's bachelorette party to be bothered."

I clenched my fists at my sides while choking back a string of expletives. She had to be kidding me! *Breathe, just breathe.* Closing my eyes, I silently counted to five. I had bad news to deliver, and screaming at my client wasn't going to make it any easier.

"Mrs. Abernathy, I'm doing everything I can for you. Rest assured, you have my full attention. Just think of it as something I did on my lunch break. Anyway, we went to the church to find Father Villarreal, only he wasn't there."

"That reminds me," said Nicole. "We should really send him a thank-you note."

"Yes, dear, you really must. Just because you're married now doesn't mean you can forget your manners."

Brody and I exchanged a quick look. "I don't think that will be necessary," I said.

"Of course it's necessary," said Mrs. Abernathy, staring at me in disbelief. "We're not going to be gauche."

"You can certainly write it," I said, "but he won't be able to read it." They stared at me quizzically, trying to figure out if it was some sort of riddle. "Father Villarreal is dead."

That got their attention. There was a shocked silence as they absorbed the news. Kirk hadn't known him, but even he looked a little shaken.

"I'm sorry to have to tell you all. The police are looking into it."

Nicole's eyes welled up with tears. "Why does everyone around me keep dying?"

I knew exactly how she felt.

I had planned on attending Father Villarreal's funeral, but what I hadn't planned on was arriving with an entourage. As it turned out, Nicole had insisted on coming, and Vince and Mrs. Abernathy wanted to pay their respects, too. Although we'd only known him briefly, Father Villarreal had played an important role in Nicole and Vince's lives. In fact, marrying the two of them had probably been his last official act before he died.

I only hoped it wasn't the *reason* he had died.

We arrived early and filed into the church, following a procession of people down the center aisle toward the casket, which was draped with a blanket of gladioluses and surrounded by enough candles to light the room on their own. One by one, the mourners stopped and said a quick prayer.

I wondered if I might be able to learn more about how Father Villarreal had died, and tried eavesdropping as we inched our way slowly past the packed pews. My Spanish wasn't good enough to catch anything other than an occasional noun, and I quickly realized that I didn't even know the word for "murder," much less any of the terms for the various ways a person could die. I wondered if it would be rude to whip out my phone and open up my Spanish-English translation app. Probably.

Nicole and Vince were in front of me, and as we got closer to the front of the room, I heard her let out an audible gasp. She turned and grabbed my arm, her face white as a ghost.

"Nicole," I said, "what is it?"

She pointed mutely to the open casket, where the priest's body lay peacefully, his hands folded over his chest, holding a rosary. Had she not expected an open casket? The sight of him must have been too much for her. I put my arm around her reassuringly. "It's all right, Nicole," I whispered. "You can do this."

Vince was nudging me in the shoulder, trying to get my attention. "What?" I said, allowing a little bit of irritation to creep into my voice. If anyone should be comforting his wife, it should be him.

"Kelsey," he whispered, his voice tense. He pointed at the casket. "Who the hell is that?"

I stood on tiptoe and leaned to one side so I could get a better glimpse of the gray-haired man in the casket, who looked particularly unlike the man we were here to say good-bye to.

I shook my head as my voice caught in my throat. I looked at the couple, my eyes wide.

"I have no idea."

CHAPTER 18

This could not be happening. I felt the blood rushing to my face, making my cheeks hot as I looked at Nicole and Vince. Mrs. Abernathy was a few seconds behind, but she quickly caught on.

"Who is that man?" Mrs. Abernathy hissed, grabbing me by the arm and squeezing harder than was entirely necessary.

"I don't know," I said, my mind a complete blank. The three of them stared at me expectantly, waiting for answers, but I had none. The man in the coffin was a good twenty years older than Father Villarreal, and nowhere near as handsome; I could see that, now that we were right in front of him. I wanted to run out the church doors and into hiding, but since we were still standing in the front of the church with a couple hundred mourners looking on, I did the only appropriate thing there was to do: I pretended to pray.

I dropped down onto the kneeler and closed my eyes, my brain frantically trying to put together the pieces. *Who is that man in the coffin?*

The answer was actually fairly obvious. It was Father Villarreal. After all, it was his memorial service, at his church. If there had been some crazy mix-up at the morgue, someone would have noticed by now.

But that brought up an even more important question: *If that's Father Villarreal, then who was that man who married Vince and Nicole?*

I knew if I waited for an answer, I'd be kneeling there all day, so I whispered a quick "amen" and got up to make room for the next mourner. A church attendant helpfully gestured to some empty seats in a nearby pew, squashing my plans for escape. Not wanting to disrespect the dead man, we dutifully filed into the wooden bench and sat in stunned silence as the service began.

We stood as the priest led everyone in a prayer in Spanish. We sat while he continued to speak. We knelt when everyone else knelt, but for the most part, the service was lost on us. We were attending the funeral of a man we'd never met, which was being performed in a language we didn't speak.

A woman came to the front of the church and started singing a slow, mournful tune, and Nicole let out a loud sniff from two seats down. She'd been holding back her tears ever since our discovery, and something about the song released the flood. The tears started slowly at first, then built to gentle sobs. An elderly woman sitting on the other side of Nicole offered her a handkerchief and patted her hand reassuringly, thinking Nicole was a loyal congregant in mourning.

Mrs. Abernathy, of course, was shooting daggers at me with her eyes. I was glad the funeral gave me a chance to prepare for the confrontation that was sure to come. Even if it was just delaying the inevitable, it allowed me a few minutes to figure out what I was going to say.

There had to be some simple explanation, some sort of miscommunication caused by the language barrier. Maybe there were two Father Villarreals. A father and son? That didn't make sense; priests don't have kids. A nephew who'd been inspired by his uncle to go into the clergy? I scanned the room to see if our guy was among the congregation. Mrs. Abernathy gave me a sharp elbow to the ribs. "Sit still," she hissed. "This is bad enough already."

I slunk down into my seat, wishing I could disappear.

After what felt like hours, the funeral was over and everyone slowly started making their way to the back of the church. I started to get up, but the others were frozen in their seats. Mrs. Abernathy sat on one side of me, Vince and Nicole on the other. I was surrounded.

"Kelsey," Mrs. Abernathy began, exhibiting an eerie calm that was more terrifying than if she'd just begun yelling right off the bat. "What have you done?"

"Let's just stay calm," I said. "I'm sure there's some explanation."

"Who was that man?" Nicole asked, her voice frantic.

"That *man*," said Mrs. Abernathy, "is Father Villarreal. It says so right here on the remembrance card. The real question is, who performed my daughter's wedding ceremony?"

"He—you—I . . ." I stammered. I was doing fine with pronouns, but I couldn't seem to get any nouns or verbs to come out. I shook my head vigorously to release more words from my head to my mouth. "I don't know!"

"Oh my God!" cried Nicole. "We were married by an impostor!"

"Now, let's not jump to any conclusions," I said. "Maybe there are two Father Villarreals."

"And my honeymoon!" Nicole wailed, ignoring my luke-warm reassurances. "I can't go on a honeymoon if I'm not even married."

You can't go on your honeymoon anyway.

"Look, let me see what I can find out. I'm sure there's a simple explanation," I said. "Why don't you guys head back to the villa and get some lunch, and I'll talk to someone at the church."

Mrs. Abernathy gathered her things to go. "I suppose if that's the best you can do, we'll just go eat some *more* Mexican food and pretend everything's hunky-dory." With that, she departed in a huff.

Vince gave me an uncomfortable smile. "Thanks, Kelsey. Let us know what you find out."

"Thanks, guys. I really am sorry about this. You deserve better."

"It's not your fault," Vince said.

"Yeah, there's no way you could have known," said Nicole.

But I could have. And I should have. And now in addition to finding a murderer, I had another mystery to solve. I had no doubt Mrs. Abernathy would ruin me if I didn't make this right.

As we were leaving, I saw the woman I'd talked to the day before snuffing out candles in the front of the sanctuary. Hoping to catch her before she left for the burial, I excused myself and hurried to the front of the church.

"Excuse me?" I said. "Remember me? From yesterday?"

She nodded. "The one who wanted to get married."

Close enough.

"My name is Kelsey. Beautiful service, by the way. I know this is bad timing, but can I ask you a question?"

She glanced toward the door and looked at her watch. "I'm supposed to be leaving for the cemetery."

"I'm sorry, I know. I'll be quick." She nodded in agreement as she continued extinguishing the candles, leaving acrid smoke behind. Now that I had her attention, I wasn't sure where to begin.

"The man in the coffin—"

She nodded. "Father Villarreal."

"That's just it. Are you sure it was him?" I hadn't meant to blurt it out like that. She was going to think I was nuts. Besides, I already knew the answer. If it weren't him, one of the couple hundred other people attending the funeral would have mentioned something. She furrowed her brow and nodded again, naturally puzzled by my question. "Of course it was him. He's been with this church for years."

"Okay, sorry. Let me start over. Remember yesterday when I said Father Villarreal had performed my friend's wedding? Well, it turns out it wasn't him."

She looked confused. "Then why did you come to his funeral?"

"We *thought* it was him, but it wasn't, and now we have to figure out who our priest was. Are there two Father Villarreals?"

She stared at me and shook her head. "No, there is only one."

"He doesn't have another family member who is also a priest? Maybe a brother or a nephew or something?"

"I'm sorry, no. It is just him. Perhaps you got the name wrong."

I was sure I hadn't. I had made the arrangements myself, and I vividly remembered being relieved when Father Villarreal agreed to step in after our original plans fell through.

"I'm sure that was the name I was given. He was supposed to fill in for Father Delgado."

Her eyes widened in surprise. "Wait, Father Delgado—are you talking about the wedding that was this past weekend?"

"Yes, in the chapel at the Instituto Allende."

"I remember it," she said, crossing her arms in front of her chest. "It was on his calendar, but then they called and canceled."

"They what? No, that's not right. I would have been the one to call, and I definitely didn't." I was pretty sure I would have remembered something like that.

"We thought you must have found someone else."

"We were expecting Father Villarreal, and in fact someone showed up and introduced himself as Father Villarreal."

"I don't know what to tell you," she said, looking as uncomfortable with my questions as I was feeling. "It wasn't him."

"And there's no chance he sent someone else in his place?"

"No, as I told you, it was canceled, so there was no need." She snuffed the last candle out and turned to me. "Is there anything else?"

There was so much else but, unfortunately, nothing she was going to be able to help me with.

"No, thank you for your time."

I retreated back up the aisle, thoroughly confused. Someone had called Father Villarreal and told him not to come? How could that be? I couldn't fathom why someone would cancel on our behalf and then show up pretending to be Father Villarreal, if that was what had happened. Was it a misunderstanding, or was the man who'd performed the ceremony an impostor?

Either way, not knowing was bad. Really bad. I had no idea what to do. I couldn't go back to the villa without answers. Nicole and Mrs. Abernathy would bombard me with questions, and this time I wasn't going to be able to get out of it by saying, "I don't know, I'm just the wedding planner." As much as I'd protested that solving a murder wasn't part of my job description, finding out who had crashed their wedding—and performed the ceremony, while he was at it—definitely was within my jurisdiction.

I dug my phone out of my bag and dialed Brody. "Pick up,

pick up, pick up," I chanted under my breath. I had promised to call after the funeral and was relieved when he answered on the third ring.

"Hi, it's me," I said. "Can you come meet me? The funeral was a mess and I have to talk to you, but not there at the villa."

There was a pause on the other end of the line. "Yes, of course. I'd be happy to give you a bid on that," he responded cryptically, a strangely formal tone in his voice.

"A bid? Brody, it's me. Can you not hear me?" My cell phone worked pretty well in Mexico, but Brody's often had bad reception.

"I'll have to look at my calendar and get back to you."

"What?" It was like he and I were having completely different conversations. "Is that some sort of code?"

"Brody, who is that?" a familiar voice in the background demanded. Mrs. Abernathy. Of course.

"Ohhhh," I said. "They're standing right there, aren't they?"

"Yes, sir. That is correct."

"Is she still pissed? Never mind, I know the answer to that already." If he was afraid to tell them it was me on the phone, then it must be bad. "Okay, come meet me at Evan's house, okay? Cough once for yes, twice for no."

"Sounds good," he said. "I should be able to get a proposal over to you within half an hour."

"Great," I replied. "See you then."

"I look forward to working with you."

I hung up and dialed Evan to let him know I was coming over, but it went to voice mail. Luckily, he'd given me the spare key to his house in case I needed it. He'd told me to make myself at home, an offer I was relieved to be able to take advantage of. If there was one thing I could use right now, it was anything vaguely resembling a home. It didn't even have to be my home, but it was good to have someplace to retreat to where I wasn't on duty twenty-four hours a day.

This whole experience had been enough to make me rethink my career choices. An occasional bridezilla I could handle, but having to travel to other countries with people I barely knew and then being held responsible for their happiness was starting to seem like a bad idea.

Maybe I should have been a funeral planner instead. Your responsibilities are finite, the expectations aren't as high, and no one's going to be happy anyway.

Besides, business seemed to be booming.

CHAPTER 19

While I waited for Brody to arrive, I perched awkwardly on Evan's sofa. I was trying to make myself at home, like Evan had instructed, but it felt odd to be in his house without him there.

Just act natural. What would you do if you were at home?

I kicked off my shoes and leaned back on a scratchy, kilim-weave throw pillow.

If I were at home, I would replace this pillow, I thought, tossing it to the other end of the couch and sitting up again. Relaxing just wasn't on the agenda at the moment.

I noticed an ancient PC on a desk in the corner. Surely it had Internet access. I could at least use my time productively while I waited, lest I start rearranging Evan's kitchen out of sheer nervousness. The connection was slow, but I was able to find a couple of new posts on Craigslist for last-minute rentals, which I jotted on a notepad I found in the desk drawer. I couldn't return to the villa without something good to report, and if I didn't have answers about Father Villarreal, I could at least distract the family by telling them to start packing.

As long as I was online, I Googled Father Villarreal and confirmed that there was only one of him in the entire state of Guanajuato. Unfortunately, it was the one in the coffin, not the one who'd performed the ceremony. If only I had Googled him in the first place, I would have known what the real Father Villarreal looked like, and then I would have known to ask more questions when Father What's-His-Face arrived. Of course, I didn't usually feel the need to run background checks on my officiants—although maybe it was time to start.

That gave me an idea. I might not be able to look up the wedding crasher's name, but I could probably find his face. I texted Brody and told him to bring the pictures he had taken at the wedding.

Moments later, there was a knock at the door, and I scrambled out of Evan's oversized leather desk chair to go answer it.

"These pictures?" Brody asked, waving his digital camera in the air as I swung open the door.

"Hooray! You read my mind."

"I did indeed." Brody came in and set his things on the painted wooden bench near the front door.

"How did Mrs. Abernathy seem?" I asked. I hoped that having a little bit of time to process the morning's events had helped her put things into perspective.

"Not that different from usual. Although she did tell me that I might as well burn all the pictures from the wedding since they were probably going to have to do it all over again anyway, but I figured she was being hyperbolic. Anyway, Nicole and Vince filled me in on what happened. I figured you'd want to look through the photos to see if we could find some evidence of fake Father Villarreal."

"Yes! That's exactly what I was thinking. Thank you."

"Actually, I uploaded them all earlier, so we can look at them online, too, if you want."

"Perfect," I said, gesturing over to the desk. "Evan is on dial-up, but I'm already connected."

"I will warn you," Brody said. "Whoever this man was, he was awfully camera shy. At the time, I thought it was kind of odd, but I guess if he was an impostor, he'd have good reason to avoid the camera."

Sure enough, our mystery priest had managed to position himself so that his face was obscured by the backs of the couple's heads for the entire ceremony. You could glimpse a forehead here or an ear there, but without Photoshop, we wouldn't be able to do anything with the separate body parts.

"Go back further, to before the wedding," I said.

Brody had taken the requisite photos of the bride fixing her veil in the mirror and the groom doing shots with his friends. There were pictures of us setting up, including one of Mrs. Abernathy scolding the florists. There were even pictures of me in there, making faces at the camera to render myself an unappealing subject, in an effort to keep Brody from taking any more.

"Wait!" I said, as he was scrolling through some shots of the guests arriving. "In the background there. That's him!" The man we had known as Father Villarreal was crossing the courtyard behind a group of cousins in sunny, flowered dresses, smiling for the camera with their arms around each other.

"You're right," Brody said, zooming in on the man in the background. "It's a little blurry, but it's him."

"If this were television, I would just say 'Enhance,' and you could magically make him be in focus and even smile for the camera."

"You mean like this?" Brody clicked a couple of buttons, and the picture got brighter and a little sharper.

"Wow, that's cool! Now make him look straight at us!"

"Ha. Nice try. I think this will help, though. You can at least tell what he looks like."

Twenty minutes later, armed with a stack of printouts, we set out on our dual missions: finding suitable accommodations and identifying the man in the picture. We stopped by the police station, but the detectives were out detecting, so we left a message. We swung back by the church but found it locked up tight while everyone was at the cemetery. We stepped into a couple of shops to see if anyone recognized the picture of the mystery priest but didn't get anything more than confused shrugs. I asked a couple of random passersby if they'd ever seen our man before, but suddenly no one spoke English anymore, and by the time I stammered out something in Spanish, they were already halfway down the street.

"Maybe we could put his face on a milk carton," Brody suggested.

"Right. With a caption that says, 'Have you seen this priest?'"

Brody shook his head. "I'm not even sure which is weirder. The fact that this isn't really Father Villarreal, or the fact that Father Villarreal is dead."

"Tell me about it," I said. "Who would kill a priest?"

Brody shrugged. "Maybe someone confessed something they shouldn't have."

I stared at the photo, studying the mystery man's features. The more I thought about it, the more sure I was that it was no misunderstanding that had placed him there on the same day Dana had died, and another idea started to take shape in my head.

"Brody, what if this guy killed Father Villarreal to keep him from showing up at the wedding?"

"But why kill him? Didn't you say someone had already called the church and canceled?"

"Yeah, but what if Father Villarreal found out? Maybe he realized somebody was planning to go in his place and he tried to stop it from happening."

Brody looked dubious. "I don't know—that's pretty far-fetched."

"I know it sounds crazy, but what about this whole thing *isn't* crazy?"

Since we weren't getting anywhere with the search for the man who had introduced himself as Father Villarreal, we turned our attention to the last few rental options remaining in the entire town of San Miguel.

We started with the most promising: a three-bedroom near the center of town that promised "incomparable views." The pictures I had seen online looked pretty nice, but in reality the house could generously be described as a hovel. The views were incomparable, but that didn't mean they were good. It just meant that you couldn't really compare the tiny slice of sky you could see out the window to an actual view. The first of the small, dank bedrooms was serviceable, but the second held a single bed with a sagging mattress centered under a bare lightbulb hanging from the ceiling.

"Where's the third bedroom?" I asked the grizzled middle-aged man giving us the not-so-grand tour.

He jerked his chin toward the foldout couch sitting sadly in the corner of the cramped living room. "No extra charge for sheets!"

"Okay, thanks," I replied, edging toward the door. "We've got some other places to check out, but we'll think about it."

"Don't wait too long! It won't last," he said, looking amazed that we were walking away from such splendor.

I was willing to take my chances.

The next place was better—although I couldn't help but notice that it smelled like a combination of freshly scrubbed mildew, Marlboro Lights, and pine-scented air freshener. Brody wrinkled his nose while I concentrated on breathing through my mouth. They'd get used to the smell after a while, right?

Sadly, I had to put it down as a "maybe."

We arrived at the third house on my list, just a few blocks away on Calle Recreo. With its plain adobe walls, it looked like every other house in San Miguel from the outside, and there was no telling what would be on the other side of the door. I knocked a couple of times and looked at Brody hopefully. "Cross your fingers."

"Can't be any worse than the other two!" he said encouragingly.

A tiny woman who introduced herself as Marisol opened the door. "Oh, you're early!" she said. She had a towel thrown over one shoulder and was holding a broom and a dustpan in her hand. "Sorry, I was just getting it cleaned up. The family that just checked out brought their kids, and they made a bit of a mess."

"Thanks for agreeing to show it to us on short notice," I said, smiling as we stepped through the wooden door into the garden. "We're in a bit of a pinch."

"Well, you're in luck," she told us. "This place usually books up months in advance, but there was a last-minute cancellation."

I felt a flood of relief as she showed us around. It was more modest than the villa, but it was nicely furnished with heavy wooden antiques. There were a few more floral prints than I would have preferred, but it was comfortable and cheerful, and it even smelled good, like mint castile soap and sunshine.

On the landscaped patio, an orange tabby lounged on the warm tile, making me miss my two fluffballs back home. Thank God Laurel was taking care of them while I was gone. I didn't know what I was going to do when she started traveling with me for work, because she was their favorite pet sitter.

"I don't know who he belongs to, but he loves hanging out here, so I guess you could say he comes with the place," Marisol told us. I knelt to stroke him and he flopped onto his side, stretching so I could scratch his tummy. Maybe I was being unduly influenced by my newfound feline companion, but I liked the place, and I thought Mrs. Abernathy would, too.

I looked up at Brody, who was giving me a big smile and a thumbs-up behind Marisol's back.

"We'll take it!" I said, relieved to have at least one thing settled. While she drew up the paperwork, I quickly called to cancel the motel outside of town, eliciting some grumbles from the surly desk clerk. He'd get over it, and much more quickly than Mrs. Abernathy would have gotten over a room with a bed that vibrated if you inserted a couple of pesos.

Feeling lucky, I showed Marisol the picture of the impostor priest, but like everyone else we'd shown it to, she shook her head. Still, I'd averted the immediate disaster and could now focus on the other pressing matters at hand: hunting down the fake Father Villarreal, dropping by the jail to visit the bride's sister—oh, and figuring out who'd offed one of the bridesmaids. A wedding planner's work is just never done.

We dashed back to the villa to share the good news, and while it didn't stop me from having to have "the talk" with Mrs. Abernathy again—the one where she demanded to know who that man who'd married Vince and Nicole was while I explained that I didn't know—it did give me a good excuse to cut it short so I could go tell the others our plan. I found the newlyweds in their room, and told them the happy news that they wouldn't have to share a motel room with the mother of the bride.

Next, I visited Kirk's room. After hearing him call, "Come in," in response to my knock, I swung the door open to find him sitting on the floor amid a sea of items, some his, some distinctly feminine. The boxes I had filled and taped shut were open, their contents spread out on the floor.

"Um, Kirk, I wanted to tell you to start packing." He was clutching the pashmina shawl Dana had brought for cool evenings, looking like he had no idea what to do next. "But on a related note, you might want to *stop* unpacking."

I dropped my bag and joined him on the floor, sitting cross-legged among the vacation necessities. Poor guy. I'd meant to check in with him to see if he needed any help getting Dana's affairs sorted out, but I'd been too busy solving everyone else's problems.

He looked at me with the saddest expression on his face. "I wasn't ready to let go of her things. I promised Dana's parents I'd send them, but then I realized I'd never see any of this stuff, or her, ever again." He thrust the silky fabric toward me. "See? It still smells like her."

I politely pretended to inhale in the pashmina's general vicinity, but it just didn't have the same effect on me it seemed to be having on him.

He hugged the soft fabric to his chest and closed his eyes. "I just wanted to feel close to her one last time."

"Why don't you keep the pashmina?" I suggested, with a gentle tone that I hoped would mask my urgent need to start packing my own belongings. "I'm sure her parents won't mind. If they do, we can tell them she left it at the church."

He nodded somberly, folding it in his lap.

I had a sudden instinct to tell him everything—including the fact that his fiancée wasn't the person he thought she was. I knew he'd be shocked to hear about the blackmail, the one-way ticket, and the condoms, but maybe learning the truth would help ease his suffering. *Or cause more of it.* Not knowing which reaction was more likely, I went for a good old-fashioned subject change instead.

"Meanwhile, I've got good news. I mean, better news, at least. I found a rental house for Mrs. Abernathy and the newlyweds, and since Brody and I will be staying with a friend, there's enough room for you, too, if you want. I mean, I'm not sure when they'll release the body to you—" His face blanched at my reference to his girlfriend as "the body." Oops. I decided to keep going rather than dwell on the moment. "But there's plenty of room if you're sticking around."

"That's awfully nice of you, Kelsey."

"No worries. You need me to help you pack these things back up? Maybe we could swing by the post office in the morning and get them in the mail."

"I can do it," he said with a sigh. "I'm sorry. I'm sure this seems pretty maudlin."

I shook my head. "No worries. I know this has been a shock. You take all the time you need." I caught myself and amended my statement: "Okay, well, all the time you need between now and ten A.M. tomorrow."

CHAPTER 20

The next morning, Brody and I made it down to breakfast early and got a head start on the *chilaquiles* Fernando had prepared. No way was I going to miss my last opportunity to enjoy his cooking before relocating to Evan's house.

"Oh, Fernando, I wish I could take you with me," I said, shoveling the egg-and-tortilla mixture into my mouth. "I'm sure going to miss this."

He smiled and ducked his head, obviously pleased by the compliment. "If you would like, I will send some tamales with you."

I nodded my head in agreement, mouth too full too speak.

Brody laughed. "You'll be lucky if she doesn't try to sneak back into your kitchen every time she's hungry. Be sure she gives you the keys before she goes."

The others trickled in gradually, having spent the morning getting ready to move out. Kirk seemed to be in better spirits than the night before. He thanked Mrs. Abernathy for the invitation to stay with them in the rental house on Calle Recreo, but he'd lucked out and found a last-minute cancellation on a single room in a small guesthouse nearby.

Too bad for him. He doesn't know what he's missing. Then again, maybe he suspects.

"All right, everyone," I said. "I hope you're all packed. I have cars coming to get us at ten o'clock."

Nicole sighed dejectedly. "I can't believe we're stuck in San Miguel," she said. "We're supposed to be on our honeymoon right now."

"Darling, your sister needs you right now," said Mrs. Abernathy, patting her daughter's arm.

"I know," Nicole said. "It's just so frustrating." I had no doubt that both she and Vince were frustrated, in every sense of the word. It was bad enough that they couldn't go on their honeymoon, but here they were stuck with Mrs. Abernathy and they couldn't even sneak off to a hotel for the night. Definitely a mood killer.

"Maybe we could just go for a day or two," Vince suggested, looking hopeful.

Nicole bit her lip and looked at her mom. "It does seem like a shame to have that hotel room on the Riviera Maya going to waste . . ."

"I could have her back by Monday," Vince said, sitting up in his seat.

Mrs. Abernathy shook her head. "No one's leaving here until Zoe can leave, too."

"I'm not talking about just abandoning her," Nicole said. "We'd come right back."

Mrs. Abernathy sighed. "Your father will return in a couple of days, and maybe then we'll talk about it. But I need you here right now."

"It's not like we're even helping," Nicole said. "We're just sitting around."

Mrs. Abernathy looked incredulous. "Don't you think that's a bit selfish, considering your sister is in jail?"

Vince jumped to his bride's defense: "Mrs. Abernathy, all Nicole's trying to say is that there's nothing we can do for Zoe. If there were, you know we wouldn't even consider it."

"Be that as it may," Mrs. Abernathy said, "it is partially Nicole's fault. The least she can do is stand by her sister."

"My fault?" Nicole stared at her mother in amazement.

"Yes. If you hadn't invited Dana to be in your wedding, none of this would have happened."

Ah, how I was going to miss these delightful family get-togethers.

"So," I said, dropping my napkin onto my plate. "Shall we go get packed up?"

Brody followed my lead. "Yes, look at the time," he said, pushing back his chair.

We hastily retreated to our rooms, where I did my checkout ritual: put my bags by the door, looked under the bed for loose items, inspected the closet, opened each drawer, then double-checked under the bed again. Granted, it was a little neurotic, but one time I left behind my favorite pair of shoes, and I've never quite gotten over it.

Satisfied that I hadn't forgotten anything, I closed the door behind myself and joined the rest of the group by the front doors right as the church bells struck ten. Packing Mrs. Abernathy, Nicole, Vince, and Kirk off into their shiny black town car was the most satisfying thing I'd done in days.

Feeling the thrill of independence, we dove into the other

vehicle—me with a box of fresh tamales warming my lap—and gave the driver directions to Evan's house. I felt slightly giddy with my escape. Even though I still had a job to do, I wasn't going to be under the same roof as Mrs. Abernathy anymore, and that lifted my spirits considerably.

When we reached our destination, Evan met us at the car and greeted me with a kiss. "Here," he said, "let me help you with your bags."

Brody followed us inside, dropped his bags on the floor, and shook Evan's hand. "Hey, thanks for letting me stay here."

"No problem," Evan said. "I've never hosted a crime-fighting duo before. Should be fun."

"It is," I said. "It's a laugh a minute. Now, about that cocktail . . ."

"Cocktail?" Evan said. "Who said anything about cocktails?"

"I did. Just now." Sheesh. Men. They never listen.

"I think I've got some wine around here somewhere," Evan said.

"I'm kidding," I said. "It's too early. However, I do have a long-running fantasy about being greeted at the door with a pitcher of margaritas after a hard day, so, you know, something to keep in mind."

"Ha. Okay, I'll see what I can work out," Evan said. "Raúl is off for a few days, but I was thinking maybe I'd cook us up some steaks tonight."

Who was I to argue with that logic?

"Sounds great." Brody nodded in agreement.

"Meanwhile," I said, "we're going to go rustle up an appetite at the police station."

We hadn't told them about Father Villarreal yet, and we needed to follow up on the LionFish data Brody had dropped off. I didn't know if they'd bothered to look at it, and I wanted to light a little *fuego* under them if they hadn't. I also wanted to check in on Zoe and see how she was holding up—not to mention remind myself of why I was doing all of this.

At the station, Officer Ortiz—having been summoned by a bored-looking receptionist whom we'd interrupted from the important task of painting her nails—met us at the front desk and led us back into the office he shared with Officer Nolasco.

"Hola," I said, giving a wave to the older cop. He responded by snapping a folder shut and shoving it in a desk drawer, then turning the notepad he'd been writing on facedown so we couldn't see it.

"What do you want?" Officer Ortiz asked, plopping down in his desk chair. We'd interrupted his lunch, from the looks of it, and I couldn't help but notice that he was more interested in his sandwich than he was in us.

Officer Nolasco mumbled something in Spanish, which Officer Ortiz helpfully translated for us: "Make it quick. We have work to do."

"Well, first of all—*primero*," I said, looking hopefully at Nolasco to demonstrate that I was trying, "we wanted to show you this. *Una fotografía.*" I pulled out a picture of the mystery priest and handed it to Ortiz.

"What is this?" he asked. "Who is this man?"

"That man impersonated a priest and performed my client's wedding ceremony," I said, stabbing the picture with my finger for emphasis.

"So?" Ortiz shrugged.

"So he claimed to be Father Villarreal!"

"You must have misunderstood him," Ortiz said. "Your Spanish, it is not so good."

I gritted my teeth as I laid out the whole story for them. When I was finished, the officers exchanged looks and shrugged. I don't know why I'd expected my announcement to be a big, dramatic moment—too many reruns of *Law & Order,* maybe—but the men were unimpressed.

Ortiz stood as if to dismiss me. "I cannot see any crime that has taken place here."

"Isn't it possible that this guy, whoever he was, had something to do with Dana's murder?" I asked.

"Anything is possible," Ortiz said. "But we don't even know who he is."

"That's what I was hoping you could help me find out." Exasperation was beginning to seep into my voice. "And what about the computer files we gave you?" I asked. "Did you even look at them?"

"We did," said Ortiz. "However, we found nothing that would exonerate your friend."

"What do you mean?" I said. "Those files clearly prove that Dana was blackmailing Ryan McGuire."

"They prove nothing," Ortiz pronounced with an air of finality.

I could feel my face starting to flush like it does when I'm flustered. "I'm telling you, you've got the wrong person. I don't know who did it, but I'm sure it wasn't Zoe, and I've given you two viable suspects."

The officers resumed their conversation in Spanish, most of which I couldn't follow. Ortiz was right: my Spanish did suck. After a moment or two, he turned back to me. "We appreciate your thoughts on the case," he said, "but we are sure we have the right person."

"What do you mean?" I said. "Aren't you going to even look at the other two suspects?"

"I don't think that will be necessary," he said. "However, you are free to go. The family, they can go, too, if they would like."

I should've known they wouldn't just toss me the keys to Zoe's cell, along with a medal of commendation for excellence in detective work, but a girl can dream.

"But what about Zoe?" I asked. "We can't leave if she can't leave."

Officer Ortiz stood from his desk. "That's your decision to make."

I'd been trying to keep my cool, but their refusal to consider any other suspects was starting to annoy me. Did they really just not want to do their job? Was tracking down the impostor too much to ask? Was hunting down Ryan and questioning him about the blackmail outside of their comfort zone?

Brody could see the ire building in me and shook his head imperceptibly, hoping I would leave it alone, but it was too late.

"Look, you two, no disrespect, but you're as bad at police work as I am at Spanish. There's an innocent girl sitting in a jail cell, and I won't stand for it. Now you need to get off your butts and look into these other suspects, because I can guarantee you, you are wrong about this."

I could feel my face flushing again, and the two policemen stared at me, wide-eyed.

No one spoke right away, so I kept talking: "I don't know why you have this vendetta against Zoe, but you can't prove she did this. You know why? Because she didn't. So why don't you stop acting like Barney Fife and start doing your job—pronto!"

I was pretty sure they hadn't caught half of what I'd said, but my tone was unmistakable. I was pissed.

"*Quién es* Barney Fife?" Nolasco asked.

Ortiz glowered at me as he drew himself up to his full height, which beat mine by almost a foot. "We got the autopsy report, and the dead girl was poisoned with the same substance we found in your friend's bedroom. So if you want to play detective, maybe you could ask your friend about that. In the meantime, we'd appreciate it if you would let us do our job while you go back to whatever it is you do."

"Lo siento," Brody said, grabbing my shoulders. "C'mon, Kelsey, let's go."

Stunned, I allowed Brody to steer me out of the police station. I'd been sure the autopsy report would clear Zoe and that whatever they'd found would turn out to be nothing, but this new development looked bad. Really bad. No matter what theories I had about the other two suspects, they weren't going to trump possession of the murder weapon.

When we got outside, I collapsed onto the curb.

"Brody, what are we going to do?"

"Let's not panic," he said. "It's not like they have an airtight case against Zoe. There's got to be a simple explanation."

After several minutes spent brainstorming, we couldn't think of a one.

"Why don't we go talk to Zoe?" Brody said. "Maybe she can help us figure this out."

We signed the visitors log, then sat and waited what seemed like an eternity for the guards to retrieve her. They finally buzzed me in—only one visitor at a time, so I had to leave Brody behind—and I settled into the cheap molded-plastic chair. Zoe looked pallid and a couple of pounds thinner than when I'd last seen her.

"Zoe, how are you doing?"

"How does it look like I'm doing?" she asked, attempting a smile.

"Not so hot," I admitted. No sense in sugarcoating it.

"Mom and I met with the lawyers earlier, and she told me about the funeral," she said. "Who was that man at the wedding?"

"I don't know, but we have to find him. Zoe, do you remember anything at all that would help us figure out who Father Villarreal was?"

"Not really," she said. "But I did talk to him quite a bit after the rehearsal on Friday."

"You talked to him? About what?" I hadn't realized he'd stuck around afterward.

"Oh, you know, the usual. Like premarital-counseling stuff. He asked me a lot of questions, but he didn't really tell me much about himself."

"What kinds of questions was he asking you?"

"Hmmm, just stuff about the family. Come to think of it, he did seem a little nosy."

This was news to me. The day before the wedding was too late to be offering any kind of fatherly guidance. What had he hoped to learn?

"I'm sorry, Kelsey, I wish I could be more helpful, but I really don't remember. I was distracted because Mom kept fussing with my dress, and, well, a lot has happened since then."

I paused for a minute, unsure how to broach my next topic.

"Zoe, remember how the detectives said they'd found poison in your room? Well, the autopsy came back positive."

Zoe looked genuinely shocked. "For poison? Kelsey, that doesn't make any sense! What kind of poison was it?"

"I don't know. They wouldn't tell me. But we need to figure out what it was and how it got there. Are you sure you didn't have anything in your room . . . ?"

"That could kill someone? No! I swear."

I could tell by her bewildered expression that she wasn't bluffing. "Okay, well do me a favor and think about it, okay? The police think they've got this thing all figured out, and we have to come up with something or they're going to stop looking for who did this."

I didn't have the heart to tell her that they already had.

CHAPTER 21

Five hours. I had gotten to enjoy five whole hours without Mrs. Abernathy around. I had hoped it would be at least another eighteen before our paths crossed again, but sometimes fate is a cruel bitch.

"Kelsey?" I heard her voice before I saw her. I was standing outside the police station, having just said good-bye to Zoe, and was checking my voice mail: one from Laurel, two from Tamara Richardson, and none from Jacinda, whom I hadn't heard from since our day of discovery at Our Lady of Perpetual Tragedy and Inconvenience.

I had my index finger crammed into my left ear in an effort to hear my messages better, so I didn't even register it at first, but she persisted.

"Kelsey? Brody? Hellooooo?"

I looked up from my phone, while Brody greeted our not-former-enough housemate. "Hello, Mrs. Abernathy. Fancy running into you here."

I hung up on voice mail and put on the best smile I could manage through gritted teeth. "Hello, Mrs. Abernathy."

"I was about to go visit Zoe, but I'm glad I ran into you."

Oh, brother. Why would she want to run into me? Maybe she missed being able to get in a dig or two before lunch.

"I just got done visiting her," I said. "Did you get settled in okay?"

"That's what I wanted to talk to you about." She pushed her sunglasses up onto her head to reveal red, watery eyes. Had she been crying?

"Mrs. Abernathy, what's wrong?" This was serious.

"I was just curious," she said sweetly, "what on God's green earth made you think I would want to shack up with a common house cat?"

"Excuse me?" I hadn't seen this one coming.

"Oh, no," Brody said, crossing his arms in front of his chest. We were about to be chastised.

"Did you think it would be *amusing* to lock me in there with that shedding beast? Did it not occur to you for one moment that I might be allergic?" She took a tissue from her pocket and blew her nose to punctuate her point.

"Allergic? Mrs. Abernathy, I had no idea."

"Well, you do now. What are you going to do about it?"

"I could talk to Marisol, but the cat kind of comes and goes as it pleases."

"Well, tell it to stop."

"I'll see what I can do."

"And another thing." There was always another thing. "Could you talk to this Marissa person about the furniture? It's simply hideous."

I hadn't expected her to love it, but I was surprised to hear such scorn. Then again, why should I ever be surprised when it came to Mrs. Abernathy?

Brody stepped in to help. "Really? I thought it was kind of nice."

"Nice?" she snorted. "It looks like it belongs in a brothel."

"I can see that," he said diplomatically, "but a really nice brothel, at least, right?"

"Ugh." She shuddered. "I can hardly stand those dark antiques and all that lace. You might as well put a corset on me and call me Miss Kitty."

Brody's gay decorating cred wasn't getting anywhere with her, and she was looking at me expectantly.

"I'm sorry you don't like it, Mrs. Abernathy, but there weren't really any other options."

"And if that isn't bad enough, what am I supposed to eat?"

Brody and I exchanged glances. Was this a trick question? "Um, food?"

"And where am I supposed to get this so-called 'food'?" She made air quotes to show her disdain for my suggestion. "There's no chef. Imagine that—no chef! I suppose you want me to just eat out of the tamale cart on the corner." Her voice was getting louder and louder, and some officers exiting the police station paused to see if this was an impending civil disturbance.

"How about if I get you a list of local restaurants for you to try?"

"How about if you find us someplace else to stay?" Her glassy, red-rimmed eyes flashed with anger as she stamped her Ferragamo-clad foot on the pavement.

I didn't care if she wanted to throw a hissy fit. I'd just about had it.

"Mrs. Abernathy, this whole town is booked up because of the festival. I looked and looked to find you the best place to stay. I'm sorry it's no villa, I'm sorry there's not a Fernando to take care of you, but life sucks all the way around, doesn't it!" I could feel my face getting hot as she looked at me with shock.

I knew I should probably stop right there, but I wasn't done. Not even close. "Instead of going around stomping your feet, why don't you try to do something useful? Your daughter's sitting in there in jail. I should be focusing on her, but instead I'm running around trying to keep you happy."

Mrs. Abernathy's eyes grew wide. She'd underestimated my capacity to have a meltdown, but after talking to the detectives, I was on a roll. "Kelsey, for goodness sake, pull yourself together. I shouldn't think it would be such a burden for you to—"

"But don't you see, Mrs. Abernathy? It is a burden. You're a burden. I'm trying to do my best to help Zoe, but I'm not your personal servant. So if you want another place so damned bad, go find it yourself!"

Mrs. Abernathy gasped audibly as I turned and stalked down the cobblestone street. I almost made it to the end of the block, too, but my heel wedged in between two stones, pitching me forward. Arms flailing, I tried to right myself, but I ended up sprawled in the street in a supremely unladylike position. Cobblestones just aren't meant for that kind of drama.

Brody rushed after me as I picked myself up and hobbled away. "Boy, two in one day," he said as he caught up to me. "Wanna tell me what you really think of me while you're at it?"

I stopped and whirled around to face him. "Brody—" I was about to tell him off, too, but he hadn't done anything wrong. It was just the adrenaline coursing through my veins. "Sorry, I'm a little hopped up."

"So I see." He was smirking, which made me want to clobber him, but he was just an innocent bystander.

Deep breaths. I leaned against the wall of someone's house, then slid down to the ground, the warmth of the adobe against my back.

Brody sat down next to me and squeezed my arm supportively. He was probably afraid to get much closer than that. "You okay?"

I could feel the tears welling up in my eyes. "I totally lost it back there."

Brody laughed. "I think you were more than entitled. You've been going above and beyond the call of duty for those people, and you know why?"

I sniffled. "Because I don't want them to cancel my check?"

"No, because you wouldn't settle for anything less," he said. "We both know you couldn't stand to leave Zoe sitting in jail for a crime she didn't commit. I just wish Mrs. Abernathy could see that."

"Still," I sighed. "I shouldn't have yelled at her."

Brody looked at me in surprise. "Are you kidding me? She needed to hear it."

"You may be right, but I like to think I'm more professional than that."

"You notice she only pushes people around when they let her? I'm glad you stood up for yourself."

He had a point. "So you don't think she's mad?"

"Oh, no—I think she's furious. But she'll get over it."

At least I didn't have to go home and have dinner with her tonight. That was a plus.

Brody stood up. "C'mon," he said, holding out one hand to hoist me up into a standing position. "Let's go pass out some more flyers."

We returned to Evan's house to find steaks sizzling on the grill, smelling heavenly in that way that only charred meat can.

"I'm back here," Evan called from the patio, where we found both him and the meat. "How was your day?"

"You don't even want to know," I said, plopping down into one of the chairs.

"That bad, huh? Hold on, I have just the thing." He disappeared into the kitchen and returned with three salt-rimmed glasses and a pitcher of margaritas.

"You remembered!" If he was trying to make me feel at home, he was doing a fine job of it.

"These are about done," Evan said, prodding the meat with a two-pronged barbecue fork.

"Can't wait. I'm starving," I said. "By the way, I think I owe you a printer cartridge."

"Yeah, sorry about that," said Brody. "We printed up some more pictures of the mystery priest and showed them around this afternoon."

Evan shrugged as he began transferring the steaks to an oval serving platter with a pair of large tongs. "That's fine. I hardly use the printer anyway. I got it free with the computer."

"Oh, and I also put your home phone number on the flyer," I added, "in case someone has information but doesn't want to spring for an international call."

"Sure. *Mi número de teléfono es su número de teléfono.* So, any luck?"

"Not really," I sighed as we moved inside to the dining room table. "We got lots of nos and some maybes, and I became all too familiar with the expression '*Yo no se.*' On the bright side, I'm now fluent in denying all knowledge of any given topic."

The table was already set: red plates and cobalt-blue glasses on red, yellow, and blue place mats, a different look from the traditional pottery I'd seen everywhere else in town. I didn't figure San Miguel had a Crate & Barrel, but then, Evan could fly wherever he wanted when he needed to pick up new housewares. Must be nice to be able to hop in your own plane and go get whatever you require. The freedom to do whatever you want to, go wherever you want to go. I could only imagine.

The steaks were a perfect medium-rare, and he served them with some decadent blue-cheese mashed potatoes and a peppery arugula salad. It took some of the sting out of losing Fernando, although it sure was going to make it hard for me to go back to the real world, where dinner sometimes meant a box of Triscuits and some tuna salad.

I wondered how Mrs. Abernathy was faring and whether she'd figured out how to get by without help.

After dinner, we retired to the living room with the intent to polish off the margaritas.

Evan turned to face me on the couch. "So this priest you're looking for—is he even a priest?"

"I don't really know," I said. "All we know is that he performed the wedding ceremony and vanished."

"And he said he was Father Villarreal?"

"Yes," I said. "My Spanish isn't perfect, but it's hard to misunderstand *'Me llamo.'* Anyway, I have to find out who this guy is and whether he's even a priest. The family wants some answers— understandably."

The margaritas were starting to catch up with me, so I scooched down enough to stretch out on the couch. Evan pulled my feet into his lap and rubbed them gently while we talked. I resisted the urge to let out a little moan.

"Besides," Brody added, "I still can't help but think he's somehow connected to Dana's death."

"Me, too. But for now, it sure is nice to have a night off." I gestured at the pitcher. "Now, margarita me!"

Tomorrow we'd have to resume our search for the impostor

priest's true identity, but at the moment, there was nothing more
I could do except sit back, relax, and speculate. We drained the
pitcher, and there was vague talk of dessert.

What a cozy way to wrap up the evening. Being able to relax
without any clients around. Yummy food. Fun conversation. I
could feel the tension of the past week draining out of my limbs.
I didn't even mind having to make nice with the scratchy kilim
pillow. I was as content as I could possibly be.

"You ready for dessert?" Evan asked. He certainly knew the
way to my heart.

I smiled up at him sleepily. "Oh, Evan, I just love you."

Evan froze. You know how on TV shows they use the sound
of a needle scratching off a record when everything comes to a
sudden halt? That would have been the perfect sound effect to
punctuate the way the mood in the room changed.

An expression I couldn't identify flickered across Evan's face.
"Um, wow."

Wait, had I just told him I loved him? No, no, no, no, no.

"You know what I mean. I love all of this." I waved my hand
around for emphasis. "Your house, the steaks, being away from
Mrs. Abernathy." Surely he didn't think I was professing my un-
dying devotion to him?

Sensing the tension in the air, Brody stood abruptly. "Excuse
me, I'm going to go visit the powder room," he said, disappearing
down the hall.

Evan picked up my feet and moved them to the floor. "Kelsey,
I hope I haven't led you to believe that you and I were . . ."

"Jeez, Evan, no! I don't mean I *love you* love you. I meant it like
'I love strawberries on my cheesecake,' or 'I love skiing in Tahoe.'"

He stared at the coffee table, nodding but not relaxing his
posture. We sat in silence for a few moments. I blamed the tequila. Evan finally spoke: "I guess I see how you meant it, and I'm

probably just overreacting, but I just want to make sure we're on the same page here. I've really enjoyed having you around this past week, but I'm not looking for anything long-term."

This was hardly news to me; I'd known that for as long as I'd known Evan. As soon as I'd told him I was a wedding planner, he'd made sure to slip into the conversation as often as he could that marriage wasn't on the table. And somehow, he'd never fully believed that that was okay with me.

How do you explain that the only reason you do what you do is because you love a great party and the money is good—not because you're secretly fantasizing about your own special day? Just because you work at the zoo doesn't mean you wish you were a giraffe.

I sighed. "Got it. No marriage. Now can we just relax and not worry about anything?"

Evan looked uncertain, but he at least leaned back against the couch cushions. "I suppose so."

From down the hall, Brody casually whistled a song a little louder than necessary, breaking through the awkward silence. Subtle. He might as well have yelled, "I'm coming back!"

Brody didn't return to his chair but instead looked at Evan, who was chewing thoughtfully on one of his fingernails. "I was thinking about taking a shower, Evan. Do you have a towel I could use?"

Dang it! I was sure he meant well and that he was trying to give us some space, but I needed him to help me dissipate this weirdness.

"Sure," Evan said, jumping up from the couch a little too eagerly. "I'll get it for you. I should probably also find you some sheets." He disappeared down the hall and started thumping around in the linen closet.

I slunk off to the half bath across from the guest bedroom to brush my teeth. How drunk was Evan? Was there any chance he wouldn't remember this the next day?

Unfortunately, I had a feeling we'd all remember it the next day.

Brody knocked twice, then poked his head in. "You okay?"

I spit into the sink and held my toothbrush aloft. "Well, now I remember why he and I broke up."

"Sorry. You wanna talk about it?"

I shook my head. "Give me a minute. I'm still processing. You can go take your shower if you want."

"Okay, but if you want to talk later, you know where I'll be." I nodded and spat again, rinsing my toothbrush vigorously as he retreated down the hall.

After pulling my hair into a ponytail and washing my face, I returned to my room and sat on the edge of the bed, unsure what to do next. It was still too early to go to sleep. Should I try to talk to Evan? Or just leave him alone and hope it would blow over? I peeked down the hall to see that his bedroom door was shut, presumably with him on the other side of it.

Leave it alone.

I padded into the living room and waited for Brody on the freshly made foldout couch, flipping through a book about San Miguel's secret gardens. In the distance, a phone rang, and I could hear Evan's voice through his closed door. He might as well have been a world away.

His door opened. Was he looking for me? Had he realized it was just a big, stupid misunderstanding?

"Kelsey?"

"In here." Oh, good. He was coming to talk to me. Maybe we could put it all behind us.

"Phone," he said, holding out the handset to me. "It's for you."

My heart sped up as I took the receiver. "Hello?"

"Kelsey, this is Marisol, from the house on Calle Recreo? I hope I'm not calling too late."

"Oh, hi, Marisol." I tried not to sound too disappointed. "What's wrong? Is it the cat? I told Mrs. Abernathy—"

"No, everything's fine at the house. It's about the flyer you left with me. You know that man you're looking for?"

My heart sped up again. "Yeah? What about him?"

"I think I just saw him."

CHAPTER 22

Thank God for Brody. I really didn't want to go on my first stakeout ever without having some sort of backup, and I wasn't about to ask Evan for anything after our little miscommunication. Brody and I got dressed in a jiff, borrowed a flashlight from Evan, and headed out into the night.

"What are we going to do if it's really him?" I asked.

Brody shrugged. "Talk to him? Ask him to give us communion? I don't know. We didn't exactly have time to think all this through."

"Yeah, I'd really pictured this being more of a broad-daylight scenario," I mused. "God, I could use a doughnut right now."

Marisol had been taking her dog for its nightly stroll when she saw a man who looked like the one in the picture going into a bar. Of course she couldn't be sure, but she'd thought she'd better call. I was glad she had. Even if it turned out to be a wild goose chase, it was a good excuse to escape the awkwardness at Evan's house.

We arrived at the address Marisol had given us and paused on the sidewalk. "Do we go in? Should we wait out here?"

"I don't know," Brody said. "It's your stakeout."

"C'mon, don't be that way. You're my partner. Just like in all those buddy-cop movies."

"Let me guess: you're the loose cannon who almost gets the other one killed."

"'Almost' being the operative word," I said. "They never actually end up getting killed. Come on."

I tugged at his sleeve, dragging him through the front door. Every seat was taken, and the small dance floor was packed, the crowd raptly focused on a lively accordion band. I wondered how many of them were chamber music aficionados living on the edge, indulging in *conjunto* music after a long day of Debussy.

We made our way to the bar, and I only got stepped on twice in the process. "What are you having?" I yelled over the music. "I'm buying."

"Club soda. And so are you. We can't get sloppy drunk in case we end up confronting this guy."

Dammit, he had a point. "Can I at least have a Diet Coke?"

"Go nuts," he replied.

Drinks in hand, we shimmied our way through the crowd and finally found a place to stand on the edge of the dance floor. I searched the room for our mystery priest. Was he still here? Was it even him?

I made the mistake of setting my drink down, which must have signaled that I wanted to dance, because a hunky Latino swooped in and pulled me onto the floor. Before my brain could even catch up to decide whether it was a good idea or not, he was spinning me around the floor in a complicated series of moves.

He pulled me close to him, breath laced with whiskey. "Are you sure your boyfriend won't mind me dancing with you?"

"Who, him?" I looked over toward Brody, who was waving mischievously at me. So much for my idea that he would cut in and save me. "No, he'll be fine. Just don't keep me away too long. He's very possessive."

Maybe I could use this to my advantage. I could cover a lot more ground this way and look a whole lot less conspicuous doing it. I scanned the faces as they whirled past but didn't see anyone who looked familiar. I was getting dizzy with the effort, and my dance partner was starting to leer at me a little. How long was this song, anyway?

He leaned in toward me, and for one panicky moment I thought he was going to kiss me, but instead of my mouth, he went for my ear. "Do you want to go to the upstairs bar, where it's quieter?"

I looked up at him, surprised. "There's an upstairs bar?"

His face lit up, and he pointed toward some stairs. "Right over there."

"It was nice meeting you!" I pulled out of his grasp and fled back to Brody's side. "There's an upstairs. Come on, let's go check it out."

The narrow staircase was bathed in an eerie red light that was probably meant to add ambience, but it made me feel like I was walking into a horror movie—one with evil clowns.

We hovered at the top of the stairs, waiting for our eyes to adjust to the lower lighting. Groups lingered at tables, singles crowded around the bar, and couples canoodled in the dark corners of the room. I checked out the faces around me: no, no, no, no, no, maybe, no, no—wait, was that him? Toward the end of the bar stood a tall man with his back mostly to us, but the glimpse of profile I caught looked familiar. I elbowed Brody in the ribs and pointed.

He squinted into the dark room. "Hard to tell. But maybe, for sure."

The man drained his drink and set the glass on the bar, then turned toward the stairs.

It was him. At least I was pretty sure it was. And he was coming right toward us.

I had to do something, quick, before he spotted us. I grabbed Brody and kissed him right there on the spot. *Nothing to see here. Just a couple locked in a passionate embrace.*

After the man passed, I let Brody go. He looked kind of dumbfounded as he wiped at his face with his sleeve. I hoped he was trying to wipe off my lipstick and that he wasn't afraid of girl cooties. "What was that for?" he asked.

"Sorry! I panicked. I didn't want him to recognize us."

It had seemed like a good idea at the time.

"No problem. It was a little weird, but . . . you're not a bad kisser." He looked as surprised to be saying it as I was to be hearing it.

"Thanks. You feel anything?"

"Nope, still gay. You?"

"Nope, nothing. I mean, no offense . . ." He wasn't a bad kisser, either, but I've never been particularly attracted to people who aren't attracted to me. Brody had nothing to worry about.

"That's good. So we're all . . . good?" First Evan, now Brody— what was it with these boys?

"Jeez, Brody, I'm not going to propose or anything. Now let's go follow him!"

We scrambled down the scary red stairs and followed the man toward the door. With his extra height, it was easy to keep an eye on him as he traversed the crowd. A woman in a tight green dress stopped him, and we pulled back and watched as she introduced him to her friends. As he turned his head to greet each one, we got a good look at his face.

It was him all right.

I looked at Brody, and he nodded.

"So what now?" I asked.

Brody shrugged. "I say we go talk to him."

"Here?" I squeaked. I hadn't meant for my response to sound so shrill, but I could feel the adrenaline starting to pump through my body.

"Better here, where it's crowded. If he leaves, we'll be out on the street with him alone."

"Good point." We pushed through the crowd until we were right behind him, and I tapped him on the shoulder. He turned to greet me, not recognizing me at first. *"Hola,"* he said, a charming smile in place. He must've thought it was his lucky night.

"Father Villarreal?" Whatever he'd been expecting, it wasn't this. His face registered shock as he looked back and forth from me to Brody. Panic filled his eyes, and he turned and ran toward the door.

"Stop!" We dropped our drinks and ran after him. *"Alto! Ladrón!"* In addition to asking where the library was, my Spanish classes had taught me how to yell, "Stop! Thief!" and right now that was coming in way more handy.

Hearing my cries, a burly doorman grabbed the fleeing man and held him, giving us time to catch up. *"Hay problema?"* the bouncer asked.

"Please," I said to the man who had so eloquently performed the wedding ceremony. "We just want to talk to you." The man shrugged uneasily and nodded, saying something to the bouncer in Spanish a little *más rápido* than I could follow.

The bouncer released his grip as Brody took the impostor's other arm and led him out into the street.

"Don't run, okay? We just have a couple of questions. Obviously, you're not really Father Villarreal . . ."

"No."

"Are you even a priest?"

He looked inside the bar, then back at me as if to say *Well, what do you think?*

"No, I am not." He wasn't exactly opening up. Maybe I should try not asking so many yes/no questions.

"So then tell us— I'm sorry, what was your name again?"

"You can call me . . . Leo."

"So, Leo, if you're not Father Villarreal, and you're not a priest, how is it that you ended up performing a wedding ceremony last Saturday night?"

He shrugged. "It was just a job. It wasn't my idea."

"A job?" I understood that it was a job, but since he wasn't a priest, he was horribly underqualified. "What do you mean?"

Leo tilted his head and smiled. "I am an actor. A man saw me, an American. He offered me six hundred dollars. Easy money, he said."

"Wait, who?" said Brody. "Who paid you?"

"I don't know. He didn't tell me his name. Not his real one, anyway."

"Okay," Brody said. "Keep going. Why did he want you to perform the ceremony?"

"He said he'd give me a hundred dollars to do the ceremony, and another five hundred for information. He told me to get close to the family, find out some things. The wedding party, too."

I couldn't believe what I was hearing. "What were you supposed to find out?"

"He had a list of things he wanted to know. He wanted me to get them talking."

"But why you?" I asked. "That doesn't make any sense."

Leo shrugged. "Priests know things. People tell them things."

I wondered what Dana had told him. Had it contributed to her death?

"Did he ask you to talk to the bridesmaid? The one who died?"

His eyes grew wide. "I had nothing to do with that!" He took a couple of steps back.

"But you did talk to her, right?"

"I've said too much." He waved his hands at us to indicate the door was closing.

"Wait, please!" I took a couple of steps toward him. There was so much more we needed to know, but Leo was clamming up on us.

"I'm sorry," he said, shaking his head. "I'm sorry about the girl."

What could we do? If he didn't want to talk, we couldn't hold him down and make him. We had no upper hand.

"Just tell us who hired you," I asked, reaching out to touch his arm.

"It's too late," Leo said, backing away. "He's already gone. You'll never find him." And with that, he turned and bolted down the street.

"C'mon," Brody yelled over his shoulder, as he took off after the man. "Let's see where he goes." But we were no match for Leo. Within a couple of turns, he'd lost us. Turns out steak and margaritas are not a good way to prepare for a foot race. Winded and out of good ideas, we stood in the middle of the street. There was no use continuing our search. He could be anywhere.

My pocket buzzed and emitted a muffled ringtone. I pulled out my phone. Evan. I sent it straight to voice mail. Whatever he had to say could wait.

I turned to Brody. "What now?"

"I don't know. Want to go back to the bar and make out?"

Brody always knew how to make me laugh, even in a tense situation. "You wish. I guess let's head back home. Or whatever you want to call it."

We didn't hurry. I wasn't anxious to deal with Evan, and besides, I was still a little amped up from the chase. I wasn't going to be able to sleep anytime soon.

My pocket buzzed again, and again I let it go to voice mail. Was he worried? Let him worry.

"Was that Evan?" Brody asked.

I nodded.

"You want to call him back?"

"Not particularly." I set the phone to Silent and turned off Vibrate mode, too.

"C'mon, Kelsey, you can't blame the guy for being kind of freaked out."

"You're supposed to be on my side!"

"I am on your side. But what's he supposed to think? I mean, you moved into his house and then you said you loved him."

"It wasn't like that! You know me. I'm . . . affectionate. I tell you I love you all the time, but it doesn't *mean* anything."

Pretending to sulk, Brody scrunched his face at me. "Thanks a lot."

"Oh, stop." I gave him a playful shove. "You're know you're my favorite. Anyway, this whole thing has been a good wake-up call. Evan and I weren't meant to be. There were lots of good reasons we broke up the first time around, and I don't need to go down that path again."

Brody put his arm around me and squeezed. "Well, don't call it quits yet. Maybe he's calling to apologize."

"Hmmph." It would be great if Evan realized how silly the

whole thing was, but I still wasn't sure I could forget the look on his face. Would it really be that awful if I had feelings for him?

"Anyway, *I* love you," Brody said, drawing out the "I" for dramatic effect.

I laughed. "You know I'm not looking for anything serious, right?"

We circled the *jardín,* which was strangely quiet now that the mariachi bands had all gone home, and headed toward Evan's house. I couldn't tell if the lights were on inside, so I slipped the key quietly into the lock. No sooner had I stepped inside the door than Evan came rushing in from the kitchen. "Kelsey, thank God!"

I rolled my eyes. Look who was all serious now. "Oh, you're up," I said breezily, handing him his flashlight.

He hugged me tightly to him. "I was so worried about you."

I furrowed my brow, puzzled. "Really? Why? We were only gone just over an hour." Even Brody looked surprised by Evan's sudden change of heart.

Evan walked to the door and slid the dead bolt closed. "You didn't answer your phone. I thought something had happened."

"Something did. We found Father Villarreal. Well, not the real one, of course. We knew where he was."

Evan looked exasperated. "But why didn't you call me back?"

Hadn't he heard me? I had really expected a little more reaction to my news. "What do you mean?"

"Didn't you even listen to your messages? Kelsey . . ."

"I was kind of busy chasing someone at the time. What's the big deal?"

"The big deal is this." He walked over to his answering machine and pressed Play, and a man's muffled voice filled the room: "You need to back off and mind your own business, or you are going to end up like the dead girl."

Beeeeeeeeep.

CHAPTER 23

*I*f there was one way I definitely didn't want to end up, it was "like the dead girl."

My stomach lurched as I pressed the Play button again. It was a man's voice, older, from the sound of it. Despite his heavy Mexican accent, his point was all too clear. He knew what we were up to, and he was more than mildly disgruntled.

But who was he? It couldn't have been Leo, whatever his real name was. If he were the bloodthirsty type, he wouldn't have run away from us like a scrawny third grader being chased by the class bully.

Goose bumps prickled my arms as I thought back on our evening. We'd been out traipsing around the empty streets of San Miguel in the dark. Had the man who left the voice mail been following us?

"First thing in the morning," Evan said, "I want you to go to the police."

Brody and I exchanged looks. "I'm not exactly in good standing down at the station," I said sheepishly.

"I don't care," Evan insisted, his voice emphatic. A vein in his temple throbbed as he clenched and unclenched his jaw. "Talk to someone different if you have to. I'll give you my friend's name, and you can ask for him. This is serious."

Brody nodded in agreement. "He's right, Kelsey. This guy could be dangerous."

I nodded my consent. Even if Ortiz and Nolasco weren't interested in hearing my theories about the case, they'd have to take a threat against my life seriously. I mean, wouldn't they?

We all headed off to our respective beds, pretending we'd be able to sleep. But sleep was hard to come by. The long, dark shadows in the guest bedroom took on ominous shapes, and every unfamiliar sound put my central nervous system on high alert.

I rolled over and punched my pillow into shape, trying yet again to get comfortable. This little sleepover was not at all what I'd hoped it would be. Brody was on the foldout, I was in the guest room by myself, and instead of a good-night kiss, I'd been sent off to bed with a death threat.

How serious was the man who'd left the message? Was he just trying to scare me, or was I actually in danger? My mind buzzed as I replayed the evening in my head again and again.

I must have drifted off eventually, because the shadows had dissipated and bright morning sunlight was streaming into my room.

In search of caffeine, I stumbled out to the kitchen, where I found Brody working on his laptop. "Morning, cupcake. You missed Evan, but there's coffee ready for you."

I poured myself a cup, then dumped in some cream and sugar. Maybe it was the sunshine, maybe it was just a strong case of denial, but I felt a little better this morning. "I don't suppose the fact that Evan is gone means I can skip going to the police station?"

"Nope," said Brody, closing his laptop and sliding it a few inches away. "I promised him I'd make you go first thing."

"All right, all right." I slurped the lukewarm brew and wrinkled my nose. How long had it been sitting in the pot? I stuck my cup in the microwave and pressed some buttons until it started to go. It still wouldn't be fresh, but at least it'd be hot. I slumped against the counter. "I just don't want to have to talk to those detectives again."

Brody laughed. "Yeah, especially after you compared them to a bumbling sitcom deputy."

"Yeah, I'll try to avoid that this time."

After getting myself properly caffeinated, I threw on some clothes and hurried to the station. I insisted Brody stay and get his work done. I'd disrupted his life enough already, and besides, I didn't need an escort in broad daylight. That's not to say I didn't look suspiciously at every person I passed on the street.

No one was paying much attention to me, though, and by the time I got to the police station, I was starting to wonder if maybe we were getting ourselves all worked up over nothing. Nonetheless, I pushed through the double doors and approached the uniformed woman who was manning the front desk.

"*Hola.* Hi. I need to talk to Officer Castillo," I said, slipping her the piece of paper on which Evan had scribbled his friend's name.

"*Porqué?*"

"*Habla inglés?* I got a death threat. *Cómo se dice 'muerte'* . . . threat?"

The desk clerk creased her forehead in disbelief and looked me up and down. "Really? Why?"

Now, why was it so hard to believe that someone wanted to kill me? "Could you just—?" I pointed at her phone to indicate that now would be a good time to use it.

She not-so-subtly rolled her eyes and picked up the receiver. "Okay, *momento*."

I settled into a plastic chair as she rattled off some Spanish into the phone, then hung up. "Okay. Wait there. Someone will be with you eventually."

"I'll wait," I said, scrunching down in the seat to show my resolve.

After about ten minutes, my phone started ringing from inside my purse. The woman at the desk flashed me an annoyed look as I fished it out of the side pocket and checked the caller ID.

Tamara Richardson.

Again.

She had left me a couple of messages, but I hadn't had time to call her back. I gestured to the clerk to let her know I'd be right outside, then braced myself with a plastered-on smile I hoped would convey enthusiasm over the phone line.

"Hey, Tamara, what a coincidence. I was just about to call you." Okay, so I wasn't, but I felt bad that I'd been ignoring her.

"Kelsey. *Finally.* I've been trying to reach you. I was worried you might be dead or something."

"I'm so sorry, Tamara. I'm sure Laurel told you, but I'm dealing with . . . a family emergency." I glanced in through the doors to make sure no one had come to retrieve me, but the lobby was empty and the clerk was absorbed with some paperwork on her desk. I really should have been waiting inside so they wouldn't have to hunt me down.

Tamara sucked in a breath. "I hope everything is okay . . ."

Feeling a little bad about my white lie, I waved one hand to dismiss her concern. "Thanks, it is. I just—"

". . . because my wedding is next weekend, and frankly I'm kind of freaking out here."

For a split second I'd actually let myself believe she was worried about my well-being, but her only concern was whether I'd be back in time for her wedding. I couldn't be too offended; I hadn't exactly been giving the bride-to-be my full attention. But at the moment, I had much bigger problems than her impending nuptials.

"Tamara, don't worry: I will be there next Saturday. Meanwhile, Laurel is doing a great job of getting everything ready. And if there's anything she can't handle, I'll make sure it gets done."

"Really?" Tamara asked, her voice hopeful.

I had won her back over. Sometimes you just have to know the right things to say to make it all better, and I patted myself on the back for possessing such a skill. "You have my word."

"I'm so glad to hear you say that," she gushed, "because I had the greatest idea. I was watching some really fun wedding videos online, and I want to do a flash mob!"

"That's . . . great," I lied. The last thing I wanted to do was plan a flash mob. Well, the last thing I wanted to do was be stuck in Mexico investigating a murder with someone leaving me threatening messages, but planning a flash mob was second on the list.

Did Tamara really not get that an emergency usually indicates something bad is happening? I fake-smiled again to cover my irritation. "Who's going to choreograph it?"

"That's why I called you! I want you to do it!" Tamara sounded as giddy with excitement over the news she'd just delivered as if she'd asked me to be her maid of honor.

Not this, not now. I really didn't have time to think about a dance number, what with my impending death and all.

"Tamara, I'm not a choreographer; I'm just a wedding planner."

I'd been repeating variations on that phrase a lot lately. *I'm not a detective; I'm just a wedding planner. I don't want to get married; I'm just a wedding planner.*

"But you said you'd help!" She sounded incredulous about my lack of excitement.

"I will—I want your day to be perfect—but you don't know what you're asking. You only have a week. These things take time, planning, practice."

"Well, I'm asking you to make the time. You said I was your priority."

Had I? I always want my clients to feel special—they don't call it "your special day" for nothing—but right now my priority was talking to a police officer.

"Tamara, look, I'm sorry, but you're not my only client. And unfortunately, I have way worse problems than some misguided conga line!"

As soon as the words were out, I let out a little gasp. I shouldn't have gone there. But I had.

What was I thinking? I couldn't go around yelling at my clients, no matter how stressed out I was. Biting your tongue is an essential skill for a wedding planner, and apparently I needed a refresher course.

I opened my mouth to apologize, but it was too late.

"Well, I'm sorry to be such an inconvenience!" Tamara yelled into the phone. "You know, in case you hadn't realized, my wedding is kind of *important*."

I rubbed my forehead, trying to stave off the headache that was barreling down on me. I felt terrible. She was totally right. "Tamara, look, calm down. I didn't—"

"Calm down? Calm down? You don't even care, do you? It's my special day—MINE!—and you're ruining *everything*!" I had to pull the phone away from my ear to keep her from splitting my eardrum.

I couldn't take it anymore. She was right. When it came down to it, I didn't give a rat's ass about her stupid flash mob. A girl was dead, and all Tamara could think about was herself. Not that she could have known, but I had way bigger issues to deal with. Life-and-death issues, as a matter of fact. "You know, Tamara, it's not all about you."

"*Excuse me?* What did you just say? My wedding isn't all about me?"

Okay, so it was a low blow. That's the one thing you should never tell a bride; it's pretty much all about them.

"I don't mean your wedding isn't all about you. It totally is. I just mean that not everything in the *world* is about you."

My clarification didn't help much.

"I hope you'll be very happy with your other clients, and I hope they're paying you a lot of money, because you're fired!"

"Tamara, look— hello? Hello?" Dang it. She'd hung up on me. I tossed my phone back into my purse and buried my face in my hands.

I'd just lost a client.

I should have been distraught, I should have called her back, but I just felt numb. I didn't have time to deal with happy, fluffy wedding plans, not with everything that was happening here.

One of the doors swung open and a heavyset man in a black uniform motioned for me. "*Señorita?*"

I nodded.

He looked a little gruff, but he greeted me with a tight-lipped smile. "I'm Officer Castillo. Come on inside."

I followed him to an interview room and filled him in on the events of the night before as he jotted furiously in his notebook, furrowing his brow in concern. I told him about Dana's murder, our search for the priest, our conversation with Leo—all the way through coming home and finding the message on Evan's machine.

"That sounds serious. I'm going to need you to fill out a report," he said, standing up from his chair. "Wait here."

I sat quietly, swinging my legs back and forth. I didn't know what kind of muscle he could wield, but at least he was showing the proper concern. While I waited for him to return, I texted Laurel:

Veruca just fired us. Correction: just fired me.

She texted back:

I know. I'm on the phone getting an earful from her right now.

Damn. Poor Laurel.

After a couple more minutes, the door swung open again, but instead of the nice officer I'd been talking to, Officer Ortiz stepped into the room, clutching the file the other man had started.

Uh-oh.

"Officer Castillo tells me you've been busy," he said, settling himself onto the edge of the table, his mouth a grim line. "After our conversation yesterday, I hoped you'd start minding your own business. Going behind my back and talking to another officer isn't going to help anything."

"But this isn't about that!" I said, jumping from my seat.

"Someone threatened my life. Did he mention that?" I couldn't believe Castillo had ratted me out.

"And why do you suppose someone would want to threaten you?" he asked calmly, as if talking to a small child.

I don't take well to being patronized, and I could hear my voice go up an octave. "Because they didn't want me to—oh, I see what you're doing there." If I had minded my own business like he'd told me to, this never would have happened. Talk about blaming the victim.

Maybe I could try a different tack. "Look, I know you think Zoe is guilty, but if she were, why would someone be after me? Don't you think that means I'm onto something?"

"Then that's all the more reason for you not to be involved," he said with an air of finality. "You let us do our job, and you won't have anything to worry about."

"Yeah, nothing except the wrong person being convicted," I huffed, plopping down in my chair and crossing my arms in front of me. I wasn't getting anywhere with this man. "May I please speak to Officer Castillo again? I would like to finish filling out my report."

Officer Ortiz stood and put both hands on the table, leaning down to look me in the eye. "A report isn't going to help you if you don't back off. You're pissing off the wrong people, and you need to mind your own business, you got it?"

"But—"

"I mean it." He slid the folder across the table to me. "You can file a report, but if someone really wants to hurt you, this piece of paper won't protect you." He turned to leave. "You want to know what you can do if you want to stay safe?"

I nodded. Of course I did.

"Go home."

CHAPTER 24

How did it go?" Brody asked as soon as I walked through the door.

I went to the hall closet, where I had stashed my empty suitcase less than twenty-four hours earlier, and pulled it out with a yank. "Does this answer your question?" I asked, holding it up for him to see.

"Whoa. Okay," Brody said, scrunching his face in concern. "What happened?"

"Brody, the police can't help me. I filed a report, but their advice was to butt out. And I think they might be right."

Brody let out a low whistle and followed me as I dragged my suitcase into my room, tossed it onto the bed, and unzipped the zipper. Whatever my job description did or did not include—and it had been stretched to its limits over the course of the past week—I was done with the whole mess. If the police couldn't help me, I had no business being here. It was time for me to hang up my badge.

I opened the dresser drawer and started scooping up my clothes, dumping them unceremoniously into my bag. "If I keep pursuing this, I might be putting us both in danger."

Brody nodded pensively. "I hate to say it, but that message did leave me kind of shaken."

I went to the closet to retrieve the clothes that were hanging there. "Even if you take that out of the equation, I still have no idea what I'm doing. This whole thing is a disaster. I told Zoe I'd help her, but I'm not helping at all. I'm just antagonizing the police. They're sure Zoe did it, and they won't even listen to me anymore."

I slapped the empty hangers back onto the rod with such vigor that they continued swinging back and forth while I scooped my shoes up off the closet floor. "Mrs. Abernathy is going to be mad at me, but she's just going to have to be mad. Oh, and did I tell you? I lost a client today! I'm supposed to be working on her wedding, which is next weekend, but instead I've been neglecting her while I play private investigator. She called me today, and I lost it. She fired me, and frankly, I don't blame her one bit."

"Wow, yeah, that sucks pretty bad. This thing has really taken over your life."

I knelt down and checked under the bed for shoes, then sat up again and looked at my friend. He'd been so patient, and I was exceedingly grateful that he'd stuck by me these last few days. "Yours, too," I acknowledged. "I know you have a life you have to get back to."

"What? And miss out on all this?" Brody laughed.

"So, anyway," I said, ducking my head to the floor to check under the bed again, "I say we get out of here."

Brody nodded, but I noticed he was chewing on his lip thoughtfully. He didn't seem as enthusiastic about my suggestion as I'd thought he'd be. "What?" I said. "Spill it."

He shook his head and shrugged innocently. "What do you mean, 'spill it.' Spill what?"

"You're thinking. What are you thinking?"

He studied my face. "No, I think it's the right thing to do. And believe me, I want to sleep in my own bed tonight as much as you do. I just don't want you to regret it later, that's all."

"Regret it? How do you mean?"

"Well, yeah. You like to finish what you start. You're going to get back and you'll worry about Zoe, but you won't be able to do anything about it. And you're going to start wondering, 'What if I'd stayed?' "

I closed the lid of my suitcase and zipped it up. "I can't say that's not going to happen. You're probably right; I'm sure I'll second-guess myself. But ever since the wedding, exactly *nothing* has gone right, and every cell in my body is telling me to run away."

Brody offered me a hand, pulling me up from the floor. "Okay, then. It's settled. So what's the plan? Bus to Mexico City, then catch the next flight out?"

I nodded. "I have enough frequent-flier miles to get us both home."

"That's perfect," Brody said, "so long as I'm in first class."

I could tell he was kidding, but I thought it sounded like a terrific idea. Let someone take care of *us* for a change. "If I have enough miles, we're totally doing that. Now go get packed."

"What about Evan?" Brody asked.

"I'll leave him a note." I didn't know where he'd gone, and I didn't want to wait for him. Besides, he hadn't bothered to say good-bye before he left, so I didn't feel too bad.

I grabbed a purple highlighter I'd scrounged from my purse

and flipped over one of the flyers with the grainy picture of Leo on the front. I chewed on the end of the marker for a second, trying to decide what to say. Was I being too hasty? I hated to leave things like this, but after last night it was probably for the best. I'd seen the look on his face when I'd said I loved him. If anything, he'd probably be relieved to come home and find me gone.

> *Dear Evan,*
> *Thank you for offering us a place to stay, but Brody and I*
> *are heading back to the States. E-mail me if you want to*
> *talk, but I think we both know this is for the best.*
> *Love,*
> *Kelsey*

Dang it! There was that word again. I wadded up the paper and stuffed it in the side pocket of my carry-on, then rewrote the message and signed it, "Cordially, Kelsey."

I left the note on the coffee table so he'd be sure to see it, then took one last look around. *Hasta la vista, Evan.*

There were no cabs to be found on the street, so we bumped our way down the hill, suitcase wheels clacking loudly on the cobblestones. The bus station wasn't that far, and the adrenaline was enough to keep me going.

The tiny station was stuffed with people. We bought tickets for the bus, but an hour and a half seemed like an eternity to wait. I looked at the clock on the pale, industrial-green wall. If I hurried, I had time to run over to the jail and say good-bye to Zoe in person. I hoped she would understand, and that she would pass on my apologies to Nicole and Vince. I felt terrible for leaving without saying good-bye to the newlyweds, but I just couldn't face Mrs. Abernathy. She would be furious with me, of course, and might threaten to withhold my final check, but my crime-fighting days were officially over. I just prayed Nicole and Vince would forgive me.

I nudged Brody, who was listening to a podcast. "What?" he said as he took the tiny headphones out of his ears.

"Will you watch my stuff? I'm going to run to the police station to say good-bye to Zoe."

"Of course. I'll be right here."

The police station wasn't far, so I took off on foot. I had to hurry if I was going to make it in time.

"Kelsey!" Someone was shouting my name from down the street. Brody? I turned and squinted into the sun to see a man running toward me. It was Evan.

"Kelsey, I got your note. What's up? Why are you leaving?" He looked genuinely confused, maybe even a little hurt.

"Oh, Evan, what's the point? Everything I've touched has turned to disaster. That phone message was just one thing too many."

"What about the police?"

"They can't help me. They told me to go home. And that's exactly what I intend to do. Good-bye, Evan." I turned and walked away.

"Kelsey, wait." He caught up to me and matched my stride. "Can you stop?"

I turned to face him. "What?"

"I wanted to say I'm sorry about last night. I got kind of freaked out. But I don't want it to end this way."

Dang it, how was I supposed to storm off in a huff of self-righteous indignation when he was standing there saying he was sorry? It didn't change anything, except maybe make me like him a little better.

"I appreciate you saying so, Evan, but I have to get out of here. You can call me if you want, and we'll talk."

He pulled me in and hugged me close. *Stop smelling good!* I thought, allowing myself to enjoy it for a moment before pulling away.

"At least let me fly you to Mexico City," he said.

I searched his face. "Really?" I couldn't even pretend I was too mad to take him up on his offer. I'd been dreading the bus ride, and if we hurried we could catch an even earlier flight out to San Francisco.

"It's the least I can do."

It was. It really was.

Evan flagged down a cab, and I directed the driver to the bus station. I hurried inside and found Brody right where I'd left him. "C'mon, let's go," I said, gathering up my bags. "Our getaway car is waiting."

"We're driving?" he asked.

"Even better. I hitched a ride on a Cessna, and I think we can make our flight back to SFO."

"What about Zoe?"

I checked my watch. "I really don't want to miss that flight and have to spend the night in Mexico City. I feel terrible about it, but I'll just have to call her later."

I did feel guilty about not saying good-bye. Maybe I'd write the family an apology letter and send it back with Evan, or send Zoe a nice floral arrangement. Some orchids would really spruce up her cell.

The private airport where Evan kept his plane was about half an hour outside of town, and Evan called ahead to have them start the paperwork for our flight manifest. When we finally arrived at the airport, the cab dropped us off right in front of the hangar. My stomach was doing flip-flops as I thought about the flight ahead. I would never let on to Evan, but small planes make me nervous. Still, I was glad to be leaving, and my stomach would just have to deal.

"Wait here," Evan said as he went to check in at the office. "I have to make sure we're okay to go."

We lined our bags up next to the luggage hatch and waited. A few minutes later, Evan came striding back into the hangar.

"They're not quite ready for us, but let's get loaded up." He opened the door to the storage compartment under the plane and started hoisting our bags in one by one.

Had we not had our heads inside the compartment, rearranging our bags, we would have seen the two cars coming before they squealed to a stop outside. The sound made Evan jump, and he narrowly missed hitting his head.

I whirled around to see who had made such a dramatic entrance. Four police officers had guns pointed at us, and they were yelling something in Spanish. I didn't know what they were saying, but judging from the context I was pretty sure it was somewhere in the neighborhood of "Freeze!"

What now? Officer Ortiz had cleared me to go. Had Mrs. Abernathy found out I was leaving and had me arrested for—what? Failure to get her daughter out of jail? I was pretty sure that wasn't a thing.

Brody and I looked at each other wide-eyed. I turned to Evan, who had his hands up. What must he think? I'd brought nothing but drama into his life.

The police officers were directing all their questions at him, and they spoke so rapidly I couldn't follow what they were saying at all. I knew I'd screwed up plenty, but I didn't think I'd done anything illegal. What was happening? Where were subtitles when I needed them?

The policeman who was talking to Evan turned him around, frisked him, then slapped a pair of handcuffs on him.

What was going on here? What had Evan said to the man to get himself arrested? Evan glanced back at me as an officer led him to one of the patrol cars. I frantically mouthed the words "I'm sorry!" at him, but I wasn't sure he'd understood. An officer who spoke English attempted to question me and Brody, as the squad car containing Evan turned on its sirens and sped away.

Where were you flying to?

Why was the flight manifest filed at the last minute?

How do you know the pilot, Evan Reilly?

Passports?

I waited nervously as they checked our passports, radioed in to the station, and waited for a response.

"Okay, let us check your bags, then you're free to go," the English-speaking officer said as he handed our passports back.

Wait, what? Evan was in custody but we were free to go? Not that I wanted to argue, but what had just happened?

"Brody," I whispered, as the policemen started searching the plane. "Did you catch any of that?"

Brody nodded as he stared at me wide-eyed. "A little. I'm not sure, but it sounds like Evan has a drug problem."

"What? That's crazy. Evan doesn't do drugs."

"No, not a problem with doing them. A problem with smuggling them."

CHAPTER 25

I should have been thirty thousand feet in the air, feeling anxious about the tiny aircraft but excited to be on my way home. Instead, I was still standing on Mexican soil, watching policemen rifle through my luggage and wondering what my next move should be. If they thought they were going to find a kilo of coke among my underthings, they were sadly mistaken.

Drugs? Was that how Evan was supplementing his income? He did seem to live rather comfortably, but I'd figured it was just because of the advantageous exchange rate. In fact, I'd assumed he'd moved to Mexico because it was less expensive, but maybe it was a better base of operations for drug running.

I was having trouble letting the information sink in. I couldn't believe he'd kept this from me. Not that our week of romance meant that he owed me full disclosure, but that was a pretty big secret.

The officer had said we were free to go—but go where? By the time we got back to the bus station, we'd have missed the last bus for Mexico City. All the hotels were full; we'd established that already. Mrs. Abernathy had room at the house on Calle Recreo, but I wasn't about to walk right back into her clutches.

That left Evan's house. "What do you think?" I asked Brody. "Should we go back to Evan's place? I still have his key. I meant to drop it through the mail slot, but we left in such a hurry I forgot."

"Surely he won't mind." Brody sighed. "Two steps forward . . ."

"One step back into San Miguel."

We must have looked pretty pitiful, because the policemen offered us a ride back into town. On the way, I tried Evan's cell, but it went to voice mail. I pictured it sitting in a plastic baggie along with his car keys and wallet. I decided to take his lack of an answer as tacit permission to go back to his house, but I left him a message just to be sure.

As we rolled our suitcases back through his front door, I couldn't help but feel defeated. It had only been a few hours earlier that I had left with a sense of triumph, and now here I was again.

"Home sweet home," Brody said, dropping his bags on the floor.

"I guess we should be grateful we have someplace to go," I said, "although I'm not sure I feel entirely comfortable here now."

"I know. I keep thinking the police are going to come bursting through the door any minute to search the premises."

That hadn't even occurred to me. "Thanks for that image."

Having all those guns pointed at us had been every bit as stressful as the threatening message I'd gotten. If they did have a warrant to search Evan's house, I didn't want to be there when it happened. "You wanna go get some food?"

"You read my mind," Brody said.

We walked down the hill for the second time that day, toward the *jardín,* where we found a café and settled in.

"So," Brody said, after we'd properly creamed and sweetened our coffees, "you didn't know *anything* about Evan's extracurricular activities?"

"I swear, Brody! I had no idea. I never would have accepted his offer for us to stay with him if I'd known, let alone agreed to get into a plane with him." I had trusted him so completely that I'd even had him fly in several members of the wedding party the week before the ceremony. Had it really been almost two weeks ago? God, it seemed like a year.

Brody smiled sheepishly. "I'm sorry I pushed you to go out with him again. I just want you to be happy."

I waved my hand in the air as if to dismiss his guilt. "It's okay. I'm the one with the questionable taste in men, not you."

"But I was the one egging you on." The waiter slid two sandwiches onto our table, and Brody and I ate in silence while I replayed the events of the day. I'd gotten myself into this mess, whether Brody had encouraged me or not. And besides, I had much bigger messes than Evan to deal with.

That morning, after the police had told me they couldn't help me, all I'd wanted was to run away. But now that I'd been forced to pause for a minute and think about things, I knew I owed Zoe an explanation as to why I couldn't help her. I also owed Nicole and Vince the truth about Leo posing as Father Villarreal. Call it fight or flight, but my survival instincts had been overriding my sense of duty. Luckily, my conscience had kicked back in, and I knew I couldn't leave again without talking to them. Surely the man on the answering machine wouldn't begrudge me that.

But what was I going to tell them?

I set my sandwich down. "Brody, will you go with me to visit Zoe?"

"Sure. Of course." I hadn't really thought he'd say no, but I'd asked so much of him already.

"I feel so bad leaving her here, but what else can I do?"

He leaned in and covered my hand with his, giving it a squeeze. "I'm sure she'll understand."

"That's good, because I'm not. Sure, that is."

"I'd lead with the phone message you got," said Brody. "Surely she'll understand that."

"I guess so," I said, nibbling on a radish that was probably only meant to be a garnish. I should have been ravenous, but I didn't really feel all that hungry.

"And then you can explain to her that you've exhausted all the possibilities."

I poked at my potato chips, rearranging them on the plate. "Yeah, I know. It's just . . . I guess it's not really true."

Brody raised his eyebrows. "Yeah?"

I stared at my plate as I turned things over in my mind, then looked up at Brody, who was watching me expectantly. "Maybe we should look at everything one more time and make sure."

Brody's eyes crinkled as he smiled. "I knew it."

"What?"

"I knew you couldn't leave it alone."

"So?" I shrugged. "You know me. If I didn't feel invested, I wouldn't be doing my job."

"I believe I might have mentioned something to that effect earlier today."

"Okay, Mr. Know-It-All. So you were right. Big whoop."

He smiled in satisfaction. He was loving it.

"Let's go back to the beginning." I fished through my bag and

found the list of suspects I had made with Brody wedged in between the pages of the paperback I'd been saving for the flight
home. "This list had Zoe, Trevor, Fernando, and—well, Mrs. Abernathy, of course, but I just added her to humor you. After Father
Villarreal's funeral, I was sure he was the key, but all that led us
back to was Leo."

Brody turned the paper sideways so we both could look at the
list. "I don't think Leo had anything to do with it, do you?"

I shook my head. I doubted the killer was still hanging around
drinking in bars, and besides, if Leo had killed Dana, he wouldn't
have been so afraid of us. "Yeah, I doubt it. But it could be whoever hired him."

"True. It sounds like whoever sent him was looking for information on the family."

A sudden thought occurred to me. "You know, with all the
Father Villarreal nonsense, we're forgetting something."

"What's that?"

"Ryan McGuire."

"You're right! The dead priest kind of sent us off in another
direction, but Ryan was looking pretty guilty before all that."

I added Ryan's name under Leo's and drew an emphatic circle
around it. "Motive? Well, that's easy enough. Dana was trying to
ruin his life. And doing a pretty good job of it, from the sounds
of it."

"Is there any chance he had something to do with Father
Villarreal's death, too?" Brody asked.

"I wondered that," I said. "But there's no way to know without
talking to him."

"Well, at the risk of stating the obvious," Brody said, "maybe
we should go talk to him."

"Aren't you forgetting something?" I asked.

"What's that?"

" 'Mind your own business or you'll end up like the dead girl'?"

Brody nodded, brow furrowed. "I know. But think about it. The voice on the machine had an accent, which means it wasn't Ryan."

"That only makes me feel marginally better," I said. "He could have had someone else make the call."

"You really think it was him?" Brody asked.

"I don't know. But we don't even know where he is. He wasn't flying straight home, and I don't remember where he was going."

"I'm sure we could find out." Brody wadded up his napkin and tossed it onto his plate and shrugged. "I mean, you know, if you want to."

"Let me think on it, okay?" It wasn't like there was much else I could do until the next day anyway, other than curl up and relax with a good book. And we both knew that wasn't going to happen.

Things were eerily quiet back at Evan's house, which was good for concentrating, but it was hard to relax while wondering if the police were going to show up any minute wielding a search warrant. I called the cell phone number I had for Ryan, but he didn't pick up. No surprise there. Next, I dialed Vince to see if he had any idea where his best man had gone.

Vince balked at the question. "Why do you ask?" He knew there was only one reason why I would want to get in touch with Ryan, and it wasn't for a post-wedding hookup.

"I just wanted to see if he remembers anything that could be of help." I was bluffing, but I thought it sounded convincing enough.

"You don't think he had anything to do with Dana's death, do you?" Vince sounded alarmed. Maybe I wasn't as stealthy as I thought.

"No, no, nothing like that." I tried to sound breezy. Best not to play all my cards up front. I didn't want Vince calling up Ryan and warning him about what we knew.

"Look, Kelsey, he hardly knew Dana. I don't think he'll be able to help you."

"I know, but I'm doing this for Zoe, and I'm running out of options here. Now, if you hear from him, can you have him call me? I need to ask him some questions."

Vince sounded dubious, but he said he'd see what he could do.

Right as we were hanging up, I heard a noise at the door, and my body stiffened. Were armed policemen about to come bursting through? I was being silly. Surely they'd knock first. Wouldn't they?

Brody looked up at me and gestured toward the front door. "Did you hear that?"

I nodded, and neither of us spoke.

The scrape of a key in the door lock ended the speculation. The doorknob twisted slowly, and Evan walked into the room. Wasn't he supposed to be in jail?

"Kelsey! I'm so glad you came back." He rushed over to the couch and hugged me, but I pushed him away. I was in no mood to cuddle.

"Evan, what the hell? Drugs? Seriously?"

"I'm so sorry. I can explain."

Explain? I was incredulous. What explanation could there possibly be for him breaking the law, lying to me, and putting me, Brody, and my business in jeopardy?

"How are you even here?" I asked. "They let you go already?"

He shrugged. "Castillo helped me out. Released on my own recognizance, but I am going to have to get a lawyer."

Brody sat awkwardly in Evan's black leather Ibiza chair, leaving the talking to me.

I was fuming. "Evan, do you realize you could have gotten us arrested?"

"There was never any danger of that. I swear to you, there were no drugs on that plane."

"But you're not denying it, are you?"

"It's complicated. And you don't really want to know." He tried to take my hand, but I pulled it back and crossed my arms in front of my chest.

"It's a pretty simple question, Evan. Have you been smuggling drugs or not? Yes or no."

"No." He stared at me levelly to drive his point home.

"Then what was that whole scene at the airport about?"

Evan sighed and rubbed his hand over his head. "I'm a pilot."

"I believe we've established that."

"A private pilot. Which means I don't work on salary. I rely on repeat customers who need to be flown places, and what they do while they're there, and what they bring back with them—it's their business. Do you understand?"

"So you don't smuggle drugs, you just help other people do it?"

"I fly people. Not all of them are nice people. Part of my job is not asking questions."

"Well, that sounds like a pretty lame job, if you ask me."

The three of us sat in silence for a moment. I didn't know what to say. Evan was staring at me intently, and Brody was busy studying his cuticles.

"Anyway," Evan said at last. "I'm sorry. I know you wanted to go home tonight, and I'm sorry I made you miss your flight. What can I do to make it up to you?"

I was about to suggest something involving a cliff and him

jumping off it, but Brody intervened. "We're going to need a place to stay. Is the foldout still available?"

"Of course," Evan said. "I insist. That is, if Kelsey is okay with it."

What choice did I have, other than begging Mrs. Abernathy to take us in or sleeping on a hard plastic chair at the bus station? If there had been another option, I would have taken it, but there wasn't, so I gave a half shrug, half nod to indicate that I agreed, even if I wasn't happy with it.

Evan slapped his hands on his knees and stood. "It's settled, then."

I had to get out of the house for a while and clear my head. "I think I'm going to go visit Zoe."

"I'll come with you," Brody said. "We should ask her what she knows about the best man."

"You're still investigating?" Evan asked. "I thought you were done with all that."

"We are," I said. I mean, I wasn't, not entirely, but I didn't particularly feel like sharing.

Brody, however, was feeling chatty. The guy just can't hold a grudge. "We want to talk to the best man, Ryan. There's a chance he might know something. It may be nothing, but it's kind of our last hope. Problem is, we're not sure where he went."

"Wait," said Evan. "Ryan who?"

"Ryan McGuire. He was in the wedding."

Evan went to his desk and opened a drawer, pulling out a dog-eared calendar. He flipped it open and ran his finger down the page, then looked up at us, excitement lighting his eyes.

"I may be able to help with that."

CHAPTER 26

*A*s it turned out, Evan had flown Ryan to San Diego right after the wedding to meet with some potential investors. During the course of the flight, Ryan had even told Evan that he was staying through the weekend to attend a tech conference, which meant he should still be there. Say what you will about Evan's business practices, he had turned out to be a great informant.

Best of all? It was only a couple of hours' flying time—that is, if you flew directly from San Miguel to San Diego. And thanks to the massive favor Evan felt he owed me, I now had a direct flight that was leaving whenever I wanted.

It was the perfect solution. I'd still be helping Zoe, just not from Mexico.

But before we could go, I had to figure out where to find the best man. After all, I couldn't exactly walk around San Diego with a stack of flyers.

I tried the hotel where the conference was being held, but the crisp-voiced operator on the other end of the line was no help. "I'm sorry, ma'am, but there's no one registered here by that name."

"Shoot," I said, hanging up the phone.

"No luck?" Brody said.

"Nope," I said. "Maybe he decided not to go to the conference after all."

"Or he could be staying at another hotel," said Evan.

Suddenly, a lightbulb went off in my head. "Wait!" I said. "I think I know where he is."

Brody and Evan exchanged puzzled looks. "Where?" Brody asked.

"When I was making hotel reservations in San Miguel, I remember he made a really big deal about staying at a Hilton because he's a member of their rewards program. I told him he'd be out on the outskirts of town, but he didn't care. Apparently, he was close to earning a free stay and really wanted the points."

I grabbed my laptop and searched for the hotel chain in San Diego. Then, armed with phone numbers, I started dialing. I struck out at the first property, but at the next location the operator said those three little words I longed to hear: "I'll connect you."

No one answered, but that didn't matter. I had confirmation that he was still in San Diego. The next morning we would leave bright and early for the two-hour flight, and if I couldn't find him at the conference, I'd stalk him until he returned to his hotel room.

In the meantime, I had some business to take care of.

First stop, the house on Calle Recreo. It was still early enough that the family wouldn't have eaten dinner yet, so I stopped into an Italian restaurant Evan recommended and loaded up on takeout.

I even picked up a couple bottles of red wine, in the hopes of keeping things civilized.

Nicole and Vince were enthusiastic about my peace offering, but Mrs. Abernathy's frosty greeting told me it was going to take a lot more than pasta Bolognese and Sangiovese to get back in her good graces. While the young couple went to the kitchen to fetch plates and glasses, I sat down next to Mrs. Abernathy and tried to look dutifully contrite.

"Mrs. Abernathy, I'm really sorry about yesterday, what I said. This whole thing has been hard on all of us, and I let the stress get the best of me."

She still looked miffed, but she didn't instantly shred me to bits, so I continued: "I've been trying my best to help. In fact, I just lost a client because I'm here helping you instead of there doing my job."

She sighed and folded her hands in her lap. "Perhaps I expected too much of you."

I waited for the follow-up, the one where she offered a reciprocal apology, but after several moments passed, I realized that was all I was going to get. I couldn't take the silence, so I kept talking: "Anyway, I'm sorry if I've let you down. And I'm sorry I lost my temper."

Nicole poked her head in from the dining room to interrupt our Hallmark moment. "Come on, Mom. Kelsey brought us dinner, and it looks delicious."

Mrs. Abernathy grudgingly rose, and the four of us gathered around the table and spooned steaming mounds of the pasta onto our plates. I gave everyone the chance to dig in before I delivered my real news.

"Nicole, Vince, we have to talk." The chewing stopped, and I heard at least one audible swallow. "I found the man who performed your wedding ceremony."

Nicole set her fork down and stared at me anxiously. "And?"

"As you know, it wasn't actually Father Villarreal."

Mrs. Abernathy's wineglass froze in midair. "The dead man? Well, I should think not."

"It was a man named Leo, an actor. Someone hired him to play the role of a priest."

"What?" said Vince, dropping his fork to his plate with a clatter. "Why would someone do that?"

Nicole's mouth made a perfect, round O.

"I wish I knew." If only Leo had stuck around long enough for me to figure it out.

"An actor? Well done, Kelsey." Mrs. Abernathy shook her head.

Nicole's eyes welled up with tears, and she held on to Vince as if someone were going to take him away from her. "I don't understand. Did someone want to keep us from getting married?"

"I don't know, Nicole. This whole thing is so bizarre. But don't worry, everything's fine. Remember, the civil ceremony is the one that counts."

Nicole and Vince looked mollified, but Mrs. Abernathy was seething. "Everything is *not* fine. You know how I feel about this, Kelsey. The law might recognize the civil ceremony, but as far as I'm concerned it's the church wedding that counts. Otherwise, what's the point of doing it at all? If they're not married in the eyes of God, these two might as well just live in sin."

I didn't agree with her assessment—married is married, and the two were legally wed—but I knew better than to try to dissuade her from her beliefs.

Mrs. Abernathy threw her napkin on the table in disgust. "You're lucky I don't ask for a complete refund."

"That's not entirely fair, Mrs. Abernathy. You hired me to plan the wedding, and I did. It's not my fault this happened."

"Oh, isn't it?" She fixed me with a pointed stare. "I would think that seeing to it the couple is actually married would be equally as important as suggesting floral arrangements."

Things were going poorly. I did a quick calculation of my chances of winning this argument and came out with exactly zero. I needed to watch my step before things got out of hand. Deep breaths. Deep breaths. "Okay, tell me what you want to do. Do you want me to find a priest who can perform a do-over on the ceremony?"

"I think you've done enough already," Mrs. Abernathy said, then got up abruptly and left the room. The angry clicks of her heels on the tile floor receded as she walked down the hall, and she slammed the door to her bedroom.

There was an awkward silence as Nicole busied herself by arranging her silverware neatly on the plate.

"I'm really sorry, Nicole, Vince. I hope you're okay."

"We'll be fine," said Vince.

Nicole smoothed out her place mat and looked at her husband. "It *is* weird, knowing he wasn't a real priest, but I guess it doesn't matter. Not really." She smiled at me. "The service was beautiful, and it'll make a great story for our grandkids one day."

"Except they'll be illegitimate, apparently," joked Vince. Even Nicole laughed.

Phew. I felt better knowing they were okay.

"I have some more news," I said tentatively, folding up my napkin and laying it next to my plate. "I have to fly back to California tomorrow."

I still wasn't ready to tell them about Ryan, so I blamed the wedding I'd just been fired from. I felt bad about lying to them, but there was a good chance Vince would try to convince me that his best friend was innocent, and nothing he could say would sway me. There was also a chance he'd warn Ryan that I was coming to talk to him, and I was relying on the element of surprise.

"I get it," said Nicole, although she looked a little glum. "I don't know what I would have done if you hadn't been there for me on my wedding day, so I can't exactly ask you to skip someone else's wedding."

"Thank you for understanding," I said. "And I'm sorry I can't stay here and help, but I think I've done everything I can. I'll definitely stay in touch though, and I'll help Zoe's lawyers however I can."

Nicole got up from the table and came over to give me a hug. "I appreciate everything you've done already."

"Tell your mom . . ." I paused, not sure how to finish the sentence.

Nicole smiled. "We will. Don't worry about her. When all this settles down, I'm sure she'll see things differently."

I wasn't so sure, but I smiled and nodded.

My next stop was the jail, where I waited while they brought Zoe to the visitation room. Although happy to see me, she looked gaunt and exhausted. Jail time did not seem to suit her.

After we exchanged pleasantries, I got down to the reason for my visit. "I wanted to let you know I'm flying to San Diego in the morning."

Her eyes grew wide with fear. "What for? You're coming back, aren't you?"

I stared at the table and shook my head noncommittally. "I don't know. You know Ryan, the best man? There's a chance he might have information that could help us, and I want to go talk to him."

"What do you think he knows?"

I had to watch my step. I couldn't exactly let all my suspicions go spilling out, since I was just operating on speculation. "It's complicated. But listen: I need you not to mention this to Nicole or Vince, okay?"

"But—"

"I know it's a lot to ask, but I need to make sure nothing messes this up, so please, don't say anything, at least for a day or two. Can you do that?"

"Okay," she said finally. "I can keep my mouth shut."

"Good. Thank you. And there's one more thing." I reached across the table and took her hand in mine. "If this doesn't go anywhere, Zoe, I will have done everything I can do."

Her eyes welled up, and she nodded. "I get it. I mean, you have a life and all."

"It's more than just that," I said. "I knew I was putting my life on hold when I decided to stay. But this has gotten bigger than I can deal with. The police have told me to back off, and I'm getting death threats."

Zoe gasped. "What?!" She said it so loud it drew stares from the people sitting at the next table. "Why didn't you tell me?"

"You have enough to deal with," I said.

"Kelsey, that's awful!"

"I'm not trying to make you feel bad; I just wanted you to know this isn't a decision I took lightly."

"Wow. Yeah, I get it," she said, shuffling her feet against the concrete floor. "I'm sorry, Kelsey. You've done so much for us already. I really appreciate it."

"I'll let you know if I figure anything out, but I did want to at least tell you what was going on."

There was an awkward pause as we both searched for something to say.

"So . . . I guess this is good-bye," Zoe said at last.

"I hope not," I said, rising from my chair. "But it very well may be."

CHAPTER 27

The trip to the airport was uneventful, especially compared to last time. Although Evan swore he had permission to leave the country, I couldn't calm my jitters until the plane took off. Once we'd gotten aloft with no one drawing guns on us, I felt better, but I still would have given up all my frequent-flier points for a flight attendant to stop by with some tiny bottles of cocktail makings.

While Evan and Brody made polite chitchat, I pressed my face against the window and watched Mexico drop away from us. Somewhere down there, Zoe was sitting in a jail cell, Nicole and Vince were wishing they could go on their honeymoon, and Mrs. Abernathy was keeping herself busy, probably by scolding someone or fashioning a new coat from Dalmatian puppies. And here I was, jetting off to San Diego to confront Ryan. I had no idea what I was going to say to him, but this was my last shot.

I must have dozed off, because I awoke with a start as we began our descent. Sleeping through the flight was an amazing feat,
considering the amount of adrenaline that had been coursing
through my body. Then again, airplanes have always made me
semi-narcoleptic.

Brody turned and smiled at me. "Good morning, sunshine.
You ready to go fight some crime?"

I wasn't feeling very sunny, but I was ready to get some answers.
"Ready as I'll ever be."

The plan was simple: Brody and I had looked up the conference schedule online and would get there right as the eleven o'clock
session ended. We'd use the element of surprise to our advantage,
and Ryan would have to talk to us. Okay, well, maybe not, but at
least he couldn't totally ignore us.

We got to the hotel in plenty of time, and Evan pulled the rental
car up to the front door.

"Are you coming in?" I asked.

"Oh, well, I just thought I'd . . ." He motioned toward the
parking lot as an awkward look passed between us.

I didn't particularly want him edging in on my interrogation,
but it would have been nice if he'd offered. (I'm complicated that
way.) I was pretty sure he didn't want Ryan to know he was the
one who had given up his location. Oh, well. I shouldn't have been
surprised that he was letting me down again.

"I'm only a phone call away if you need help or anything," he
offered.

Some help he was. But then again, what had I expected?

Brody and I climbed out of the car as Evan called after us:
"Let me know when you're ready to go back to the airport." He
quickly pulled away as the automatic doors into the lobby swooshed
open.

Downstairs, a sign propped on an easel welcomed us to the

Data Solutions West Conference. The hall was deserted except for a table bearing the picked-over remnants of the morning break. I helped myself to a blueberry muffin as Brody plopped down on an oversized velveteen chair under a potted palm.

"Yuck," I said, spitting out my first bite of the overprocessed pastry. "You can practically taste the trans fats."

Right at noon, the doors to the ballroom swung open and hundreds of conference attendees poured out of the room, heads full of data solutions. I scanned the crowd anxiously, Brody by my side; we hadn't been prepared for the hordes of lanyard-wearing geeks we'd have to fight our way through to find the best man.

As I craned my head to get a better view, Brody elbowed me in the ribs.

"Ow!" I yelped. "What was that for?"

"Over there," he whispered excitedly, pointing to three men huddled near the coffee carafe. Ryan was at the center of the group, talking animatedly about the new app LionFish was developing. After we crept up behind him, I tried to give him a moment to finish—just because I was there to accuse him of murder, there was no reason to be rude—but he spoke with such enthusiasm, I was afraid he'd keep going until it was time for the next session.

I took a deep breath and tapped him on the shoulder, interrupting his long-winded speech, which had no doubt been perfected for just such an occasion. Ryan turned to us with a big smile, ready to share his elevator pitch with a new audience. He scanned our faces, and I caught the way his eyes flicked downward toward my chest for a conference name tag, his smile in place the whole time.

"It's me, Kelsey, from the wedding."

"Oh, Kelsey! Sorry, of course," he said, his face registering recognition. He looked puzzled, but certainly not alarmed to see us. "Small world." He reached out to shake hands with Brody. "And you're the photographer, right?"

"Brody," said Brody.

The two men Ryan had been talking to took their cue and wandered off into the crowd.

"So," Ryan began, "you're not here for the conference, are you?"

"No, actually, we came to see you. Is there someplace we can talk for a second?" I asked, trying to sound casual.

"Sure," he replied. "What's up?"

We walked back to the lobby and settled into a cluster of chairs in the corner, away from the prying eyes of the data solutions community.

"So, Ryan," I began, "we wanted to talk to you about Dana."

His face darkened. "Dana? What about her?"

"As it turns out, I'm trying to help the Abernathys figure out what happened to her."

"I don't know anything about that; I flew out first thing Sunday morning. I didn't even know she was dead until Vince sent me a text message." He fidgeted distractedly, bouncing one leg up and down while he talked.

I was trying to formulate a good follow-up question when Brody jumped in to help: "Ryan, we know about the blackmail."

Ryan's eyes grew wide. "Blackmail? I don't know what you're . . ."

Brody rolled his eyes. "Dude, c'mon, I just said we know already."

Ryan sighed and fell back in his chair. "How did you find out? Who else knows?"

I looked cautiously at Brody. I didn't want to tell Ryan everything we knew, at least not yet. "Let's just say Dana left behind some evidence."

"Where? We looked everywhere for—" He stopped abruptly.

He might as well have clamped his hand dramatically over his mouth.

Aha!

"So it was you who trashed her room?"

"Okay, yes, I went through her room, but I didn't kill her. You have to believe me!"

I wasn't sure what I believed, but I've watched enough crime shows to know that the killer always says that. Maybe Brody and I should have worked out a good cop, bad cop scenario before we started.

"Okay, yes," Ryan said. "Dana was blackmailing LionFish, but we were cool. I didn't want her dead. I just wanted the whole thing to go away before everyone found out about . . . well, you know."

"About LionFish tanking?" Brody suggested. He wasn't quite a bad cop, but maybe he could be the "slightly testy cop."

Ryan checked to make sure no one was within earshot. He leaned in toward us and lowered his voice. "Look, the company went through a rough patch, okay? And, yeah, we lost some money. I won't lie: I was really angry that Dana took advantage of the situation. But it was being handled."

"But you said yourself you needed the problem to go away," I said.

"Well, sure, but I gave her everything she wanted. I wasn't trying to permanently silence her, if that's what you're thinking. I figured I'd give her the cash, she'd give me the data, and we'd go our separate ways. No harm done."

"But," Brody persisted, "you were looking for the flash drives, which means Dana didn't hold up her end of the deal."

"She was going to give me everything after the reception that night, but then she collapsed in the church and I didn't see her again. I went to her room a couple of times, but she never answered the door."

"So you broke in?" Brody asked.

"Yeah." Ryan looked uncomfortable. "I mean, sort of."

I had a quick fantasy of Brody jumping out of his chair, grabbing Ryan by his collar, and screaming in his face, spittle flying, *"Which is it? Yes, or sort of?"* I waited a beat, but it didn't happen. Was I going to have to do everything myself? I cleared my throat. "So which is it? Yes, or sort of?"

"Let's just say I had some help," he said, fiddling with his lanyard and refusing to meet our eyes.

"Look, Ryan," I said, "you're going to have to help us out here, or I'm going to have to go to the cops with everything I know, including LionFish's"—I looked around furtively—"*situation.*"

"No! Please, I can't let that information get out." I hadn't really meant to, but I could see I'd struck a nerve. "We screwed up our first round of funding big-time, and if people find out, it's over."

"I'm serious, Ryan. I'm done playing investigator, and after I'm done talking to you, I'm going to turn everything I have over to the police. If you're not guilty, you're going to have to convince me, or I'll hand the files over to them as evidence."

That got him talking.

"Look, the other partners insisted I bring a team from CIS with me—Corporate Intelligence and Security. They didn't trust Dana to turn over the information, and they wanted to make sure nothing got out. It would be a disaster for our company, okay? When I told them I hadn't gotten the information yet, they went and searched her room themselves."

"You mean to tell me two complete strangers crashed the villa?" I'd had to deal with uninvited guests before, but they didn't usually wreak such havoc. "That was an awfully big chance they were taking. Why didn't they just have you take care of it?"

"I know! I told them I'd handle it," said Ryan, "but they didn't trust me. Maybe they thought I was in on it, too."

The thought hadn't occurred to me, but I could see why they might have suspected him. After all, he and Dana were friends long before she'd started blackmailing them; for all they knew, he'd been the one who'd given her the data in the first place. I could see why they'd want to take matters into their own hands.

"Wait a minute!" I said. "How do we know *they* didn't kill Dana?"

"I don't think they would have killed her," Ryan said. "I mean, they wouldn't . . . would they?"

I rolled my eyes; no wonder cops on TV always seem so irritable. "I don't know—that's why we're asking you."

He shook his head. "I don't think so. I mean, why would CIS have let me give her the money if they were just going to kill her anyway?"

"Good point, I guess." I wasn't entirely convinced, but I hadn't prepared a rebuttal.

"Maybe the plan all along was to kill her and steal the money back," Brody offered.

"No," Ryan replied. "It's not like it was in a messenger bag full of unmarked bills. They deposited it in an offshore account somewhere. It would have been impossible to recall the deposit, and they knew it."

I stared at the ceiling over Ryan's head, momentarily absorbed by the ornate wallpaper border. I made a mental note of the cobwebs in the corner. Yech. I would never hold a wedding reception here. I sat up suddenly. "Maybe they thought she was going to blab. You know, they wanted to shut her up?"

Ryan thought for a second. "Why would she talk after we gave her what she wanted?"

"Or maybe she already had," I continued. It made sense. They gave her the money, she talked, and they wanted to make sure it stopped there.

"No, she definitely hadn't told anyone," Ryan replied, looking pensive.

"But how do you know that?" I persisted.

Ryan's demeanor shifted suddenly. Had he said something he hadn't meant to say? Lucky for me, he was as bad at interrogations as I was. "I just know, okay?"

"Okay," I said as I gathered up my bag and stood to go. "If you're not going to tell me—"

"Wait!" he pleaded, jumping up after me. "They had someone keeping tabs on her, someone who could get close to the wedding party."

"Ooh, a spy?" asked Brody. "This is getting good."

Suddenly, a piece of the puzzle fell into place. "Ryan, who was the spy?"

"Just . . . someone."

I jumped out of my chair, propelled by a vision of Leo the actor dressed as a Mexican priest. "It was Father Villarreal, wasn't it! They wanted someone who everyone would trust, someone they'd open up to."

Ryan didn't have to answer; his look said it all as he sank back down into his chair and rubbed the side of his head in what must have been a major Excedrin moment.

Damn.

If LionFish's security team had sent a fake priest to perform a wedding ceremony, then was it such a stretch to believe they could have killed Dana? Because, come on, who screws with a wedding? Okay, maybe that was just the wedding planner in me talking. Clearly I was taking the deception kind of personally.

I fished through my bag for a notepad and pen. "Ryan, we're going to need some names."

He sighed, looking defeated. "Sam Fortney and Naomi Cutts."

"Naomi Cutts? Why does that name sound familiar?" Before

he had a chance to reply, I remembered. "You mean the same Naomi who was Trevor's date?"

"Yep," Ryan said.

"But she's missing!" I exclaimed.

"She's not missing. She e-mailed me this morning."

"But when I asked Trevor about her, he clammed up. He was acting really suspicious and we thought—"

Ryan held his hand up to stop me. "That's because she wasn't really his date. He needed someone to keep Dana away from him, and she needed a cover. I set the whole thing up."

"Wait, so you're telling me Naomi was from LionFish?"

"Yep."

"And she and this Sam guy were the ones who tossed Dana's room?"

"I'm sorry. I should have said something earlier. I thought maybe if I kept my mouth shut, no one would find out. But if they really did this, our financial data is going to be the least of my worries."

Well, that was a relief. Everything was starting to make sense. LionFish was in trouble, Dana was blackmailing them, Ryan wanted to pay up, someone else wanted to shut her up, and the company had sent a security team to finish the job.

Naomi was no missing person; she was a suspect. Everything was falling into place, and I couldn't wait to go hand over her and Sam's names to the police. This was news I was going to enjoy delivering in person—even if it did mean flying back to Mexico one last time.

CHAPTER 28

*T*axi?" the doorman said, as we planted ourselves near the hotel's revolving doors to wait for Evan.

"God, I wish." I smiled. "I mean, no, thank you."

It was tempting to jump into a Yellow Cab and hop the next flight to San Francisco, but I still had one piece of business left: turning over the information Ryan had given me to Zoe and Mrs. Abernathy and washing my hands of this business once and for all.

I paced back and forth, borderline giddy, clutching the notebook containing the names of my two prime suspects. The team from LionFish had had plenty of opportunity, more than ample motive, and, well, I didn't know about the means, but I was sure someone more experienced than me could figure that one out. Mrs. Abernathy could take the information to the police or she could pass it on to her attorneys, but my work here was done.

After an excruciatingly long wait—in reality probably no more than seven or eight minutes—Evan rounded the corner in the rental car and Brody and I piled in.

"How'd it go?" Evan asked.

"It went well," I answered. "I'll fill you in on the way back, but do you mind if we drop Brody off at the main airport first? He's going to go ahead and fly back to San Francisco."

"Sure," Evan said. "Does that mean you're coming back with me?"

"Yeah. Call me old-fashioned, but I want to deliver the news in person."

We pulled up to Terminal 2, and Brody and I got out of the car.

"Are you sure this is okay?" Brody asked, pulling his luggage out of the trunk.

"Of course! Go, go. I'll be fine. I'll be right behind you, as soon as I retire from my accidental career in law enforcement."

"Okay," he said, scooping me up in a big hug and planting a peck on my cheek. "Let me know when you get a flight. I can pick you up from the airport."

"You mean you haven't had enough of me yet?" I punched him playfully on the arm.

"Almost, but not quite," he joked.

"Well, you should get a medal," I said, handing him his camera bag. "Thanks again for everything. I really don't know what I would have done without you."

We finished saying good-bye, and I climbed back into the car with Evan and rolled down the window. "Don't forget to bill your return flight to Mrs. Abernathy," I called after Brody as he walked away.

"Oh, don't worry!" he exclaimed, smiling broadly. "I even booked myself in first class!"

I buckled my seat belt as we exited Lindbergh Field and headed toward the private airstrip where Evan's plane was waiting.

"You hungry?" Evan asked. "We could stop at In-N-Out Burger."

I shrugged in response. My stomach was starting to grumble, but I wasn't eager to spend any more time with Evan than I had to.

"C'mon, it's not like the plane can leave without us." He smiled winningly. If I hadn't known better, I would have thought he was trying to charm me into forgetting about the other night. It didn't matter. I was still miffed.

"I can wait till later," I replied. "I want to get back to San Miguel and wrap things up."

Evan looked hurt, but he left it at that.

After riding in silence for a bit, I flipped on the radio, trying to find something to fill the void in the conversation. Why was there nothing but Spanish-language stations? Probably because we were only fifteen miles from Tijuana. After the last couple of weeks, I was ready for a break from all things Mexican. I scowled and turned the radio back off.

"What are you thinking about?" Evan asked. He never had been comfortable with silence, even if he'd caused it himself.

"Just that I can't wait to be back in my own bed."

He sighed, then pulled into the parking lot of a strip mall and turned off the ignition.

"Look, Kelsey, can we talk about the other night?"

"There's nothing to talk about." I crossed my arms in front of my chest and stared out the window at a pawn shop next to a Chinese restaurant.

"I'm sorry about what I said." He reached out to take my hand, but I refused to unfold myself.

"I don't care that you said it. I'm just upset that you seem to believe it."

"Well, I mean, c'mon . . ." He wasn't exactly leaping in with a well-articulated explanation. "You're around weddings all the time. I assumed . . . I mean, surely you must want to get married yourself."

I kind of wanted to smack him. Good thing we were having this conversation in a parked car and not in midair, in case I decided to act on the urge.

"Maybe," I said, "someday, but not right now. Weddings are my job, not my *goal*. I'm not acting out some secret fantasy I doodled in my spiral notebook in eighth grade."

"But you can understand how a guy might feel pressured, right?"

"What?" I turned in my seat to look at him. "No, I really can't."

"It sets an impossible standard. All day long you're immersed in true love and long-term commitments and all that fairy-tale, happily-ever-after crap."

"Well, sorry, but I can't exactly be a wedding planner without going to some weddings, and I'm not going to change careers simply because it makes you feel uncomfortable."

He sighed and stared out the window. "You're right. I'm sorry."

I grunted noncommittally. It wasn't that I didn't forgive him. I did.

But it didn't change anything.

He reached over and took my hand, and we sat in awkward silence for a moment. "Can't we forget that this whole thing ever happened? Believe it or not, I've really enjoyed getting to spend time with you again."

I wanted to say yes. But that was exactly what had gotten me into this predicament: I had conveniently chosen to forget every-thing that had happened the last time we were together, back in San Francisco, and now the same old problems were popping up all over again.

I sighed. "I think we both know this isn't going to work out. We should have just left it alone."

He opened his mouth to speak, but nothing came out, and he shook his head instead.

"Besides," I said, "let's be realistic. We live in different countries. I mean, what's the point?"

As a rebuttal, he pulled me toward him and kissed me. I'd be lying if I said I didn't still swoon a little at the feel of his lips on mine. He wound his fingers through my hair, and for a moment I forgot where I was—but then I remembered we were in the parking lot of a pawn shop and I pulled away from him, breaking the spell.

"Kelsey, we're so good together," he murmured. "Don't you want to see where this goes?"

"Right now the only place I want this to go is to the airport," I said impatiently. I checked the passenger mirror for smudged lipstick and wiped at my mouth with my hand.

He looked dejected as he started the car; then his face brightened momentarily.

"Hey, ever wanted to join the mile-high club?"

I turned and looked at him, scrunching up my eyebrows in bewilderment. Was he really hitting on me? I had a list of things to do, but having a midair farewell quickie wasn't one of them.

"I'm kidding," he retracted. "I mean, unless you really wanted to . . ."

Any doubt I'd had about my decision evaporated. "Just drive."

It was late afternoon by the time we got back to San Miguel, and I couldn't wait to tell the newlyweds and Mrs. Abernathy what I'd learned about the security team from LionFish. The more I thought about it, the more I was sure that they'd killed Dana. They'd been sent to protect the company's interests, and Dana had been in direct conflict with those interests. Even if she'd turned over the data, she still could have blabbed to someone that the company was in trouble. What better way to keep her from talking than to silence her permanently?

The only thing I couldn't figure out was, how had the real Father Villarreal played into all of this? Whatever had happened, I felt terrible about it. To some degree, Dana had been responsible for her own death, but Father Villarreal had never been anything more than an innocent bystander.

I tried calling Mrs. Abernathy and the newlyweds, but all I got was voice mails, so I decided to swing by the jail to see if I could find them there. At the very least, I could report what I'd learned to Zoe, who no doubt would be thrilled at the news. On the way, I stopped at the coffee stand near the *jardín* for a mid-afternoon pick-me-up. Not that I needed the caffeine—I was too excited for that—but I had to have one more *café con leche* before I left town. Who knew when I might be back this way again?

As if in answer, my cell phone buzzed with an incoming text from Jacinda Rivera, whom I hadn't seen since that day at the church when she had practically fled after learning that Father Villarreal was dead.

Are you still in town? Have time to meet?

I did a little happy dance in spite of myself. As much as I was ready to spend some quality time apart from San Miguel, I couldn't bear the thought of missing out on a potential client, especially since I had already hit it off with the bride-to-be. I eagerly texted her back, making plans to meet a little later.

What can I say? I love my job.

I slurped down the rest of the coffee as I made my way back

toward the center of town. I pondered stopping by and talking to the two detectives, Ortiz and Nolasco, but I'd had enough of them. Nope, best to leave it in the hands of Mrs. Abernathy. She could tell the lawyers, and they could take it from there. The suspects— or soon-to-be suspects—were surely back in the States by now. I had no idea how that all worked, but luckily I didn't need to. This job was officially out of my hands.

At the jail, a guard buzzed me in, and I hurried into the visitation room to see Zoe.

"You came back!" she exclaimed. "Does that mean you have good news?"

"I think I might," I replied, sitting across from her. "So I talked to Ryan."

She sat a little straighter in her seat and looked at me expectantly. "Yeah?"

"And I think I have a really solid lead on who killed Dana."

Her eyes welled up at the news and she swiped at them with her right hand, the handcuffs dragging her left hand along, too. "Oh my God, Kelsey, that's amazing. Who? How? Tell me everything!"

I filled her in on what I'd learned from Ryan, and her smile grew bigger and bigger.

"Have you told Mom yet?" she asked.

"No, I called but they didn't answer, so I came straight to you."

She bounced up and down in her chair a little. "Oh, I can't wait to tell them. Or for you to tell them. I don't care—I just want this to be over with."

Poor Zoe. She'd gone from being a maid of honor to a murder suspect in just one day, and I could tell her incarceration had really started to wear on her. Despite the fact that Mrs. Abernathy had bullied me into this job, the reason I'd stuck with it was sitting right in front of me. I was as happy for Zoe's impending freedom as I was for my own.

"Don't worry, Zoe," I said, reaching across the worn wooden table and taking her shackled hands in mine. "We'll get you out of here in no time."

CHAPTER 29

I swung by the house on Calle Recreo, but nobody was home yet, so I left a note and headed to Jacinda Rivera's house. She greeted me at the door in a long, pale green dress embroidered with tiny flowers, her tousle of curls pulled effortlessly into a wedding-worthy 'do.

"Look at you!" I gushed. She was going to make one gorgeous bride. I only hoped I hadn't scared her off.

"Kelsey, come in." She swung the door open and beckoned me inside. "Sorry I didn't call sooner. I was a little freaked out when we found out that priest had died, but I realize I was being silly. It's not like it was your fault."

"I understand. I was a little freaked out myself. I've never had anything like that happen before. For what it's worth, we have a good, solid lead on who did it." It was a relief saying those words, reassuring her that the two deaths weren't the work of some crazed serial killer who only targeted weddings planned by me.

"Who did what?" Jacinda looked at me with a puzzled expression.

"Killed Father Villarreal? The priest? And Dana, the bridesmaid? I mean, I don't know exactly what happened, but I feel pretty confident that we've found their killer."

"*Their* killer? What do you mean?"

I paused, uncertain how to proceed. "I mean, I found out who had a motive to kill Dana—she'd made some pretty powerful enemies—and I don't know how Father Villarreal got caught up in the whole mess, but I'm sure the police will be able to figure it out."

She cocked her head to one side as if she was unsure what to say. "So I guess you haven't heard."

Now it was my turn to be puzzled. "No, heard what?"

"Nothing happened to Father Villarreal. A friend of mine goes to his church, and apparently he had a heart attack. That's what I meant when I said I was being silly."

Oh, man. Now instead of thinking I was dangerous, she probably thought I was nuts. "Oh, no, I hadn't heard." Good thing she was interested in my services as a wedding planner and not a detective.

She smiled uncertainly at my reaction. "That's good, right? I mean, better than having *two* murders linked to your wedding."

Jeez. Well, sure, when you put it that way. "Yes! I'm sorry. I'm a little embarrassed. I just assumed—well, anyway, let's talk about your wedding, shall we?"

"Yes. I guess this got off to kind of a weird start, but I'd still like you to submit a proposal. I mean, this wedding's not going to plan itself, is it?"

I was glad she saw it that way. I wanted the job and would do whatever I could to prove that I was the right person to plan her wedding. Thank goodness she knew that Father Villarreal's death hadn't had anything to do with me. Besides, it made the case against the security team from LionFish even stronger. I hadn't been able to explain their connection to Father Villarreal or why they'd want to hurt him, and now I wouldn't have to.

". . . and so I just wanted to see what you thought."

Jacinda was holding out a stack of photos, staring at me expectantly. Had she been talking this whole time? I had to stop letting the Abernathy case interfere with my real job. It was time to focus.

"These are gorgeous," I began, flipping through some pictures she'd printed off the Internet. Lots of rustic charm but with plenty of crisp, modern elements thrown in. My mind was already buzzing with ideas.

"Have you thought about a color scheme? I can tell from these photos that you're not afraid of color."

She pointed to the large painting I'd admired on my first visit. "No, I love color. And I wouldn't mind if we could incorporate some of my artwork."

"I think that's a great idea! That will really make it unique."

"That's what I was hoping," Jacinda said. "I want it to be really personal."

"Absolutely," I replied. "That's my favorite part."

"Oh! But there is one idea I want to steal." She turned on her phone and started flipping through the pictures. "Remember how I said I saw them setting up for your bride's wedding? I absolutely loved what you did with the old fountain in the middle of the courtyard, filling it with flowers like that." She zoomed in on the center of one of the photos and handed it to me so I could see.

It really had been the perfect centerpiece. Using the fountain had been the florist's idea—I couldn't take credit, as much as I'd have liked to—but it was definitely easy enough to replicate. I zoomed out a little to admire the setting.

Wait. Something had caught my eye. I tapped my finger on the screen to zoom in again. There in the background was a man wearing an orange shirt that looked an awful lot like a *guayabera*. Hadn't Fernando, the chef at the villa, said that whoever had visited Dana's room had been wearing an orange *guayabera*? Fernando had thought it was Vince who'd gone to her room, and later we assumed it was Ryan, but the man in this picture didn't look like either of them. Could it have been the security guy from LionFish? Was this the evidence I needed to convince the police? Maybe they'd even let Zoe out of jail!

"Jacinda, can I have a copy of this photo for reference?" I asked excitedly.

"Sure. It's not very good, but I can e-mail it to you. Of course, I'd want different flowers. I mean, I don't want it to be *exactly* the same."

"Of course." I handed the phone back to her, and she forwarded the photo to me with a satisfying *swoosh* noise. I could have kissed her, but I didn't want to let on that this was about anything other than her wedding. "All right, let's talk about your guest list. How many people are you thinking?"

Although I could hardly sit still, I fought with every cell in my brain to stay focused on her wedding for the rest of the meeting. We talked food, flowers, venue, all of it, and I promised to send her an estimate ASAP.

At last we were done, and Jacinda showed me to the door. "Thanks again for coming, Kelsey. I'll be on the lookout for your proposal."

"Thank *you*, Jacinda. I really appreciate it." She had no idea how much I really meant it.

As soon as she closed the front door, I scrambled for my phone to retrieve my e-mails. Yep, there it was. I shot off a copy to Ryan with a message asking if he could identify the man in the photo, then texted it to Brody, too. Underneath I wrote, "Orange guaya-bera man?"

I really wanted to see what Fernando thought, and I was only a few blocks from the villa. I walked straight there in the hopes of catching him and asking if this was the same man. The maid es-corted me to the steaming kitchen, and my stomach growled audibly at the smells coming from the stove.

"Kelsey!" Fernando greeted me. "How is it you always know when I am cooking?"

"*Hola,* Fernando. I didn't come to eat—although I wouldn't say no. I mean, come on, who am I kidding?"

"Here, taste this," he commanded, handing me a forkful of the fragrant pork that was simmering in the skillet in front of him.

"Oh my God, that's good!" It was so tender and delicious I almost forgot where I was for a second, but I was there for busi-ness, not Fernando's incredible cooking. I swallowed and re-trieved my phone from my purse. "And while I can't deny the lure of your cooking, I actually had a question for you."

I pulled up the picture from the courtyard and showed it to him. "You said you saw a man in an orange *guayabera* entering Dana's room the night before she was murdered. Can you tell me if this was him?"

Fernando studied the picture on my phone. "It's hard to say because this picture's so small, but it sure looks like him." The phone chimed, and he handed the phone back to me. "Here, it looks like you got a message." A text from Brody was superim-posed over the photo:

this looks like kirk?!?!

Kirk? Dana's fiancé? No, it couldn't be. I peered more closely at the photo, but the tiny man on my phone's screen could have been anybody.

"Can you excuse me for a second, Fernando?" He nodded, returning to his cooking, and I stepped into the dining room and called Brody, who didn't even bother to greet me with a proper hello. "Where did you get this picture?" he asked.

"Jacinda took it. What do you mean, it looks like Kirk?"

"That's his name, right? Dana's fiancé?"

"Yeah, but you think it looks like him?" My voice was getting a little shrill.

"Did you see it on your phone, or on a computer?"

"On my phone," I admitted, trying to remain calm. "My laptop's still at Evan's."

"Well, I'm looking at it up close on my computer monitor, and I'm telling you, it's Kirk."

"Hold on." I held the phone at arm's length, squinting. It was hard to tell on the tiny screen, but the guy in the picture did bear some resemblance to Dana's fiancé. "Maybe," I said, "but that doesn't make any sense! Kirk didn't arrive until a couple of days after the wedding."

"Well, if this is him, that changes everything."

I told Brody I'd call him back and hung up, my mind racing. Surely this was a coincidence. As I tried to decide what to do next, my phone chimed again. It was Ryan:

Nope, sorry, whoever that is wasn't with us

I sank back against the doorway for support. What could this mean? If it was Kirk, not only had he been here before Dana had even died, but Fernando had seen him going into Dana's room *while she was still alive.*

I was getting ahead of myself. Maybe Dana had kept him on the down low. Mrs. Abernathy would have given Dana hell for having an uninvited guest at the villa. Still, why would he pretend he'd just arrived instead of telling us he'd already been here?

After saying a hasty good-bye to Fernando, I exited through the back. Then I sat on the curb for a few moments, contemplating my next move.

I called the hotel where Kirk had been staying. The front desk girl didn't speak English much better than I spoke Spanish, but she was able to tell me that Kirk had already checked out. At least I thought that's what she said; she might have been recommending a restaurant. I really needed to brush up on my Spanish.

On a hunch—and not wanting to attempt any more bilingual conversations over the phone—I looked up the address for the morgue and headed straight there.

"Hi, *hola, habla inglés?*"

"*Sí?*" the front desk attendant answered.

"I wanted to check on a body. Dana Poole?"

"*Momento.*" He walked to the back of the room and thumbed through some files on his desk. "*Sí.* She's ready to go."

"You mean she's still here?" I practically shouted.

"*Sí . . . ?*" he replied, confused by my reaction. "Aren't you here to take her?"

I sank down in the metal folding chair near the desk. Kirk hadn't picked up the body? He'd said he would take care of it. Had there been a change of plans?

I held up one finger as I searched for the directory on my phone. "*Momento.* I need to check on something." I dialed Dana's parents, and her mom picked up after a couple of rings.

"Hello?" she answered.

"Mrs. Poole, hi," I said. "This is Kelsey. I was wondering if you had heard from Kirk?"

There was a pause. "I'm sorry?" she replied.

"Dana's fiancé, Kirk? He was supposed to make arrangements for . . . you know . . ." I could hear her whispering to someone in the background. *Please let this all be a big, fat misunderstanding.*

Mrs. Poole came back on the line after a second. "Kirk? I'm confused, Kelsey. We don't know anyone named Kirk."

CHAPTER 30

I wish I could say I handled the situation with aplomb and made up a good cover story while I got my wits about me, but I mumbled something approximately like, "Um, he, well, I—I have to go!" At least I didn't make static noises and say I was about to go through a tunnel.

Who was this guy? We had taken him in without a second thought. We'd fed him dinner. Heck, we'd even comforted him for his loss. And what did I know about him? Even less than I know about Japanese battleships or the mating rituals of warthogs. That is to say, very, very little.

Here's what I did know: He'd said he and Dana were engaged and that she was going to have his baby, but her parents had never heard of him. He said he'd arrived in Mexico the night we met him, but if Brody was right, Kirk had been in town for several days before that. He'd claimed to be devastated; he'd even sat in

Dana's room and unpacked all her things. Had he been looking for something? Like the flash drives?

I hesitated for a moment, trying to decide whether to call Mrs. Abernathy. I wasn't sure which would be worse: getting her, or not getting her. I certainly didn't want to start rambling nervously into her voice mail.

I called Brody back instead.

"Tell me I'm letting my imagination run away with me," I said as soon as he picked up.

"Oooh, fun game. Okay, you're letting your imagination run away with you."

"Except what if I'm not?" I asked.

"What you *are* doing is being cryptic," he said. "Tell me what's going on."

"Oh, sorry. I talked to Dana's mom, and they've never heard of Kirk."

"Whoa, seriously?"

"Yep. Kirk never picked Dana's body up from the morgue, either. I guess that's a good thing, since he wasn't sent here by her family."

"Wow. So who the hell is this guy?"

"I don't know! Do you remember Kirk's last name? Or if he even gave us a last name?"

Brody paused for a second. "He must have, but I couldn't tell you what it is. It's not like he gave us his business card."

My mind raced, trying to figure out what Kirk's role had been in everything that had happened. Clearly he wasn't who he'd said he was, but could *he* have been the killer, dispatched by the security team from LionFish to do the dirty work? Or had they simply sent him to the villa that night to have another go at searching her room? "Brody, this is crazy! Are you sure it's him in the photo?"

"Well, no, his head is kind of turned to the side, and it's blurry when you blow it up." Brody paused. "But I have to tell you, when I saw the photo, my immediate gut reaction was that it was him, and when you put that together with everything else you found out . . ."

I sighed, letting out a long puff of air. "So what should I do?"

"I think you should go to the police."

"The police? And say what? 'I met a guy who is super suspicious but I didn't catch his name and he's probably left town'?"

"You're right, that's not likely to get you far. But remember, you also have Naomi and Sam from LionFish, which means you at least have one solid lead for them to go on."

"I know, I know. I'm afraid they're not going to take me any more seriously than they did before. I really dread going to that police station again and getting more abuse from those two. They seem to kind of hate me."

"Then why don't you talk to Mrs. Abernathy. She can tell her lawyers, and they can deal with the police."

"You're right," I said. "That's actually a really good idea."

"What do you mean, 'actually'? I have lots of good ideas!"

"Awwww, look at you and your fake indignation. I gotta go, smarty-pants."

Still unable to reach Mrs. Abernathy by phone, I walked back to the rental house. There was no answer at the door, so I dropped my bag on the ground and leaned against the wall. Where could they be? It was starting to get dark. Surely, they'd be home soon. Visiting hours at the jail were over, and Mrs. Abernathy usually insisted on dining early.

After waiting what felt like a really long time, I started to get impatient. I checked my watch. I'd only been there for three minutes. *Aaaarrgghhhh!* It had been a ridiculously long day, and I desperately wanted to sit for a while. Plus, I couldn't be sure that I was alone as long as I was standing out on the street. The more I thought about it, the more I didn't feel safe.

I checked my messages. Nothing. But I did have Marisol's phone number. If she was still at the office, maybe she could help.

"*Bueno?*"

"*Hola,* Marisol, it's me, Kelsey. Thank God I caught you!"

"Hi, Kelsey. Is everything okay?"

"Yes. Well, sort of." It was too long a story to get into over the phone. "I have a favor to ask. Mrs. Abernathy called, and she needs me to pick up something for her at the house. Can I swing by and borrow your spare key?" Okay, so I was totally lying, but it was far from the worst thing that had happened that day.

"No problem. I'm just finishing up some things. I'll be here a little bit longer."

Right after I hung up, a text message lit up my screen.

Should I expect you for dinner?

Evan. I hesitated a moment. My things were still at his house, so I had to go back eventually, but I didn't really want to spend my last evening in town making awkward chitchat with him.

No, thanks. Finishing up some things. Don't wait up.

If I stayed out long enough, maybe I could sneak in and avoid seeing him altogether, at least until the next morning.

By the time I got back to the rental house, it was fully dark outside. I knocked on the door again, in case they'd gotten back from dinner while I was gone. Then, for good measure, I grabbed the brass knocker and banged it against the heavy wooden door loudly and repeatedly. *Sorry, neighbors.* I waited an appropriate amount of time, then let myself inside.

I hoped Mrs. Abernathy wouldn't mind my intrusion. But

surely any annoyance she might feel would be forgotten when I told her my news.

As I slid the key into the lock and opened the door, I felt something brush past my leg. It was the orange tabby that had set off Mrs. Abernathy's allergies. Indignant at having been locked out all week, he jumped straight up onto the couch and started cleaning himself. *Good boy.*

I turned on the lamp next to the couch, then wandered into the kitchen to search the refrigerator. Clearly buying groceries or saving leftovers was for commoners.

Returning to the living room, I picked up the cat. "Mind if we share the couch?" I lay down and set him on my stomach, where he stretched out and began purring contentedly as I scratched his head. "What a handsome boy. I shall call you Guapo." Soon enough, I'd be back home with my own cats, but for now, my tabby *gato* was a nice surrogate.

Man, it felt good to relax for a second. I had barely slowed down all day. I closed my eyes, enjoying a moment of peace.

A sudden noise from somewhere outside startled the tabby. He hissed and jumped off me, racing across the floor and hiding behind a chair.

"Owww!" I cried, rubbing the rising welts on my stomach where his claws had dug in for traction. "What was that about?!"

I heard the noise again, but it wasn't coming from outside. It was coming from somewhere down the hall. Was Mrs. Abernathy home? Why hadn't she answered the door when I'd knocked? My entire system went on high alert. Maybe it was someone else. After all, Mrs. Abernathy would have had the common decency to come out and scowl at me after I'd let myself in.

I raced to the kitchen and looked around for something to arm myself with. Riffling through the drawers, I found a large knife, but it looked like it could hardly slice a banana. Typical for a rental; heaven forbid they stock proper cutlery. It was the best I was going to do on short notice, though, so I grabbed the heavy black handle and closed the drawer quietly behind me.

Damn it, how do you dial 911 in Mexico? *Nueve uno uno?* As a wedding planner, I was used to handling emergencies on my own. I was woefully unprepared for what to do in the case of an actual emergency.

I knew 911 wasn't right, but I tried it anyway. Nothing. I quickly dialed Marisol, but the call rolled over to the after-hours recording. She must have already gone home for the evening.

Stubbornly undaunted, I crept down the dark hallway clutching my knife, while Guapo stayed in his corner, flicking his tail furiously back and forth. At the end of the hall, I found three closed doors and paused, unsure which one to try. I listened as hard as I could, but all I could hear was my own heartbeat pounding in my ears.

I slowly turned the knob to the first bedroom and swung open the door, peeking inside. I couldn't see anything at first, but as my eyes adjusted I could make out the furniture and Nicole and Vince's suitcases. Nothing appeared to be amiss, unless someone was hiding.

I snuck up on the door to the master suite, pausing to listen for any noises coming from inside. I couldn't hear anything. I reached out, but my hand paused just short of the knob. What if someone really was in there? What exactly was I planning to do with a dull kitchen knife, anyway? I pulled back. *What am I thinking? I have to get out of here!*

And then, well, I'm not exactly sure what happened next: Did I hear the loud *crack* first or feel the searing pain across my skull? I do know what happened after that, though: everything went to black.

CHAPTER 31

No matter the reason, waking up on the floor is never a good thing. It invariably leads to all sorts of existential questions, such as "Where am I? And how did I get here?"

I started to open my eyes, but the light hurt my head and I shut them again quickly. I reached up to rub the knot that was swelling on the back of my head but was having trouble moving. How long had I been out? I had no idea. I could barely remember my own name.

I heard movement and opened my eyes to see a dark figure hovering over me. I squinted, trying to focus, but things were still a bit blurry.

"You're awake," Kirk said matter-of-factly. His eyes were dark, his friendly demeanor gone.

"Kirk . . ." I began. Was that even his real name?

I tried to prop myself up on my elbows, but I still couldn't move my arms—which were inconveniently bound together with rope.

Where was I, anyway? Cold, concrete floor, a beat-up washer and dryer, stairs leading up—ah, the basement. I hadn't paid much attention to it when Marisol had showed me around, but then I hadn't figured anyone would be spending much time down here.

Kirk yanked me up into a sitting position. "Sorry I can't offer you a chair."

Somehow I didn't think he was really sorry, as evidenced by the click of the gun he had pointed at my right temple. I leaned against the wall for support, closing my eyes for a second. My head felt like it was splitting open. Even my eyelashes hurt.

"Today must be my lucky day," he said, kneeling on the floor next to me. "I came here to ask that nice family where I might be able to find you, and here you are."

"Me? Why did you want me?"

"Because I'm looking for something—and I have a feeling you might just know where it is."

My mouth was so dry it was hard to speak. "What do you mean?"

He leveled a cold stare at me. "Don't play dumb. You cleaned out Dana's room. She had some information with her. Information I need to get back. Sound familiar?"

I knew exactly what he meant, but tried to feign innocence. "But I don't have any of her stuff. I turned it all over to you."

"Not everything." He looked me dead in the eye. "Where are the flash drives, Kelsey? They weren't in her things. Believe me, I looked."

My head was throbbing, and I scrunched my eyes shut to stave off the pain while I came up with an answer. Kirk, however, wasn't prepared to wait. He leaned over me and put the gun right under my chin. "Answer me!"

"Look, Kirk, we did find the information you're talking about, but we gave it to the police."

He looked surprised, like the possibility had never even occurred to him. "I don't believe you! Now, where is it?"

"I'm telling you, I don't have it. Once we realized what it was, we handed it over."

Kirk didn't like my answer. A vein on his left temple throbbed as he punched his left fist through the basement drywall.

I winced. Add that to the list of things Mrs. Abernathy was going to be mad about. Speaking of Mrs. Abernathy, where was she? Where were Nicole and Vince? For all I knew, they were tied up somewhere, or even worse—no. I refused to believe he'd harmed a bunch of innocent bystanders, because if he had, that would mean I was next.

Who was this stranger we had let into our lives without a second thought? Had he even known Dana, or had he been sent by someone else to retrieve the company's information?

My head had started to clear, and I angled my back away from him. I thought it best not to let on that I knew about Dana's plan, but I wanted to keep him talking while I worked to loosen the rope around my wrists. "What do you need it for, anyway?"

"That's none of your business."

"If you work for LionFish, I can tell you right now that the police aren't going to go digging into those financial records. It's over. You can go home and tell everybody their secret is safe."

"What are you talking about?" he asked, rubbing the bloodied knuckles on his fist and staring at me with contempt. "I'm not from LionFish. This is about the money."

I kept trying to pull one wrist free but wasn't succeeding at much more than giving myself rope burn. Stupid knots. *Keep him talking.* "What do you mean? What money?"

"The money LionFish was giving us to keep us quiet. If the investors found out how much trouble the company was in, it would all be over."

I feigned surprise, but it was just an act. In the short time I'd known him, he'd lied to me, bonked me over the head, and tied me up in a basement. Surely he wasn't above blackmail, too. "So you were in on Dana's blackmail scheme?"

"In on it? It was my idea! Dana and I were supposed to be partners. Fifty-fifty, but then she decided to take all the money for herself."

"Why would she do that? I thought you two were a couple."

Kirk laughed bitterly. "We were. But I guess she had other plans."

"What do you mean?" The binding around my wrists hadn't budged one bit, and my wrists were starting to feel raw from the effort.

"She'd been bugging me to come to the wedding with her, but I couldn't get the time off from work. She was pretty pissed. Said there was no way she was showing up without a date."

"But she changed her mind?" Obviously she had, or she wouldn't be dead and I wouldn't be tied up in a basement, but the real question was *why?*

"She didn't have a choice. Ryan said that LionFish was prepared to give her what she wanted, but that she had to bring everything to him in person. So she booked a flight. Things were pretty tense between us, and I felt so bad after she left that I decided to follow her down to Mexico to surprise her."

"You just showed up?" Man, no wonder things had gone poorly.

He sucked in a deep breath and held it in for a second before continuing. "I thought she'd be happy I came, but apparently not. She told me I could stay, even snuck me into the villa, but she said she didn't want me to come to the wedding with her. She claimed it was too late to change the RSVP or something stupid like that."

I was tempted to tell him that RSVPs are not stupid, they're a vital part of the planning process, but this was no time to stand on etiquette.

"When I asked her about the money, she said not to worry about it, that it was all taken care of. But I knew there was something she wasn't telling me. Then, when she was in the shower . . ." He stopped and shook his head angrily.

"What?" I asked. "What happened?"

"I decided to search her room to see if she already had the money. And you know what I found in her bag? A bank deposit slip and a plane ticket to Barbados! She wasn't planning on coming home at all. She was going to take the money and disappear."

"Oh, I'm sure she wouldn't have done that!" Actually, I was totally sure she would have done that.

He spun around, eyes flashing. "Of course she would. She was lying to me all along!" Kirk's fists clenched at his sides, and his eyes darkened even further. "Do you really think I was going to stand for that?"

"So you killed her?"

He gave me a look of surprise, incredulous that I didn't get it. "She left me no option."

I could think of some other options, but unfortunately, it was too late to offer them.

"After she left for the rehearsal dinner, I started making some calls. Turns out, it's not as easy to buy poison in a foreign country as you would think. Luckily, there's an auto parts store on the edge of town that set me up with a little ethylene glycol." His expression had turned smug as he recounted this small victory.

"Ethylene glycol?"

"The main ingredient in both antifreeze and one very special margarita I made for Dana before she left for the bachelorette party that night."

"Why go to all that trouble? Why not just shoot her?" I asked, jerking my chin toward the gun in his hand.

"Too many people around. No way I would have gotten out of that house when everyone came running. Besides, a cocktail seemed like a much more civilized way to go."

Ugh. I'd warned the girls about drinking. If only I'd been more specific.

One detail was still bothering me. "I'm curious: Why did you pin it on Zoe? The police said they found poison in her room."

He shrugged. "It was nothing personal. When I was leaving, I heard someone coming, so I ducked into one of the rooms and hid the bottle under the sink. I didn't know whose room it was, but I didn't want to get caught with it."

I glared at him openly. "I know you probably thought Dana got what she deserved, but doesn't it bother you even a little bit that an innocent girl is sitting in jail right now?"

Kirk smirked as he folded his arms in front of his chest. "If you see her, be sure to pass on my apologies."

Just then, we heard the sound of the front door opening. Thank God! They were back. *About damn time.*

Kirk held a finger up to his mouth and looked directly at me. "Not one word or I shoot you."

We paused for a minute. I could hear Mrs. Abernathy, Nicole, and Vince above us, settling into the living room. Kirk didn't seem especially daunted by their appearance; then again, he had a gun.

"I'm going to go upstairs and say hi," he said in a low voice, waving the gun in the air in a gesture that would have seemed friendly had it not been for the weapon. "I think you know more about those files than you're letting on. There might even be an extra copy floating around."

"Kirk, I'm telling you—"

He cocked the gun and pointed it straight at my face. Oops. Okay, I was just going to let him do whatever he felt like he needed to do.

"You make a noise and I'm going to kill your friends. Then I'm going to come back down here and kill you. You got it?"

I nodded mutely. The guy with the gun gets to call the shots.

He walked up the stairs, tucking the gun into the back of his jeans. "Hello!" he called out cordially. "Sorry to startle you, but you said if I needed a place to stay I could come here. I hope that's okay. I was just doing some laundry." The door closed behind him, so I couldn't hear how his arrival was received. Hopefully Mrs. Abernathy wouldn't say something stupid and make him mad.

I realized with horror that they had no idea he was dangerous. They didn't even know he'd broken in; for all they knew, he had just sweet-talked someone at the rental company. I had to find some way to get free. I closed my eyes to concentrate, frantically working at the knots. Too bad I didn't have my wedding emergency kit with me.

I heard a soft meow and opened my eyes. Guapo the cat was staring right into my face. He must have slipped past Kirk when he went upstairs.

"Hi, kitty," I said quietly, still tugging at the rope with an urgency the cat did not share. He butted my face with the top of his forehead and started purring.

"Good boy! Be like Lassie—go get help!" In response, the tabby started licking my forehead in short, raspy strokes that actually kind of hurt.

"Ewww, that's not helping," I said, moving my face away from his, but he was persistent. "Stop that!"

Bored, he walked several feet away and began cleaning himself.

"Thanks a lot, cat."

I looked around the room to see if there was any means of escape. I could hear the cat playing with something in the corner of the room, and I twisted around to see what it was. My knife!

"Don't suppose you know how to fetch?" I asked, scooching across the floor toward him without waiting for an answer.

With my back to the knife, I twisted my body into a position for which I have yoga to thank and managed to take hold of the handle. The cat batted playfully at my fingers, happy that I was joining him in his game. "Sorry, kitty, this is mine now."

It took some maneuvering, but I finally managed to wedge the knife against the rope with my wrists bent backward in an awkward position. A lot of good it did me. I could barely manage to move the blade back and forth; at this rate, it would take forever to get free.

I could hear the sound of muffled voices coming through the door, the tone sounding more urgent than before. What was happening? I resumed my sawing with greater intensity. If Kirk returned before I got free, it would all be over.

Finally, I felt the rope start to give. I had frayed it enough to loosen my wrists. I dropped the knife and began frantically working my hands around until—success!—I managed to get one hand loose. I quickly freed my other hand and then my feet, and I scrambled to stand. The cat followed me up the stairs, whapping playfully at my heels as I went.

I paused at the door. I didn't have much of a plan. I cracked it open a hair and peeked out. Kirk had the family lined up on the couch where I'd been attempting to nap not all that long ago.

". . . so are you sure no one made a copy or anything?" He was chatting amicably with them, trying to learn what he could without the use of the gun.

As I swung the door open a few more inches, I caught Nicole's eye and held one finger up to my lips. Her eyes grew big, but she didn't say anything. She nudged Vince and somehow did some secret look at him, then me, then back at him, and he nodded imperceptibly. How did couples do that?

I spotted a heavy ceramic vase on a table a couple feet from the basement door. Maybe I could grab it before Kirk noticed me.

Mrs. Abernathy caught sight of me right at that moment and opened her mouth to speak. "Kelsey—"

"—is supposed to join us a little later for a glass of wine," Nicole interrupted with surprising force, giving her mother a pointed look. "In fact, Kirk, maybe you could ask her about the files. You know, she planned the most beautiful service. I'm so glad I trusted her, because she always knew exactly what to do." Mrs. Abernathy looked confused, but Nicole continued with her monologue, providing the distraction I needed.

I darted for the vase, and Kirk spun around at the movement, pulling the gun out of his waistband. Right as he lunged at me, the cat zipped across his path, causing him to look down for a split second.

"Kelsey, what are you doing?!" Mrs. Abernathy cried, jumping from the couch. But it was too late. I swung the heavy vase with all my might, landing a blow squarely on the back of Kirk's head and sending shards of Mexican pottery flying and the gun skittering across the floor.

Nicole was on it before anyone else. She scrambled across the floor and grabbed the gun, holding it victoriously over her head. "Got it!"

In the meantime, Vince had pounced on Kirk, who was lying on the floor, not quite knocked unconscious but looking pretty woozy. "Yeah, how does it feel having someone smash you over the head?" I yelled at his prone figure, still hopped up on adrenaline.

"Kelsey, what in heaven's name were you thinking?" Mrs. Abernathy demanded, nostrils flaring.

"Mrs. Abernathy, it was Kirk! Kirk killed Dana. He was in on the blackmail with her and he poisoned her and he had me tied up downstairs." I was out of breath and not sure if I was making much sense.

Nicole tossed me the gun. "I knew it!" she exclaimed. "I thought it was weird when he was asking all those questions, and then when I saw you on the stairs, I knew something was up."

Kirk was starting to come to, but Vince shoved him down on the floor while I held the gun on him, hands shaking.

Vince looked up at me. "What do you want me to do with him?"

"Feel free to punch him in the face if you'd like." I figured the groom probably had a lot of pent-up frustration from spending his honeymoon with his new mother-in-law. "In the meantime, does anyone remember how to dial 911?"

Mrs. Abernathy let out an exasperated sigh. "Well, did you absolutely *have* to break my vase in the process?"

"Your vase?" I sputtered. "I thought it came with the house."

She knelt to pick up one of the larger pieces off the floor. "It was a wedding gift for the kids. It's one of a kind, made by a local artist who's earning quite a name for himself. It wasn't technically for sale, so you wouldn't believe how much it cost me." She added an eye roll for dramatic flair.

We all stared at her, not sure what to say.

She tossed the jagged shard back onto the floor and sighed. "Well, this is clearly beyond repair. I suppose you can reimburse me."

CHAPTER 32

*T*hanks to a roll of duct tape Vince remembered seeing in the hall closet, we were able to subdue Kirk until the police came. It was going to hurt when they removed the tape later. They'd probably end up pulling his arm hair out by the roots. I hoped he'd think of me fondly when that happened.

"Let me go! You can't prove anything!" Kirk spat, writhing on the floor while we all watched from the couch. "I'll have you arrested for assault!"

"Oh, please," Mrs. Abernathy snorted. "Kelsey, will you be a dear and tape his mouth shut?"

"Glad to oblige, Mrs. A." I applied a piece of the sticky silver tape with a satisfying slap to make sure it stuck. Mrs. Abernathy cocked her head to one side. Had I really just called her Mrs. A? My triumphant mood was making me a little brazen.

Soon enough, a couple of officers arrived to take away our

bound suspect, followed moments later by Detectives Ortiz and Nolasco.

As Nicole led them into the living room, I greeted the officers enthusiastically. I was genuinely glad to see them, although it was a bit difficult restraining myself from dancing around the room like it was a college football end zone, chanting, "I told you so!" at the top of my lungs.

"Kelsey," Ortiz said formally, as Nolasco merely nodded to me by way of greeting. I noted the lack of astonished appreciation in their tone. I was going to miss them.

Okay, no, I really wasn't.

They took our statements separately, starting with Mrs. Abernathy. Although they were in the other room, she managed to raise her voice just enough so we could hear her mention the "very expensive vase"—pronounced *vahzzz*—that had met its untimely demise.

"Don't listen to her," Nicole said, smiling warmly at me. "You were amazing. You may have even saved our lives."

"I don't know about that," I demurred.

"Besides," Nicole said, "you caught the bad guy! I wish I were as brave as you." Her look of admiration made me feel proud inside. *I am pretty brave, aren't I?*

"Yeah," Vince agreed, almost in response to my unspoken thought. "You were a total badass."

Nicole brightened. "And now maybe we can actually go on our honeymoon!" She leaned over and kissed Vince—just a peck at first, but then I swore I could see a little tongue. *Ewww. Get a room, people.*

I was waiting outside the jail, catching up on my e-mails and phone messages, when Zoe emerged into the early afternoon sun, flanked by her mom, sister, and new brother-in-law. She wore a flowered dress her mother had bought her in one of the boutiques near the plaza, a definite improvement on the prison uniform she'd been forced to wear, and she broke into a huge smile when she spotted me.

"Kelsey!" she exclaimed, and she rushed over and tackled me in an enthusiastic hug. She pulled back and looked at me, eyes tearing up with emotion. She brushed at the tears and started laughing at the same time. "Nicole told me everything. I don't know how to thank you!"

"Oh, no need to thank me," I said modestly. "Just doing my job."

"Are you kidding me?" she said. "I'm pretty sure your job duties don't normally include smashing bad guys over the head."

"Well, I'm glad it all worked out." I glanced at Nicole sheepishly. "Although I think I owe your sister a vase."

"Now, don't you think you're being a tad overdramatic?" Mrs. Abernathy said. I opened my mouth to protest but saw a hint of a smile creep over her face.

Nicole and Vince laughed as Zoe pulled me in for another hug.

"That's enough, girls," said Mrs. Abernathy. "People are starting to stare."

Zoe snuck in an extra squeeze, then pulled away. "I thought you had a plane to catch?"

"And miss all this?" I beamed. "No way!" I was leaving with a clear conscience, and that was all that mattered.

"Why don't you fly back with them?" Vince asked, jabbing a thumb in the direction of his new in-laws.

"Yeah!" said Zoe enthusiastically. "Dad's flying down on the company plane to pick us up."

"I didn't want to have to spend one more night in this awful little town," Mrs. Abernathy said, fluttering her hand dismissively toward San Miguel in general.

"Although you have to admit, Mom—" Nicole was stopped dead by her mom's stare. Mrs. Abernathy didn't have to admit anything.

"Anyway," Nicole continued, "we're leaving for our honeymoon, like, right now, so it seems a shame to waste all that extra space on the plane."

Mrs. Abernathy offered a tight-lipped smile. "I suppose there's room for one more."

"Great!" said Nicole. "It's settled then."

Mrs. Abernathy reached out and pushed a strand of hair behind Nicole's ear. "Honey, don't think I don't want you kids to go have fun. I do. But this has been such an awful ordeal. And if you think about it, it wasn't even a real wedding. Don't you want to try again?"

Looking confused, Nicole took Vince's hand protectively. "What do you mean, try again?"

"We could do a *real* wedding in Napa, like we had planned. Wouldn't that be lovely? I could invite all of my friends."

Laughing, Vince held up his hand to stop her. "Please, no more weddings! Once was enough."

"Yeah, Mom," said Nicole, "I think we're done with weddings. No offense, Kelsey."

"None taken, believe me!" I was ready to move on with my life, and I was sure they were, too. Not that Mrs. Abernathy would have hired me to plan Nicole's "real" wedding. Or maybe she would have, just so she'd have another shot at firing me.

We said our good-byes, and I hurried back to Evan's house to get my things. In a couple of hours, I'd be heading home. On the way, my cell phone buzzed again to let me know I had a voice mail, so I dug it out of my back pocket and pressed it to my ear to listen.

"Hi, Kelsey, this is Jacinda. I got the strangest call this morning from a Mrs. Abernathy?" *Oh, dear Lord. What had she said?* If she had blown this job for me, I was going to strangle her with my own two hands. Although perhaps I'd wait until we were back home to do it, because I'd quickly grown accustomed to the idea of hitching a ride on their private plane.

Jacinda continued: "I'm not sure how she got my number, but then again, San Miguel is a pretty small town. Anyway, Mrs. Abernathy recommended you very highly. In fact—what was it she said? Oh, yeah. She said I'd be a fool not to hire you."